"Who's there?" Rhiannon murmured as he picked her up in his arms, snuggling against his chest, but not waking.

"Hawk."

"Hawk…ah, yes." She curled her hand around his neck. "Where are you taking me?"

"My bed."

"I see." She was quiet until he crested the top of the stairs. "Is this you getting creative, Mr. Jackson?"

He might be dead tired, but he wasn't dead. "Don't tempt me," he muttered, and swung her onto his bed. He stood there for a moment, bent over her, arms still clutching her body. Just to catch his breath.

She gazed up at him, her hands splayed against his chest. "Where are you going to sleep?"

He had the strangest feeling if he said, "With you," she might just have slide over to make room for him.

Crazy.

Dear Reader,

I don't know about you, but September makes me miss buying pencils and notebooks for school. Under cover of night (the only way for an Intimate Moments gal to go), I'll creep into a drugstore and buy the most garish notebook I can find, along with colored markers and neon erasers. Because you deserve to be pampered, why not treat yourself to September's fabulous batch of Silhouette Intimate Moments books, and at the same time maybe buy yourself some school supplies, too?

USA TODAY bestselling author Susan Mallery delights us with *Living on the Edge* (#1383), a sexy romance in which a rugged bodyguard rescues a feisty heiress from her abusive ex-husband. While cooped up in close quarters, these two strangers find they have sizzling chemistry. In *Perfect Assassin* (#1384), Wendy Rosnau captivates readers with the story of a dangerous woman who has learned how to take out a target. And she means to kill those who hurt her father. What happens when the target is the man she loves?

Hard Case Cowboy (#1385) by Nina Bruhns is a page-turning adventure in which two opposites have to run a ranch together. Can they deal with the hardships of ranch life and keep from falling head over heels in love? And in Diane Pershing's *Whispers and Lies* (#1386), an ugly-duckling-turned-swan stumbles upon her schoolgirl crush, who, unbeknownst to her, is investigating the scandalous secrets of her family. Their new relationship could be the biggest mistake ever...or a dream come true.

I wish you a happy September and hope you'll return next month to Intimate Moments, where your thirst for suspense and romance is sure to be satisfied. Happy reading!

Sincerely,

Patience Smith
Associate Senior Editor

Please address questions and book requests to:
Silhouette Reader Service
U.S.: 3010 Walden Ave., P.O. Box 1325, Buffalo, NY 14269
Canadian: P.O. Box 609, Fort Erie, Ont. L2A 5X3

NINA BRUHNS

HARD CASE COWBOY

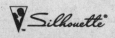

Silhouette®

INTIMATE MOMENTS™

Published by Silhouette Books

America's Publisher of Contemporary Romance

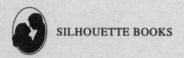 **SILHOUETTE BOOKS**

ISBN 0-373-27455-6

HARD CASE COWBOY

Visit Silhouette Books at www.eHarlequin.com

Printed in U.S.A.

Books by Nina Bruhns

Silhouette Intimate Moments

NINA BRUHNS

credits her Gypsy great-grandfather for her great love of adventure. She has lived and traveled all over the world, including a six-year stint in Sweden. She has been on scientific expeditions from California to Spain to Egypt and The Sudan, and has two graduate degrees in archaeology (with a specialty in Egyptology). She speaks four languages and writes a mean hieroglyphics!

But Nina's first love has always been writing. For her, writing for Silhouette Books is the ultimate adventure. Drawing on her many experiences gives her stories a colorful dimension, and allows her to create settings and characters out of the ordinary. She has won numerous awards for her previous titles, including the prestigious National Readers Choice Award, two Daphne Du Maurier Awards of Excellence for Overall Best Romantic Suspense of the year, five Dorothy Parker Awards and two Golden Heart Awards, among many others.

A native of Canada, Nina grew up in California and currently resides in Charleston, South Carolina, with her husband and three children.

She loves to hear from her readers, and can be reached at P.O. Box 2216, Summerville, SC, 29484-2216 or by e-mail via her Web site at www.NinaBruhns.com or via the Harlequin Web site at www.eHarlequin.com.

For my favorite doctor, Dr. Harley Freiberger,
and all his lovely, wonderful staff.
Thanks for everything, gang!
You're the best!
Love, Nina

Chapter 1

There was a dead cow in the road.

"By the saints," Rhiannon O'Brannoch muttered as she slammed on her hired car's brakes before hitting it. Dust from the dirt track billowed around her in a huge, gritty cloud. *What on earth...?*

Was there no end to the savagery of this country?

Rhiannon gripped the steering wheel tightly and peered out at the strange Arizona landscape all around her. Harsh, desolate, forbidding. And red. The gnarled trees that stood crooked and hunched over like old men were green, but everything else was the color of a flaming sunset. The ground, the mountains, the rocks, were all so red she only now noticed the dark shadow of blood pooling under the dead cow's side.

"Oh!" she exclaimed aloud. "What'll it be next? Wild Indians?"

She closed her eyes and wiped a bead of sweat that trickled down her temple. This was a sign. Coming to Arizona had been a colossal mistake.

Last week's letter from her late father's long-lost brother had seemed like a godsend, with its mysterious scrawled message, "Rhiannon, love, your uncle Fitz needs you," and its one-way ticket to America. It was exactly what she'd needed—a way out. Away from her ex-fiancé Robbie, away from Da's—her father's—farm that should have been hers but now belonged to her aunt Bridget and uncle Patrick, away from the hurts and betrayals those she loved had dealt her one after the other. Away from Ireland.

She'd thought coming here would give her a new start and help her set aside the pain of the past several years. Help her forget, and forgive.

But now she wondered what she had got herself into.

She opened her eyes. *Dust, uncivilized wilderness and dead cows.* It was like something out of a bad spaghetti Western.

Suddenly, the cow's tail twitched up.

It was *alive!*

Should she try to help it? Instinctively crossing herself, she opened the car door and prepared to take her first step onto Irish Heaven, her uncle Fitz's primitive, sprawling ranch.

At least, she hoped it was Irish Heaven. Lord knew with the crazy directions she'd gotten at that last petrol station and the unholy distances in this country, she could easily have driven clear to Montana and be none the wiser.

She slid out of the car and heat hit her like a foundry furnace. Warily, she inspected the surroundings for snakes, coyotes and mountain lions. One couldn't be too careful. Something had attacked that cow, and she didn't intend to be its next victim.

After two steps, her sensible suede pumps were covered in red dust. Good job she hadn't put on tights this morning.

She hesitated just before reaching the animal. Rhiannon knew about cows. She'd had fifteen Guernseys on the farm back home. But they were milch cows and looked nothing like this massive beast lying on the ground. Did American cows bite?

Then she heard its breath. Coming in short, shallow pants, each puff accompanied by a soft grunt.

"Ah, you poor thing," she murmured, and knelt by its head. Its eye opened and regarded her in a glazed stupor. "There, now," she said, and ran her hand lightly over the hide of its neck. It felt stiff and matted. And hot. Very hot.

Its legs and side were covered with long, ugly scratches, oozing blood. Whatever had inflicted these had been vicious. A mountain lion? She glanced around again nervously, imagining every shadow was a predator about to leap out at her.

She shook herself and looked back at the cow. It needed medical attention, and quickly, or it would die. Unfortunately, it was blocking the entire road. To get around it and continue toward the ranch house, she'd have to drive off the road's packed dirt path out onto the soft desert verge.

She'd never driven in this kind of sand before. She'd never even *seen* this kind of sand before. She could get stuck. Out here in the middle of nowhere with only a dying cow and whatever had attacked it for company. She'd brought no food and there was just one bottle of water left.

The only other alternative was to turn around and drive the approximately thirty-five miles back to the petrol station.

The cow gave a low, exhausted moo, the sound tugging at her heart. She knelt down again and stroked its silky ears. Its mournful eye followed her, as though it knew she could ease its suffering. Making a quick decision, she fetched her last bottle of water from the car and returned to the animal.

"Are you thirsty, then?" she asked, and dribbled a small stream into the side of the cow's mouth. Its tongue slowly stroked at the liquid.

When the bottle was empty she stood and looked desperately down the ribbon of dirt track, first in one direction, then in the other.

The cow mooed again.

She stood paralyzed with fear and indecision.

What on earth should she do?

"Damn it, not again!"

Redhawk Jackson let out a nasty curse. Blood-matted cowhide clung to the curls of barbed wire dangling from a perimeter fencepost that had been in perfect repair just last week.

The cattle thieves were back.

Redhawk swore again and spurred his horse across the breached fence. This was the third time this year. And it was only July. If the rustling kept up at this rate, Irish Heaven would be bankrupt by Christmas.

With an angry roar he urged his horse Tonopah into a gallop, charging across the high desert, dodging piñon pines and sagebrush, heading for the road that led out to the highway.

He would catch these bastards. No way was he going to let thieves too lazy to do an honest day's work force the ranch under and ruin his future. Not a chance in hell. After a lifetime of losing—his mother, his rodeo career, his health and nearly his sanity—this was one war he was determined to win. Or die trying.

Nothing and nobody was taking Irish Heaven away from him.

He sped over the rocky ground.

Nobody.

How many head had the rustlers gotten this time? Four? Five? They never took more cattle than would fit into the truck they'd have waiting in a secluded section of the road. They were smart. But he was smarter.

Tonopah flew over the last rise before the road. Redhawk couldn't believe his eyes. A car! Parked in the sand. And someone was still there.

Filled with rage, he spurred his mount down the slope like a madman. This guy was dog meat.

Except it was a woman.

Reddish-blond curls flowed around a shapely figure with long legs standing in the middle of the road. She looked up at him in surprise as he bore down on her at top speed.

That's when he noticed the steer. Down on the ground and hurt, blood everywhere.

"What the hell are you doing?" he yelled in outrage.

The woman's mouth dropped open. She stared at him for a split second, then turned and ran for the car.

Oh, no. No way was she getting away.

"Stop!" he yelled.

She ran faster and stumbled. "No!"

He swooped down on her, grabbed her by the waist and lifted her into the saddle in front of him.

"Let me go!" she screamed, kicking and thrashing in his grip, pounding him with her fists.

"I ought to string you up," he growled, yanking her hard against his chest as he reined in Tonopah.

Her eyes went wide and she struggled even harder. "Don't hurt me. Please!"

With difficulty, he hung on to her and turned the horse back toward the injured steer. "Wasn't it enough to *steal* my cattle? Now you have to slaughter them, too?"

"I did none of that!" she cried, still squirming. "I was trying to help. I even gave it my last bottle of water. Let me down!"

She sounded funny. Not her voice, but the way she talked.

Like Fitz.

Hawk looked down at her, searching her features for the first time. And got a weird, tingly feeling in his scalp.

He didn't let her go, but loosened his grip a bit. "Who the hell are you, and why are you trespassing on my ranch?"

Her fists stilled and she met his gaze. "*Your* ranch? Devil take it, I knew I was lost."

Tonopah stopped next to the steer, but Redhawk didn't move except to shift a little in the saddle, sliding the woman more firmly onto his thighs and off the uncomfortable saddle horn. "Did you get a look at the rustlers?"

"What rustlers?"

Suddenly he noticed her hands were splayed on his chest, where a moment ago they'd been beating on him. She was wearing a skirt which had ridden up her thighs, and her short-sleeved blouse had pulled out. His arms were around her, one touching a narrow band of skin at her waist, the other circling her slim shoulders.

He shifted again, uneasily.

"Yeah. Rustlers. If it wasn't you, who do you think did this?" He jerked his chin at the steer.

Her gaze dropped to it hesitantly, then returned to his. "I…I assumed it was an animal who'd mauled it. A wolf, or mountain lion."

The way her voice lilted, and how she pronounced *mauled* and *wolf*—definitely Irish.

He had a very bad feeling about this woman.

"You've answered none of my questions," he said, pulling his face into a scowl. She moved, and her breast brushed his forearm, scalding it with unwelcome softness. Unwelcome because of who he was beginning to suspect she was. "Who are you, and what ranch are you looking for?" he demanded.

Her eyes, green as juniper against the snow, sought his. In them he saw a growing awareness of their bodies pressed together, and he watched her lingering fear turn to a different kind of apprehension.

She tried to back away from him, but perversely he held her fast. Clinging to his last vestige of power over her.

There was only one person on earth who could come between him and Irish Heaven, and he had a sinking feeling that instead of being safely thousands of miles away in Ireland, for some unknown reason she was right here, sitting in his lap.

He hoped he was scaring the hell out of her. Enough so she'd turn tail and run right back to where she belonged.

"Who are you?" he repeated, and prayed she wouldn't say—

"Rhiannon O'Brannoch, Fitz O'Brannoch's niece. And I'm looking for Irish Heaven."

Redhawk ground his jaw and held Rhiannon O'Brannoch prisoner in his arms as the news sank in. Once more everything he'd worked for was about to be taken from him.

You'd think he'd be used to it by now, but each time it happened, it hit him with the same inevitable force of unfairness. Luckily, this time he had something else to focus on, so it wouldn't bring him to his knees. Not in front of witnesses, anyway.

Without warning, he swung her from the saddle, holding her up until she got her legs back, then slid off after her, favoring his bum knee.

He grabbed his saddlebag and canteen and strode to the injured steer. He had to get it together. He had no idea why she was here. It might have nothing to do with wanting the ranch.

"I'm Redhawk Jackson, Fitz's foreman," he said without looking at her. "Is your car stuck in the sand?"

In his peripheral vision he saw her glance back at the vehicle and nod. "I tried to get around the cow. To go fetch help."

"Steer," he corrected, gratified when she blinked and her cheeks turned pink. He yanked his Stetson down over his eyes and added gruffly, "Sorry I mistook you for a thief."

She folded her arms under her breasts, watching him pull his medical emergency supplies out of the saddle bag. "Do you always shoot first and ask questions later, Mr. Jackson?" Her tone was noticeably annoyed.

"Always. If someone is trying to steal something that's mine," he answered pointedly.

She didn't even have the grace to look guilty. "What if they're innocent?" she asked, moving in closer.

He paused in his inspection of the steer's injuries, doing his best to ignore her bare legs under that skirt. "You think whoever did this was innocent?"

"But why would rustlers harm an animal they're attempting to steal?"

He shook his head. "I doubt it was deliberate. The steer probably spooked when they tried to load him into the truck, ran into the barbed wire fence and sliced himself up. It happens."

"And they just left him here to die?"

Redhawk shrugged, pouring disinfectant onto the worst wounds. "No use to them like this. Can't sell an injured animal."

"That's appalling."

"Yep."

They fell silent as he worked, which was just fine by him. He needed time to wrap his mind around this unexpected development. He just wished she would take her long legs out of his damn line of vision. The last thing he wanted was to be attracted to the woman who could turn his life upside down and send him packing from the only real home he'd ever known.

"I need to get the doc," he announced when he'd done all he could do, and awkwardly rose to stand. He shook the numbness from his knee and whacked the dust off his pants. "This animal needs antibiotics and an IV, hopefully get him on his feet long enough to load him into a truck. He'll die out here otherwise."

She nodded and backed away. "Can you phone someone to pull the car out of the ditch for me?"

"Call yourself. You're coming with me."

"But—" She looked around and caught sight of Tonopah. "Ah, no," she said, waving her hands in front of her. "I'll wait here if it's all the same to you."

"Sorry. I don't leave Fitz's guests stranded in the desert." He whistled and Tonopah trotted over. "Climb on. You can even have the saddle."

She took another step backward. "Thank you, no. I'll walk."

He glanced down at her inappropriate footwear. "In those?"

She twirled a high-heeled foot. "They're sturdy enough."

"Forget it. You'll have blisters the size of the Grand Canyon." His gaze traveled up to her skirt. "You got a pair of jeans in your suitcase?"

"I don't wear blue jeans," she said.

So, maybe she wasn't out for the ranch, after all. You couldn't own a ranch and not wear denim. Maybe she was only here for a visit.

Yeah, right.

"Guess you'll just have to hike up your skirt. Ever ride a horse?"

"Not for several years. Mr. Jackson, I really don't think—"

"Redhawk. Don't worry, it's like riding a bicycle. You never forget." He gave her a long, even look. "You've ridden a bike before, haven't you, Miz O'Brannoch?"

Her lips parted a fraction and she swallowed. Her chin lifted slightly. "Never in the dirt, Mr. Jackson."

He chuckled and turned to his horse, making sure the cinch was tight. She had spunk, had to give her that. "Dirt's about all you'll find around here, so better get used to it. And you should probably call me Redhawk. Considering the circumstances."

"And what circumstances might those be, Mr. Jackson?"

He smothered a grin at her tone. With her melodic Irish accent, the words sounded more mischievous than prim, though he was sure she was aiming for the latter.

He tipped back his hat and closed the distance so they were standing nose to nose. Well, chin to nose. "Wasn't too long ago in these parts when a man and a woman shared a saddle, they had to get married."

Her nose went up even further. "How quaint. Well, as I have no intention—"

Before she could react he'd swung her onto Tonopah's back and jumped up behind her. "You were saying?"

She gasped, tugging at her skirt, which was now bunched up

around the tops of her thighs. It was no use. That skirt wasn't going anywhere but further up her hips. And it was a hell of a view.

"Kick off your shoes," he advised as he slid the toes of his boots into the stirrups and clicked Tonopah into motion.

"They're my best pair."

"You'll lose them," he warned as he urged the horse into a canter. Sure enough, the left one dropped off when she grabbed for the saddle horn. A huff followed, then the right one flew off as well. "We'll get them later," he assured her. "Hang on."

Tonopah picked up the pace. To Hawk's surprise, she didn't fall off. He didn't even have to steady her. She held the saddle horn, but her back was straight and her knees gripped the horse expertly. Her back didn't once touch his chest. She obviously remembered a thing or two from a few years ago.

Just as well. Putting hands on her again could prove dangerous. His imagination didn't need any more fodder to egg it on. Bad enough her long, pretty legs were snugged up against his like sardines in a can. Thank God the saddle had a high back on it to separate the sardines where it mattered most.

"Redhawk," she said above the clatter of hooves on rocks and gravel. "That's an Indian name, isn't it?"

He pursed his lips and reminded himself she was a foreigner. "Yep," he said, refraining from any of two dozen retorts. With his complexion and facial features, only a blind man could mistake him for anything else.

"What kind?"

"American," he replied.

She turned to look at him. "No, I meant—" But his expression must have scared her off. "Sorry. Didn't mean to pry."

"Worried I might carry you off to my teepee and scalp you, Miz O'Brannoch?"

There was a pause, then she said, "I'm sure you could come up with something more creative than that, Mr. Jackson."

There was that prim-mischievous tone again. He couldn't help but grin. Was it sarcasm…or a challenge?

If she'd been anyone else he might make it his business to find out. He'd been a good stretch without a woman's company, and though he steadfastly avoided relationships, he didn't generally avoid an attractive, willing woman.

But despite the clichés, sleeping with the enemy was never a good idea. And she might well be the biggest enemy of his life. Best let it go.

His biceps brushed against her shoulder, setting off a chain reaction in his body.

Let it go, he told himself.

At least until he found out for sure why she was here.

"Don't even think about it," Rhiannon said when she felt Redhawk's hands circle her waist, preparing to hoist her off the horse like a sack of potatoes. "I am perfectly capable of dismounting by myself."

His hands dallied on her for a moment, then he said, "All right," and took them away again. He swung off the horse with practiced ease and stood there watching her with an expectant expression on his face.

His deadly handsome face. Dark eyes, square jaw, largish but nicely shaped nose, wonderfully high cheekbones. All below a classic black cowboy hat that set it off to perfection. It was all she could do not to stare.

His lips quirked. "Well?"

"Turn around, then. I'll not give you more of a show than you already got."

He grinned but did as he was told. A nice trait in a man, and all too rare.

"You'll be sorry," he said.

Wasn't she always when it came to men?

She harrumphed and dismounted. "Ouch!" she cried when

her bare feet hit the rocky ground. She'd forgotten she had no shoes on.

"Told you," he said, swept her up into his arms and carried her the dozen yards to the steps of the ranch house porch.

She considered protesting but thought better of it. She was getting rather used to being manhandled by the hulking brute. Not to say she liked it, but it had a sort of…primitive appeal. In a you-Tarzan-me-Jane kind of way.

He set her down on the smooth stone steps. "Ta," she said, and glanced up at the front door hoping Uncle Fitz would appear. She didn't quite know how to handle the unpredictable ranch foreman. One minute he was rude and broody, the next he seemed ready to seduce her.

"You're welcome," he said, and preceded her up the steps. He walked with a slight limp.

"Did you hurt your leg?" she asked, following him.

"Old rodeo injury," he replied curtly, opened the screen door and pushed open the heavy wooden entry door. "Bull riding."

Her brows lifted. "Not as easy as bicycles, I guess." She gave him a smile as she went into the house, trying not to think about the type of man who would ride angry bulls for amusement.

He hung his hat on a rack by the door. "You've definitely got your uncle's sense of humor," he said, heading for the back corner of the room, where a small cluttered desk stood.

"How's that?" she asked, looking around. The place was enormous. And none too tidy. Large leather furniture was dotted with newspapers, used cups and the odd bit of clothing. Built-in bookshelves were crammed with volumes willy-nilly. The crowded mantelpiece was covered in dust.

He picked up the phone on the desk. "A real smart aleck."

She glanced over at him. She was pretty sure she'd just been insulted. But his expression as he dialed was more one of affection than condemnation.

"Where *is* my uncle?" she asked, but he raised a finger and spoke for a few minutes with the veterinarian about the steer and arranged to meet him there in half an hour.

"Fitz is probably taking a nap," Redhawk said after hanging up. "Listen…" He put his hands on his hips and regarded her. He looked as though he had something to say but wasn't sure if he should say it. "I know you've been exchanging letters with him regularly, so you've probably noticed…" His words trailed off.

Alarm flashed through her. "Noticed what? Is he ill?"

She hadn't seen Uncle Fitz for twenty-four years, not since he'd fled Ireland when she was eight, the day after her da was thrown in prison. But because of their long letters, she felt close to him despite the distance and the years.

And he was the only family she had left, besides the aunt and uncle who'd taken the farm from her.

If this was bad news, she really didn't want to hear it. But she forced herself to say, "What's the matter? Please tell me, Mr. Jackson."

He pushed a hand through his thick black hair. "Only if you stop calling me Mr. Jackson."

"Redhawk, then," she said impatiently. "What's happened to Uncle Fitz?"

He sighed. "There's no easy way to tell you, so I'll just come right out and say it. He's been diagnosed with Alzheimer's disease."

Rhiannon just stood there staring at him in shock. How was this possible? In his letters Fitz had always been vibrantly alive. She'd loved reading his rambling descriptions of life in America. Arizona had sounded like another planet to her untravelled Irish ears. His adventures, both the good and the bad, had fascinated her, making her own dreary life pale by comparison.

Redhawk walked over and led her to an oversize easy chair, pushed off a couple of magazines and urged her into it. "I simply can't believe it," was all she could manage.

"I couldn't, either, at first. I thought he was just being forgetful." He sat on the arm of the sofa across from the chair. "I figured the doctor would prescribe ginseng or something." He laughed humorlessly. "But he did some kind of psychological test instead and it indicated advancing dementia."

"When was this?"

"A few months ago. Since then, he's gone downhill fast. He still has some good days," Redhawk said, obviously reluctant to complete the thought.

She dropped her head in her hands. The déjà vu felt like a blow to the stomach. So much for starting her life anew. Instead of taking a tentative step forward, if she stayed she'd be taking a huge leap backward. Back to the day her mother announced she had cancer.

That explained the one-way ticket.

Uncle Fitz had always said what a saint Rhiannon was for taking care of her mother all those years. Apparently, he was counting on her to take care of him, as well.

She knew it had been a mistake to come. To dare think she could start over.

But this was too much. Just the thought of watching another person she loved suffer, the pain and frustration of being able to do nothing about it... No. She couldn't go through that again.

"I'm sorry, Mr. Jackson," she said, standing abruptly. "I have to go."

"Where?" he asked, surprised.

"Back to Ireland. I shouldn't have come."

His jaw dropped, and she could swear she saw relief flash through his eyes. "But you just got here. Surely you could stay for a day or two. When's your return flight?"

"Return flight?" she asked with dawning trepidation. "I don't have one. He sent me a one-way ticket."

"He?"

"Uncle Fitz."

Redhawk jumped to his feet. "*Fitz* sent you the ticket?"

She nodded. "Yes. With a note saying he needed me. But—" She swallowed down the guilt and selfishness that rose in her throat. "I'm sorry. I can't—"

"You mean he paid for it?" Redhawk's face blanched pale as her own.

"Yes. I certainly couldn't afford—"

"Do you remember how much it cost?"

She thought his question rude and asking it possibly overstepped the boundaries of a ranch foreman's job, but he looked so upset she answered. "Eight or nine hundred dollars, I believe."

His throat made an odd choking noise. "Eight or nine. Hundred."

"I don't like to ask, but I'm afraid I'll need the return fare, as well. You see, I don't—"

He held up a hand, squeezing the bridge of his nose between two fingers. "Trust me, I wish I could. You have no idea. But the thing is…"

"What?" she asked. "What is it?"

He cleared his throat. "If Fitz paid for that ticket, he used nearly all of the last of our funds. Unless you've got money of your own, I'm afraid you won't be going anywhere."

She gazed at him in horror. "That's not possible. He once told me Irish Heaven is worth over a million dollars!"

"On paper, yeah, but not in the bank. I'm sorry, Miz O'Brannoch. We're dead broke. And it looks like you're stuck here."

Chapter 2

Rhiannon felt all the blood drain straight from her head to her toes. Good thing she was already sitting down or her legs surely would have collapsed.

"This can't be happening," she mumbled.

"What *is* happening, then?" came a reedy voice from a door on the far side of the room.

She turned and saw a tall, sandy-haired older man standing in the doorway looking at her with open curiosity. Suddenly his face lit up like fireworks on Guy Fawkes Day.

"Janet!" A smile blossomed from ear to ear as he hurried toward her, opening his arms wide. "Ah, Janet love, you've finally come!"

Being called by her mother's name took Rhiannon aback for the briefest second, but then she quickly rose to her feet. "Uncle Fitz!"

Fitz's steps faltered and he looked to Redhawk for guidance.

"Fitz, look who's come all the way from Ireland. Your niece, Rhiannon O'Brannoch. You remember Rhiannon, don't you? From all her letters?"

He looked confused. "But—" he took another step "—it's Janet." A frown creased his leathery face. "Tell him, love."

"No, Uncle Fitz. I'm Janet's daughter, Rhiannon." His obvious disappointment splintered her heart into a thousand pieces. "I'm sorry, I—"

"Where is she? She was supposed to come."

Odd that Fitz would be so fixated on her mother. The Alzheimer's must be to blame for his mixing them up.

Redhawk put an arm around the older man's shoulders and led him over to her. "Janet passed on ten years ago. You know that. Say hello to your niece. She's had a long trip."

Suddenly the dam broke and recognition flooded over his face. "Rhiannon! You made it! I'm so happy to see you, love! Did you get my ticket? Aye, of course you did!" He talked on and on in his twangy Irish-American brogue, hugging her in between as though his first confusion had never happened.

Over Fitz's shoulder, Redhawk gave her a shrug, as if to say, "That's just how he is." Aloud he said, "I better get going and meet the vet. Will you be okay for a while?"

"Yes, of course."

"I'll be back as soon as I can. If the sheriff calls back about the rustling, tell him I'll get with him later."

With that, Redhawk was gone, leaving her alone with her uncle, who gave her one last hug and led her into the kitchen. "Let's make some grub," he suggested. "I'm starving."

The kitchen was unusually large, done in a southwestern style with earthy colors, rich natural woods and terra-cotta tile. It would have been beautiful if it weren't in such an unholy clutter. Just like the rest of the house. What she'd seen of it, anyway. Apparently neither man who lived here overly valued cleanliness.

She sighed and went to the sink to start the dishes while Fitz chatted away and threw together some strange-but-delicious-smelling concoction, making the mess worse in the process. She didn't mind. Listening to him go on about how he'd grown the tomatoes and cilantro himself and how a lady in town made the tortillas by hand and that he'd gotten the recipe from his old housekeeper whom he'd had to let go a few years ago. His banter put her so much in mind of how her mother had talked in the same rambling drifts back when she was alive and still cooking meals for them, Rhiannon didn't even notice how many times she had to change the dirty water in the sink.

An hour and a half later the dishes were washed and put away, the cupboards and counters scrubbed, the table cleaned and set for three, and Fitz's concoction, which he called enchiladas, was coming out of the oven.

Just then, the back door swung open and Redhawk walked through it holding the shoes she'd dropped earlier. He stopped just inside, staring at the kitchen. After taking it all in, his eyes turned to her.

"You did this?"

"Uncle Fitz made the enchiladas," she said, suddenly worried he'd take her cleaning the wrong way. She hurried to take the shoes from him. "I just thought…"

"Thank you," he said, and glanced down at the floor before coming further in. "It looks great." He looked up again. "But you didn't have to. I'd have gotten to it tomorrow."

"Thursday's kitchen day," Fitz interjected with a happy smile. "Thursday's kitchen, Friday's living room, Saturday's laundry, Sunday's—"

"That's all right, old man." Redhawk interrupted the litany with a wry smile. "Miz O'Brannoch isn't interested in our cleaning schedule. I see you've made my favorite for dinner."

Fitz turned his attention to the steaming casserole dish on the table. "I'm hoping Rhiannon will like it, too."

"I'm sure I will, Uncle Fitz," she said. She gave him a kiss on the cheek before going to the fridge. "What does everyone want to drink?"

A few minutes later they all sat down at the table and Fitz said,

"Let's join hands." When they did and he said a prayer of thanks and welcome, Rhiannon suddenly knew everything would be fine.

Fitz was wonderful and he was family and he obviously cared about her. This was where she belonged. It was clear he needed her. She had worked every day for eight long years on her da's farm alongside her aunt and uncle, but Aunt Bridget and Uncle Patrick had never needed her. They'd only tolerated her presence until Da died last month and left the land to them in a move that had shocked everyone—most of all her. Aunt Bridget had been her *mother's* sister, not her father's.

She looked up and suddenly realized she was still holding Redhawk's hand across the table. He was sitting absolutely still, watching her. He didn't look happy.

She snatched her hand away with a mumbled apology.

"Looks like the steer's going to live," he said, picking up his fork. "The vet was able to revive him enough to get him back to the ranch. He's resting in the barn now."

"What steer?" Fitz asked.

"The rustlers hit us again," Redhawk said, and told him about the fence and the injured animal. "I'll ride out tomorrow and see if I can figure out how many they got this time."

"But that means…"

"It'll be a tough winter," Redhawk completed with a nod.

Fitz put down his glass and glanced back and forth a couple of times between Redhawk and her. "I screwed up again, didn't I, lad?"

"Now, Fitz—"

"Only, this time you can't fix it, can you?"

Rhiannon tried to make herself look as small as possible. They were talking about her, she realized, and the ticket he'd bought her. She'd hated when Aunt Bridget and Uncle Patrick had spoken about her as though she hadn't been sitting at the same table.

"We'll manage," Redhawk said, scraping up the last bite off his plate.

"But the money—"

"Don't worry about it. I'm sure Miz O'Brannoch won't mind pitching in until we can figure something out." He shot her a flat look. "We'll get her back home where she belongs one way or another."

Obviously, he wanted her gone. As soon as possible.

Why?

It was just as obvious he could use her help around here.

What was going on?

But she didn't get the chance to ask because he took his plate to the sink, then headed for the back door. "Got chores to do and a colt to train," he said, barely pausing to grab his hat on the way out. "If you need me, I'll be somewhere around the barn."

The door shut with a slam.

Fitz started at the noise, then looked up at her. His eyes widened. "Janet!" he cried. "You've finally come!"

With a weary roll of the shoulders, Redhawk closed the barn door and slowly limped to the water pump where he always rinsed off after working. When he was this tired, his knee bothered him worse than usual. Good thing Crimson, the colt he was training, was far enough along they could work with hand signals. Tonight he could hardly get his leg to move. What a day. He was beat. Dead beat.

Bracing himself against the split-rail fence, he primed the hand pump and let it gush a few times into a bucket sitting in the long cattle trough he liked to think of as his own private Jacuzzi. There'd be no leisurely soak tonight, though. He'd only get six hours of sleep as it was.

As he washed the worst grime off his face and arms, he tried to stretch the muscles of his left shoulder. Must have strained it pushing the steer into the truck. It hurt like hell. After dumping the bucket of water onto a scraggly cottonwood he'd planted a few years ago, he glanced longingly at the pump. Sure would be nice to have a soak.

Tomorrow he'd indulge himself. Rhiannon had cleaned the kitchen. May as well take advantage of the hour she'd freed up on his list of Thursday chores. Leaning his hips against the fence, he slowly worked the pump handle up and down, up and down, inch by inch filling the oversize trough with water. By tomorrow evening, the blazing Arizona sun would heat it to perfect bath temperature. He could hardly wait.

He tromped to the house and went in through the back door, depositing his boots outside, his dirty clothes in the mudroom hamper and his hat on the rack. Stripped to his bare feet and underwear, he grabbed a beer from the fridge on his way to the living room to shut off the TV and gather Fitz from the easy chair where he invariably fell asleep, and tuck him in.

"Damn," he muttered when he spotted Rhiannon curled up on the sofa, eyes closed and a peaceful expression on her face. He'd completely forgotten about her.

Careful not to wake the woman, he gently shook Fitz and ushered him to the bathroom and then into bed, making sure to lower the blinds before closing the door on his first-floor master bedroom.

Redhawk's own room was upstairs—the only other bedroom in the house. Because of the generous size and configuration of the ground floor, the second level of the ranch house had never been finished by the original owner, used instead as a big storage attic. The first several years Hawk lived at Irish Heaven, he'd stayed in the bunkhouse, but when Fitz's health started going downhill, his friend insisted he frame off a room and bath upstairs and move into the main ranch house. One less place to heat and clean, and the old man felt better with Hawk right there to keep an eye on him instead of in the bunkhouse out of earshot.

But there was still no place for Rhiannon to sleep.

Great. One more damn thing to worry about.

Noiselessly he padded upstairs and took his shower, then changed the sheets on his bed, silently cursing the entire time.

Why did she have to come? He and Fitz were doing just fine by themselves. He didn't need some damn woman around messing up his routine.

Regardless of how attractive she was.

Hell, her being attractive just made it worse. Made him think about things best left unthought of. Made him imagine what it might be like to have a woman in his life, warm and loving, someone to sink himself into and lose the worries of the world in for a little while. Someone who loved him.

Damn. He rolled the old sheets into a ball and pulled on a clean pair of jeans. Talk about hallucinations. He must be more tired than he thought.

Detouring past the laundry, he went into the living room, to the couch where Rhiannon was sleeping. He shut his eyes for a moment, gathered his last vestige of strength, and bent to pick her up in his arms.

She wasn't exactly light, but not too heavy, either. He'd manage, if his knee held out. She turned toward him, snuggling her cheek against his chest but not waking. Her curves pressed in against his body through the thin cotton of her blouse and the scratchy wool of her skirt, and he regretted not putting on a shirt. Halfway up the stairs he had to readjust and she stirred.

"Who's there?" she murmured, peering up at him.

"Hawk."

"Hawk…ah, yes." She curled her hand around his neck and he hardened himself against the feel of it. "Where are you taking me?"

"My bed."

"I see." She was quiet until he crested the top of the stairs. Her fingers drew small circles on his bare skin. "Is this you getting creative, Mr. Jackson?"

He might be dead tired, but he wasn't dead. He recalled exactly the bit of this afternoon's conversation she was referring to. Suddenly he felt a lot less exhausted.

"Don't tempt me," he muttered and swung her onto his bed. He stood there for a moment, bent over her, arms still clutching her body. Just to catch his breath.

She gazed up at him, her hands splayed against his chest. "Where are you going to sleep?" she whispered.

He had the strangest feeling if he said, "With you," she might just have slid over to make room for him.

Crazy.

"Couch," he answered, pulled his arms from under her and backed away. "I'll just grab a shirt."

By the time he'd whipped socks and a clean work shirt from a dresser drawer she'd fallen asleep again. Thank God.

That was one choice he didn't want to have to make. Enemy or no, she was far too tempting lying there in his own bed with her wild red hair, her long sexy legs and her sassy attitude. There was nothing he'd like better at the moment than to tame all three. Which they'd no doubt both regret in the morning.

Him, especially. He didn't want to give her the idea he'd like her to stick around. For any reason. He'd worked his butt off for over a decade on this ranch with the understanding that some-day it would be his. He didn't need some usurping niece who didn't know the first thing about Irish Heaven to come and take it from him.

Sex was a fleeting pleasure. The only thing that really mattered in his life was Irish Heaven. This land had become so much a part of him, he would feel its loss down to the last fiber of his being.

He couldn't let it happen. And he wouldn't.

Even if it meant ten cold showers a day.

Too late for that tonight, so he went downstairs and tossed and turned for a while before finally falling into an uneasy oblivion.

He woke at his usual time. Rising with the dawn had been in-grained in him for enough years to kick him out of even the soundest sleep. Aside from the lumpy, unfamiliar place he'd spent the night. He stared at the ceiling for a second, feeling as if he'd gotten maybe three minutes of sleep, max.

All was quiet, so he went to the kitchen to start the pot of coffee he'd forgotten to set the timer on before retiring. Slipping on his boots from the porch, he strolled toward the barn to feed the animals and see to the horses, the bull and the injured steer.

It was a beautiful morning. The scents of warming sage and juniper filled the air, along with the soft hum of waking insects and the soaring calls of birds of prey. The rising sun turned the whole landscape into a kaleidoscope of brilliant reds and yellows and greens, outlined with the long shadows of piñons and the nearby cliffs.

It was his favorite time of day, filled with promise, not yet marred by the dulling hardships of reality.

Turning the corner around the barn, he saw her. Rhiannon. She was sitting on a barrel, feeding the chickens. About a dozen or so surrounded her, flapping their wings, others pecked animatedly at the grain she scattered about with an elegant toss of the hand.

She blended into the morning so perfectly, with her flowing red-gold hair and her laughing face, he was forced to stop and take a deep breath.

"Good morrow, Mr. Jackson," she called with a smile when she spotted him. "I hope you slept well?"

"Hawk," he said, suddenly surly at being taken by surprise like this. She had no right being out here doing his chores, looking radiant as an angel from heaven. "And no, I slept rotten."

"I'll take the sofa tonight," she said lightly, rising from the barrel and wiping the grain dust from her hand on her plain brown skirt. The same one she'd worn yesterday.

"Not a chance. Besides, I'm up before you, anyway."

"I can see that," she said brightly.

He pressed his lips together. "You're our guest. Guests don't sleep on the couch at Irish Heaven."

Gazing at him, she held the feed bucket's handle in both hands, letting it dangle in front of her as her smile faded.

"No, Mr. Jackson. I'm family. And the sooner you accept that the easier it will be for both of us."

So there it was. Out in the open. Her challenge. And he had nothing to fight it with. Nothing but eleven years of blisters and the word of a senile old man.

"Yes, ma'am," he said roughly. "But I don't care who you are, you're still sleeping in my bed."

He turned on a heel and headed for the barn. Hell, that hadn't come out the way he'd intended. His words had sounded…possessive. Not his meaning at all. Not in a million years.

Because she was family. And he wasn't.

He stopped short when he got to the barn door. It was wide-open, sunshine pouring into the cavernous space behind it, including the stall where the steer stood munching fresh straw. She'd mucked the stalls.

Not that there was much mucking this time of year. Fitz's stud bull, Lucky Charm, and his own three horses, Tonopah, Jasper and Crimson, preferred being outside in the corral except during the worst months of winter. Still.

"How long have you been up?" he asked as she approached behind him.

"Maybe an hour."

"How did you know to do all this?"

"Farms are pretty much the same the world over. Yesterday you mentioned pitching in."

"You didn't have to do everything." He couldn't believe she'd even dared to approach the bull's stall. He was a pussycat, but with his thick neck and long horns, he looked like a real mean sumbitch.

"I didn't. I left you the pig." He turned to glare at her impish grin. "No statement implied," she added with a wayward lilt to her voice. "I've just never had a pig."

He passed his tongue over his lower lip. Never in his life had he wanted anything as much as he wanted to take her over his knee right now.

"Nothin' to it," he ground out. "Just don't let him get too friendly. You'll end up on your butt in the mud with him."

"What does he eat?" she asked, peering over at the pen where Fitz's fat Christmas pig was living out his short but exceedingly comfy life.

"Anything you give him."

Hawk stalked off, wondering vaguely what had gotten him so riled up so quickly.

Sexual frustration, he decided. He hadn't been to Jake's Saloon in a couple of months, which was where most of his friends hung out on Saturday nights—including those of the female variety. He'd have to make a point of going this week, even if he had to knock off early to do it. Rhiannon O'Brannoch wouldn't look nearly as good the morning after a long night of dancing with the local beauties, and whatever else might follow.

He fed the pig and afterward spent an hour on a shady bench behind the barn mending a pile of tack that had been growing higher and higher over the past months. As Fitz did less around the ranch, Redhawk had less time to devote to such nonessential tasks. He missed it. He liked working with the leather and latigo that smelled of horses and felt like thick butter between his fingers. A guilty pleasure.

When he finished, he reluctantly went into the house and joined the others for a hearty breakfast.

"Here he is," said Fitz as soon as Redhawk walked into the kitchen. "I was telling Rhiannon she could use my old Jeep."

"If it still runs." Hawk went to the sink to wash his hands before sitting down. "Smells great. What's cooking?"

"Rhiannon made scones. Wait'll you taste one. Melt-in-your-mouth delicious. Say, where's the strawberry jam that pretty little schoolteacher made for you, lad?"

He cringed. Apparently there was nothing wrong with the old man's memory today. "No idea," he muttered.

Rhiannon gave him a knowing grin. "Making jam for you, is she? Popular with the ladies, Mr. Jackson?"

"Some more than others," he mumbled. That pretty little school-teacher had been cute, but overly tenacious. Even when it became obvious they had nothing in common but the night in question.

"About the Jeep," he said, wanting to steer the conversation away from the topic of his pathetic love life. "You know how to drive a stick shift?"

Rhiannon poured coffee for him. "Is there any other kind?"

Figured she'd know. He had yet to hit on anything she didn't know how to do. It was kind of annoying.

"I was wondering," she said, taking her seat across from him. "Is the hired car still stuck in the sand?"

He nodded, digging into breakfast. "Didn't have time to pull it out yesterday."

"Ah." She gazed at her plate, looking uncomfortable.

"What?" he asked.

"It's just…I need to return it today before noon or I'll be charged for another day. I don't have enough money to cover that."

He paused with his coffee cup halfway to his lips, mentally rearranging his morning. For the third time since getting up.

"We can pull it out with the Jeep, and I'll follow you into town. There are some things I can pick up while we're there."

"All right," she said with a smile, and passed him the plate of scones.

Naturally they were delicious. Even without the jam.

Rhiannon tried not to stare while Redhawk was hooking the hired car to the Jeep's front winch. Honestly she did. Why would she stare? The man hadn't even taken off his shirt.

Not that he had to. The stretchy fabric of his white T-shirt molded perfectly to every contour of his broad back and muscular biceps. Almost as nicely as his tight blue jeans hugged his slim hips and thighs.

If it hadn't been for Uncle Fitz chatting on about the townsfolk he expected to run into, who he wanted to avoid, who might buy him a beer at Jake's, necessitating the occasional nod of agreement and eye contact, she'd probably just give up and ogle Hawk's posterior and not care who caught her.

Which there was little danger of Redhawk doing. The man seemed determined to avoid looking at her, or even speaking to her. What had she done to make him dislike her so?

Maybe taking his bed had made him angry. Well, it hadn't been her idea. She'd be fine on the sofa. Hadn't she slept for years on a futon in the living room at the farm? Besides, his dislike for her had started well before that.

"Watch out for Burton Grant," Fitz was saying. He leaned in conspiratorially. "He's a sheriff's deputy. Bloody sympat'izer. Turn his own grandmother in for the reward, he would."

"You don't need to worry about rewards here, old man. You're not in the IRA anymore," Redhawk said calmly, making the final adjustments to the towline. "And I doubt Burton Grant works for the British Army." He glanced at her and shook his head infinitesimally.

She ignored him, too shocked by this bit of news to let it pass unnoted. She hated the IRA. "You, too, Uncle Fitz?" she demanded. "You were in it, along with my father?"

She supported a free Ireland more than most, having been brought up Catholic in Belfast during the Troubles. But she hated the violence, and wanted nothing to do with the organization responsible for her father spending most of his life in prison. In fact, she hated the IRA so much she'd left her former fiancé, Robbie Trevalian, the same day she'd found out he'd been lying to her for years about being one of them.

Uncle Fitz put his finger to his lips and whispered, "Shhh, there's ears everywhere. Y' don't want to be talkin' too loudly, love."

Rhiannon marshaled her temper and glanced around at the stunted trees and stark landscape surrounding them. "I doubt anyone's hiding out here, Uncle."

She eased out a long breath. No sense being angry with Fitz. Whatever he was talking about resided far in the past. Dredging it up or getting upset over it would do nobody any good.

She turned back to Redhawk, who was about to flip the switch on the winch and pull the car back onto the road.

"What's that?" she asked, seeing something long and yellowish sticking out of the sand next to his boot.

He frowned and knelt down, brushing dirt and bits of vegetation away from the object. "Aw, hell," he said, sweeping aside more sand.

Both she and Fitz pressed in to see better.

"What is it?" Fitz asked.

Hawk sat back on his heels and swiped a hand over his eyes. "Perfect," he said. "This is just what I need right now."

"Tell us," Rhiannon urged, starting to worry over his reaction.

"It's a bone," he answered, his voice composed though he was clearly upset.

"Another steer?" she asked with dismay, thinking immediately of the rustlers. "Did they actually kill one?"

"No, not a steer," Redhawk said, and looked up at her, his expression guarded. "Miz O'Brannoch, you just found yourself a human skeleton."

Chapter 3

Rhiannon jumped back in horror. "Jesus, Mary and Joseph. *Human?*"

Hawk got to his feet. "Don't worry, it's probably just an old Indian burial. They turn up every now and then. I'll call the state archaeologist when we get to town."

She stared at him incredulously. "You're just going to leave it here?"

"It's against the law to disturb archaeological remains. The last thing I need is to get slapped with a fine. We'll mark the location, but leave it exactly where it is."

First dead cows, now dead humans. Rhiannon swallowed her dread and got into the hired car as Redhawk instructed. She steered as he put the Jeep into four-wheel drive and pulled her clear of the sandy verge. Fitz jumped in with her and they followed the Jeep down the fifteen dusty miles to the highway, then the twenty more to Windmill Junction, the nearest town where she could turn in the car.

Windmill Junction was no bigger today than it had been yesterday when she'd stopped at the lone petrol station to ask for directions to Irish Heaven. The highway was the main street in town. Along it were strung out a small assortment of sleepy storefronts, a seedy-looking motel, a run-down grocery store and an old log cabin set in the middle of a dirt parking lot behind a faded sign that declared it to be Pete's Gem and Mineral Emporium and Indian Trading Post.

"This is where I get off," Fitz said, motioning her to pull over in front of a place a bit further down called Jake's Saloon. This was where they'd arranged to meet Hawk after they'd all done their errands. Fitz's errand consisted of having a pint and catching up with the locals.

"You're sure you'll be all right on your own?" she asked.

Hawk had already assured her everyone who frequented Jake's knew each other, and that someone would keep an eye on her uncle if he had one of his spells of forgetfulness. But she still worried. He'd already called her Janet once that morning. What if he forgot they were picking him up?

"I'll be fine, love. See you in an hour or so."

She watched him walk in through the swinging saloon doors and shook her head at the image.

Human skeletons and swinging saloon doors.

Welcome to the wild, wild West.

After dropping off the hired car, she started walking back toward Jake's. Maybe she could find a place to buy an inexpensive pair of blue jeans along the way. Very inexpensive.

They'd retrieved her suitcase from the rental car and it was now loaded into the Jeep. But everything in it was madly inappropriate for Arizona, her tweeds and woolens too hot and itchy for the ninety-plus temperatures. Perhaps the store advertising boots and western wear in the window across the street might have something on sale.

"I'm sure we've got just what you need," said the girl behind the cash register, and led Rhiannon to the rear of the store.

She stood and gaped. The back wall was literally covered with shelves containing stacks and stacks of nothing but blue jeans. She looked at the girl with a touch of awe. "I think I'll need help."

Half an hour later she stood in front of the mirror and admired the ones she'd finally decided on that were on sale. What would Redhawk's reaction be when he saw her in them? Maybe it would wipe the scowl from his face. For a second, anyway.

"Good choice," the sales girl said. "Sexy but practical. Should last you five years of hard ropin' and ridin'." The girl shot her a wink. "Long as you keep off your knees, if you know what I mean. Now, how 'bout some boots?"

Rhiannon glanced regretfully at the long shelves filled with rows of western boots, then down at the sturdy brown shoes on her feet beneath the jeans she'd decided to keep on. "I wish I could. But not today." She'd seen the price tags. She was doing well to afford the jeans.

"You might try the consignment store down the street. Sometimes they have some real nice boots there. And they're a lot cheaper than new."

"Thanks," Rhiannon said, and decided to give it a try. She had almost no money left, but if she was going to do any real work on the ranch she'd need boots.

To her delight she found a perfect pair, pleasantly broken in but still in great shape. The fact that they were bright pink had driven the price down to the point where she could not only afford them but actually have a few dollars left over. Apparently, real cowgirls didn't wear pink.

At the cash register, a display of bandannas caught her eye. There was even a pink one.

The saleslady saw her looking and said, "What you really need is one of those." She pointed at a mannequin wearing a much larger bandanna as a top, folded like an envelope over the front and tied in the back.

Rhiannon blinked. "Oh, I could never—"

"See? You can even tie it this way." The sales lady picked up one of the patterned squares, looped it around her back then forward over her breasts, crossing in front Greek style and tying the ends behind her neck. "But only wear it this way if you're with a guy you really like." She waggled her eyebrows.

Complete exposure would be only a flick of the fabric away. Rhiannon was scandalized.

And intrigued.

How would the stubbornly disinterested Mr. Jackson react to *that* one? Not that his reaction was important. But it irked her to be so thoroughly…unnoticed.

"I'll take it," she said on a mad whim, her face instantly heating.

What was she thinking? Never mind. Too late now.

The saleslady threw in a thick pair of socks so Rhiannon could wear the boots along with her jeans. She tucked the bandanna discretely into a bag with her skirt and pumps as she left the shop. Her white blouse was a little prissy for jeans and boots, but it would have to do for now. She wasn't ready to try out the bandanna just yet. Later. When she was alone. Or nearly so.

The cowboy boots felt strange to walk in as she turned toward Jake's. Stiff, with their thick leather stovepipe sides and low wooden heels. But not unpleasant. More like…substantial. Protective. Like nothing could harm her while she wore them.

She couldn't ever remember feeling this way before. Odd that it should come in this exotic foreign place, amid people she didn't know, from something as unlikely as footwear.

She walked into Jake's, and every head in the place turned to stare. She stood self-consciously for a moment as her eyes adjusted to the darkness. The sharp smell of beer, hard liquor and an echo of cigar and cigarette smoke assaulted her, along with the sight of Redhawk leaning against the bar talking to a pretty brunette with big brown eyes.

"Over here, love!" she heard Fitz call from the other end.

She waved and walked right past Redhawk, ignoring him. What did she care if he talked to pretty brunettes?

"These are my friends Otis, Jim and Pete. And this is Rhiannon," Fitz said, taking her hand in his. "Janet's girl."

The other three men mumbled greetings and gazed at her with interest.

"Aye, the prettiest girl in County Kerry." Fitz took a swig from his glass. "But don't try to be takin' her, lads. She belongs to me brother Jamie."

Rhiannon looked at him with concern. He was doing it again.

On the other side of the room, someone dropped coins into the jukebox with a *ching-kaching-ching*. The whine of steel guitars filled the room.

Fitz focused on the swinging saloon doors. "Lower your voices, lads. That quisling Burton Grant just walked in. What's he doin' here?"

"Having lunch as always, Fitz," Pete answered, shooting Rhiannon a dry smile.

His friends must be familiar with his lapses of time and place. She still hadn't gotten used to it. Being constantly mixed up with her mother was a bit disconcerting.

"How's it goin', boys?" Burton Grant paused by their table and turned to Fitz. "Hear you had another visit from them rustlers, O'Brannoch."

"How did you know that?" Fitz demanded.

Grant tipped his sheriff's hat back on his head with a finger. "I have the sight," he said, his voice holding a hint of irritation. He scanned the table and his gaze halted on her, giving her a double take. "So who do we have here?"

"Fitz's niece, Rhiannon," Pete said.

"Janet's girl," Otis added.

"Here for a visit?" Grant asked her with an interested smile. He looked about forty, handsome in a clean-cut way.

"Helping out at the ranch for a while." She shook his hand when he offered it.

He held on to it as he said, "A pleasure, Miz O'Brannoch. Let me know if the Sheriff's Office can be of any service to you."

"Why, thank you, Constable Grant. I will."

He chuckled and let her go. "It's Deputy, actually. But please, call me Burt."

He really had the nicest smile.

"You two ready to get back? It's getting late." Redhawk's sharp voice came from right behind, making her jump.

She spun to find him scowling down at her. He was standing close. Too close. She resisted the impulse to step back from his tall frame.

Fitz scrambled out of his seat. "Aye. It's starting to stink in here."

"Uncle Fitz!"

"That's all right, Miz O'Brannoch." Burt gave her a lopsided grin. "Your uncle's got it in his head I'm some traitor from the old country. Must be the uniform."

"No doubt. Well, I'm pleased to meet you—"

"Hate to break up the party, but I've got work to do," Redhawk interrupted, putting a firm hand to the small of her back and turning her toward the swinging doors. "Let's go."

She just managed to wave a goodbye to Burt and Fitz's friends before her uncle and his pushy foreman herded her outside.

"Well, I never. That was rude!" she exclaimed.

"Your uncle doesn't like the man. Pick someone else to make eyes at."

The Jeep was parked right out front, and Hawk didn't stop pushing her until she was at the driver's side door, which he yanked open.

"I wasn't—"

"You drive." He stood, hands planted on his hips, glaring at her. Correction: at her new jeans. With an expression that warred between fury and masculine appreciation.

Whatever his game was, she wouldn't be unsettled by him.

"Like what you see?" she asked.

His flinty perusal slid down her legs. "Thought you didn't wear denim."

"Changed my mind. Since I'm staying."

He stepped in close. "And how long are you planning on staying?"

She tilted her head up to meet his gaze. There was not a spark of flirtation in it. Her pulse sped. He was trying to intimidate her.

"As long as Uncle Fitz needs me," she said. "You have a problem with that, Mr. Jackson?"

"Would it matter if I did?"

"No."

They stared at each other for long seconds, like two wolves sizing each other up.

"Hurt him and you'll have me to answer to," he said in a growl low enough only she could hear.

His threat took her by surprise. It should have made her angry. But it had the opposite effect. Redhawk's loyalty to her uncle put his wariness about her in a very different light.

"You've got nothing to worry about," she assured him quietly.

"And stay away from Burton Grant," he said, then turned to Fitz. "Let's go, old man."

The drive back to the ranch was long, made even longer by Redhawk's broody presence on the narrow rear bench of the Jeep. She drove, getting used to the feel of the vehicle, since it would be hers for the duration. Fitz slept. All the way. Even over the dirt washboard track that led up to the ranch. Maybe he'd had a mite more than a pint.

"Did you get hold of the state archaeologist?" she asked Hawk as they passed the spot where they'd marked the skeleton.

"She'll be out to investigate it in the next few days," he answered, then clammed up again.

Rhiannon wondered if he was always this terse, or if it was only with her. He hadn't seemed to have a problem talking to that brunette back at the bar. She'd even seen him smile.

Not that she'd noticed or anything.

She sighed in frustration. It wasn't as if she wanted her uncle's hired hand to make a move on her. But was it too much to ask that he occasionally spoke to her? Just to break the vast, overwhelming silence of this strange place?

She'd thought it was quiet on the farm, but by comparison there'd been a veritable symphony of noise. The bells and the lowing of the cows in the pasture, the Dublin train whistling in the distance, the chatter of Aunt Bridget's parakeet and the radio playing in the kitchen, the frogs and the seagulls and Uncle Patrick's yapping dogs outside.

Here there was none of that, save at dawn and dusk, which were the only times anything seemed to stir in this bloody heat. Only the endless, penetrating, maddening silence all around for a thousand miles. At times the sheer hugeness of scale nearly overwhelmed her.

When they got back to the ranch, Rhiannon pulled to a stop in front of the barn to let Hawk out.

Fitz woke up in the passenger seat and peered around. "Where are we?" he asked.

"We're home," Hawk told him gently. He unfolded his body from the cramped back bench and jumped to the ground. "Help Rhiannon put the groceries away, okay?"

Fitz blinked over at her. "Janet?"

"No, Uncle Fitz," she said, and introduced herself for the dozenth time.

He glanced tentatively at Redhawk, who smiled and nodded.

"Yes, Rhiannon. I remember," he said, but she was sure he once again had no idea who she was. His trust in Hawk's guidance, however, was obvious.

As she drove the few yards to the ranch house, she made up her mind. She had to get to the bottom of the enigma that was Redhawk Jackson. Find out why he disliked her so much. Dispel his mistaken belief that she somehow wanted to hurt her uncle.

Maybe then they could live together under the same roof without walking on eggshells. Have a normal conversation now and again. Maybe even become friends.

Perhaps more than friends.

She took a mental step back at the errant thought.

True, she was attracted to Redhawk. More than attracted, to be quite honest. His long, tall body was deadly gorgeous, and his face, with its dark angles and sun-creased eyes, made her ever so weak in the knees. Especially when he gave her one of those bone-melting once-overs of his. The man was walking, talking sex in a Stetson.

Okay, maybe not so much talking. Still, who needed talk when a man looked as good as he did?

No, wait a minute. She had to screw her head on right.

She *did* need him to talk.

Just talk.

So they could be friends.

Just friends.

She wasn't here for romance. She was done with romance. Robbie Trevalian had taught her you could know a man for years and still be deceived by his charming smile, believing his lies, all the while setting yourself up for heartache of epic proportions. Just as her mother had been deceived by her father. Love was for the gullible. Not her.

No, it would be a good long time before Rhiannon O'Brannoch would again trust a man, if ever. With her heart, at any rate.

But that didn't mean she couldn't look. After all, Irish women never shied away from appreciating a fine specimen of the male species. Looking was safe enough.

And talking.

As long as she kept her wits about her. And as long as the male in question felt like talking.

Which brought her back to her original quandary.

How to make the man talk?

Hawk eased down into the warm water with a long sigh. *Heaven.* After spending the afternoon stringing new barbed wire where the rustlers had cut it, the pulled muscle in his shoulder burned like fire and his knee wobbled like a one-year-old's. But all of that was forgotten the moment his body submerged into the sun-heated cocoon of his private Jacuzzi.

The day had ended, but the blazing remnants of sunset lingered on the horizon, the cobalt-blue sky oozing down onto the red earth like giant crayons melting over the distant cliffs.

His dirty clothes hung from the fence rail, his boots stood where he'd dropped them on the ground below, and three cold, dripping bottles of Colorado's finest sat in a neat line on the edge of the long, narrow cattle trough awaiting their turn to help numb his mind and the soreness of his muscles.

He'd been waiting for this moment all day.

Pulling his hat over his eyes, he let his body unfurl and relax, floating down until he could rest his neck and head on the rough metal lip of the short end. Even with his six-foot-plus frame, there was a foot or two to spare. Enough to seat a whole other person, if the occasion ever presented itself.

"Mind if I join you?" Rhiannon's voice said just above him.

With a huge splash, he airplaned his arms to sit up, sputtering water that swamped over him when he slid into the trough. He righted his dripping hat and glared at her, grabbing his sore shoulder.

"What the hell are you doing here?"

She was wearing a flimsy white dress with no sleeves. And the ridiculous pink boots she'd bought that morning.

"I saw you get in," she said, dipping a few fingers into the water. "Looks refreshing."

If she saw him getting in, she also saw him stripping out of his clothes. *All* of his clothes.

He clamped his jaw. "It *is* refreshing."

"In that case…" She pulled off her boots, climbed into the opposite end of the trough and sat down in the water, dress and all.

He couldn't believe it.

"You do realize I'm naked," he informed her, making no move to cover himself with his hat.

That mischievous smile played on her lips, but this time it was far from prim. "Shy?"

She didn't wait for an answer, but slid down under the water, intimately tangling her feet and legs with his. Too intimately for comfort. He gritted his teeth harder. She reemerged a moment later wet from head to toe and sat up again. He swallowed. Her white dress had all but disappeared.

"No, I'm not shy," he choked out. "But I thought you might be."

She winked. "I have my slip on."

"Not anymore," he said, taking in the view. Damn, she was beautiful. Slim and curvy in all the right places.

She glanced down and her eyes flared. "Oh, for heaven's sake." She plucked at the transparent fabric over her plump breasts in a belated show of modesty. "Oh, dear." She looked up, her cheeks turning pink.

"Guess you've never been in a wet T-shirt contest."

"A what?"

"Never mind," he said, leaning back against the short end again, relaxing into the beginnings of a grin. Waiting to see what she'd do. It was nice having the advantage for a change. Her legs brushing against his were even nicer. "Doesn't bother me to share," he told her, "if it doesn't bother you."

"In that case…" To his surprise, she leaned back, too. She bent her knees up, no doubt thinking it would block his view. It didn't. Just made it more intriguing.

Her breasts peeked out above her knees, round and perfect, not too big, not too small, with pretty, dusky-rose nipples that made his mouth start to water and other body parts begin to stir. He didn't dare look any lower.

What was going on here? Grabbing a bottle from the fence rail, he wrenched it open and took a really big swig. Then remembered his manners.

"Beer?" he asked, reaching for one of the spares and twisting off the cap.

"Ta," she said. She had to lean forward to take it. His parts lurched painfully.

Not good.

"Damn, woman, is this *you* getting creative?" he ground out, certain she was tormenting him on purpose. Though he couldn't for the life of him figure out why.

"Perhaps," she said, tilting her head, studying him.

He froze. Surely she didn't want to— No. This had to be a failure to communicate because of the language difference. It still happened with Fitz occasionally. She couldn't possibly mean—

"You're saying you *want* me to drag you off to my teepee?" he asked, his mind scrambling just in case she actually meant it.

Did he want to? Oh, yeah. His body was definitely ready.

Was it a good idea? No damn way.

Would that stop him…?

"Don't be silly. I know I'm safe with you, " she said with a funny smile. Not a mischievous or seductive one, but somehow sadly knowing. His budding fantasies screeched to a halt.

Safe?

Knees bent, her legs rested between his to about midcalf. It would be easy enough to reverse that and take what he wanted if he were so inclined. Which he wasn't, of course. But still.

"How can you be so sure you're safe?" he asked, feeling vaguely and unreasonably insulted, all things considered.

"Because you don't like me."

Ah.

He regarded her in the growing darkness, her wet hair curling in fiery tendrils around her face and shoulders. It wasn't true— far from true—but he'd *acted* like he disliked her since their first meeting. Spoken aloud so brutally, her matter-of-fact assessment shamed him deeply. But he wasn't willing to admit it just yet.

However… Damn, if she really wanted him, who was he to refuse?

Underwater, he curled his foot past the hem of her slip and forward, then trailed his toes lightly along the back of her bare thigh. Her mouth parted.

"I'm liking you more by the minute," he said, giving her a lazy come-and-get-me smile.

She put a hand on his ankle and set his foot away. "That's just sex," she said quietly.

He hiked a brow. "I thought that's what you wanted."

"No," she said.

Okay, miscommunication it was. He settled back again, tossing his hat onto the fencepost. Uncertain whether he should be massively disappointed or grateful for the reprieve from his own foolishness.

"If not sex, then what *do* you want?" he asked.

Like there were a lot of choices. How stupid could he get, thinking it was *him* she was interested in?

What the hell. May as well get all the bad news in one fell swoop so he could move on with his life. Or what would be left of it after she'd stolen the best part.

"I want to be friends."

Right. He sighed and tipped his beer, draining the contents in two swallows. "I doubt that's possible," he said, wincing at a painful twang in his shoulder when he set it down.

After a short pause she said, "Did you hurt your shoulder?"

"Yeah. Loading the steer yesterday."

"Turn around, then. I'll massage the muscles for you."

He gazed into her face. How could a woman be so wise and so naive at the same time? "Thanks, but I'll pass."

Lifting her own shoulder, she handed him her beer and he held it, not sure what would happen next. Cupping her hands, she scooped up water from the trough and let it trickle down onto her neck and chest. The light was almost gone by now, but he could see the silhouette of enjoyment on her face. Such a simple gesture, but the sensuality of it took his breath away.

Why couldn't it have been him she wanted?

"Tell me," she said, splashing her face, "why you don't like me."

Watching her pour, he thought about what he should say, how much, if he should say anything at all or simply take his disappointment like a man.

"It's complicated," he said.

She just looked at him.

"Fine," he said, his body humming with unwanted attraction. Maybe telling her the unvarnished truth would remind him why he shouldn't want her so much. "My mom was a drunk. My dad left when I was still a baby and she didn't deal well with being a single parent. I took the brunt of it."

He heard Rhiannon's soft murmur, felt her sympathy. But he didn't want pity. His mother had been no mother at all, and his childhood a living hell of empty liquor bottles and bare cupboards. But all that was ancient history. He was over it a long time ago. Thanks to Fitz.

"In junior high I was always in trouble. Small stuff. Joyriding. Shoplifting. Graffiti. When I was fifteen I quit school. Short time later I got arrested for possession and was given the choice of getting straight and finding a job or doing jail time. Took me two months before I found anyone willing to take a chance on a mouthy, messed-up Paiute kid with a chip on his shoulder the size of Ship Rock."

"Fitz."

Redhawk nodded. "He gave me a job mucking stables, riding fences and shifting cattle. Offered me a bed in the bunkhouse and listened to me bellyache about the unfairness of the world, all the while teaching me about the ranch. When I won the bull-riding event at the Ganado Rodeo two years running, he told me I had talent and to go out there and grab some glory in the world."

He chuckled, remembering that night. He'd been so shocked that anyone had said something positive about him, at first he'd thought Fitz was just looking for a reason to fire his ass. But then he'd realized his protector was always saying good things to him or about him.

"The next day I left Irish Heaven determined to make Fitz proud and return with a pot of money to buy the string of Irish Thoroughbreds he dreamed of raising."

Hawk put the bottle to his lips and drank before he remembered it wasn't his. He stretched it out to her. "Sorry."

"No, go ahead. I'm not thirsty."

He took another sip and fancied he could taste her on it, where she'd put it to her mouth, maybe touched it with her tongue. He closed his eyes against the unwilling rush in his groin.

"Things didn't work out the way I planned," he forced himself to say as a distraction.

"Your knee. You were injured riding."

"Yep."

"So you came back here."

"Yep."

"And you're afraid I'll take your place with Fitz."

He opened his eyes and looked at her. Her pale skin glowed, reflecting the rising moon behind him. Her nipples were hard and made small shadows on the fabric of her slip where they poked at it. It was no use. He still wanted her so badly he could taste it.

He took a steadying breath. "When I was young and he was drunk he sometimes talked about Janet, your mother. How she'd promised to come to Arizona. When I came back after getting hurt, he only mentioned her once. To say she'd died. He wrote you letters but he never expected you to come. I never expected you to come. He always said…"

He let the thought drift away and reached for the third bottle on the rail, twisting off the cap in two kinds of frustration.

They lay there soaking in the darkness together, and he willed his blood to calm. The stillness of the night was broken only by the muted lap of water against metal and a lone hoot of one of the barn's resident owls. Good thing he wasn't Navajo. The Navajo believed the call of an owl portended a coming death. Perhaps the death of a dream…

Finally Rhiannon spoke. "He expected my mother to come here, to Irish Heaven?"

Confused at first, Hawk suddenly realized while he was going through his own private agony, she'd forgotten all about him and was going through a quite different one herself.

"Yeah. I always thought—"

He stopped there. Best left unsaid what he thought. He wasn't sure it was true, anyway.

She fell silent again. He liked that about her. That she didn't feel the need to fill the warm night air with noise and chatter. That she appreciated the subtle living, breathing sense of quiet that was the desert. It was clean and uncomplicated. As he wished his life were.

"You expected to inherit Irish Heaven," she murmured.

Not a question. Not a condemnation. Just a statement by one who knew that the facts he so desperately believed in were impossible.

"Yeah." He sighed. "When I came back and decided to stay, he made me a promise. He said one day it would all be mine."

"And then I showed up."

"And then you showed up." There wasn't much more to say about that.

"He must have sent me the ticket because I wrote him my father had left the farm to my mother's sister instead of to me."

Hawk sat up. "What?" He'd heard about the farm, of course, and Jamie, Rhiannon's jailed IRA terrorist father and Fitz's brother, in countless stories Fitz had told about Ireland over the years. But the inheritance detail he'd left out. "When was this?"

"Last month."

So recently. "Why did your father do that?"

"I have no idea," she answered in an unsteady voice.

Damn. No wonder she wanted Irish Heaven. Now everything made more sense. Everything but Fitz's betrayal of his word. Except, he couldn't blame an old man rapidly losing his memory for failing to remember a promise made years ago. It was no betrayal. He'd simply forgotten. Rhiannon was family. Family inherited from family. That's the way it worked. Those who had no family were just plain out of luck.

Far away to the west a coyote howled, answered by another in the cliffs to the east. A third joined in, closer by, somewhere on ranch land. *His* ranch land.

"Does he have a will?" she asked.

"I don't know."

"We should ask him. Settle this thing so both of us know where we stand."

"No," Redhawk said, shaking his head. "He's got enough worries without bringing up dying, too."

Truth be told, Hawk didn't want to know. Not yet. If he knew, he'd be forced to act, one way or another. Give up the dream and hit the road, or live with the guilt of taking away yet another rightful inheritance from a woman he was growing to respect more by the minute…aside from wanting her so badly his whole body ached.

The whole situation sucked big-time. And there was no way to fix it.

Unless…

Toying with the beginnings of an idea, he studied the woman in front of him. In the moonlight she looked so beautiful and fragile, her white gown floating around her legs like a ghostly shroud, her red-gold hair falling over her shoulders in ringlets as it dried. He knew better; she was strong and used to hard work. She was feisty and gutsy, both traits that would serve her well in this harsh land.

And she was sexy as hell. Her curvy body had driven him crazy from the first time he'd clapped eyes on it. And he was hard as a fence post for want of her.

He could do a lot worse.

He reached over and took her hands from the rim of the trough where they lay, tugging her gently to sit up. He slid in closer, threading his legs under her knees then between her hips and the metal sides. Her feet skimmed past his waist as their bodies fit together in an ancient puzzle.

"What are you doing?"

She watched him warily but didn't pull away. He liked that about her, too. She didn't frighten easily.

He slipped his hand under her thick veil of damp hair and curled his fingers around the back of her neck, urging her face closer to his. "I'm getting creative."

Her deep green eyes widened. "Wh-what?"

He tipped his head, angling his nose next to hers, stopping just short of touching her lips with his. "I've thought of a way to solve our problem."

"Problem?" Uncertainty stampeded across her face. "What problem?"

Her wet-warm breasts brushed against his chest, tips beaded and begging for attention. *His* attention.

"The one about who inherits Irish Heaven."

"Oh?" She swallowed and made a weak attempt to draw away from him. He didn't let her.

"Yeah."

"How so?" Her hands fluttered over his ribs and up, then lightly touched down on his shoulders before taking flight again and finding his elbows. *Safe?* Her breath fanned his cheek, sweet and quick.

Not.

"We can both inherit."

This would work. It had to.

"I don't understand."

"It's simple." He eased out his tongue and drew it along her lower lip. Tasting paradise.

He felt her tremble. "It is?"

"Mmm-hmm. All we have to do is…"

The cool fabric of her slip tickled his inner thighs and he wished it were her fingers. Groaning softly, he put his free hand on the small of her back and held her still, savoring the tightness of anticipation in his throat at the thought of possessing this amazing woman.

"Is what?" she whispered.

And as he lowered his mouth to hers, he uttered the words he never thought to say in this lifetime.

"All we have to do," he said, "is get married."

Chapter 4

Married?

Utterly gobsmacked, Rhiannon stared uncomprehendingly at the man who held her in his arms. Before she could respond, his mouth came down and he kissed her. His tongue teased as his lips moved erotically over hers, then it slipped deep into her, shocking her to the core.

But he tasted so good, felt so wonderful as he surrounded her in a tight embrace, she forgot completely what they were talking about. Something about— No, she must have misheard.

An unbidden sound of need escaped her, and she looped her arms around his neck, melting into his breathtaking kiss.

Oh, how she'd wanted to taste him! Ever since that first spark of sexual awareness about five seconds after they met. Why else would she have climbed so wantonly into his bath wearing nothing but a gossamer nightshift, except to experience exactly this? She'd even carefully counted the days since her last mense, and concluded she'd be safe even if things went further than she'd planned to go.

Lord, he was every bit as luscious as she'd imagined. His naked, virile body crushed into her, making water splash everywhere, his muscles bulging and rock hard beneath smooth, dusky skin. Perched on his lap, it was impossible to miss his arousal. Long and hard, he was silk on steel as he pressed between her legs. She was giddy with blossoming sensation. It had been so long.

His strong hands pulled her closer, kneading and roaming over her as his tongue ravished her mouth.

And it had never been like this.

She kissed him back, deeply, tasting him, smelling his musky scent, touching his strong, well-knit torso. Reveling in the feeling of being truly alive, at long last. All her life it seemed she'd been waiting for this very moment, to break free of her cotton-wool shell and really *feel* something—other than frustration and disappointment.

What she felt now was the warm desert breeze on her skin as Redhawk's fingers found the row of small buttons on her slip and quickly got them open. He wrenched apart the bodice, exposing her breasts to his caress. His work-rough hands closed over them, and she gasped in pleasure, breaking their fevered kiss with a low moan.

Their eyes met, and with an expression dark as midnight he watched her, drawing his thumbs over the beaded tips, tightening the threads of desire within her so taut she bowed backward in a half-moon of need.

"So beautiful," he murmured, and eased her back against his upraised knees. He cupped her breasts and closed his mouth over an aching nipple.

"Oh!" she cried, and his name tumbled from her lips in a low keen. *"Hawk…"*

"I'm right here, darlin'."

He tugged her slip up and adjusted her on his lap until the ridge of his arousal pressed firmly against her center. She gasped his name again, as he held her hips and ground his iron length into her soft folds. His rough groan joined hers, turning to harsh breaths as he continued to rub her in erotic circles.

She threw her head back, and the stars winked at her from a black, spangled sky so vast it made her dizzy.

Or maybe it was the first glimmer of climax. "Please. Don't stop," she sobbed.

"Never," he gritted out, and took her over the throbbing edge of exquisite pleasure.

His lips briefly found hers again and then she was lifted, his arms banded around her waist. His eyes captured hers and for one breathless moment he held her there, poised above the hot, blunt tip of him. Seeking entrance.

"Yes," she whispered, and instantly he was inside her.

She shuddered, all the way to her soul. She felt filled. Complete. Safe.

Absurd, a little voice murmured in her heart. *He isn't safe.* He was the very opposite. *Dangerous.* That's what Redhawk Jackson was.

And yet, when he held her tight and began to move within her, she didn't listen to the voice. She put her mouth to his and urged him on. *Deeper. Faster. Now!* Until she shattered and he shouted and everything around them whirled into a spinning kaleidoscope of pleasure.

Long moments later Redhawk eased back to lean against his end of the trough, carrying Rhiannon with him. They were still joined, still catching their breath. Still holding each other tight.

She had never felt this good in her life.

"Oh, darlin'," he groaned.

"You were brilliant," she sighed, filled with contentment. "Ta."

He stirred under her and she glanced up to see his amused expression. "I've been called a lot of things before, but I don't believe brilliant was ever one of them," he said with a wry smile.

She chuckled. "An expression. Meaning wonderful, marvelous and amazing."

"You were pretty amazing, yourself, babe. Are all Irish women so responsive? I'm sure I counted three…"

She felt her face go warm. "Yes, well, it's been a while." She laid her cheek on his shoulder and eased her body down, the warm water covering her like a blanket. "But honestly, are all American men so skilled? And, how shall I say…well endowed?"

A low rumble sifted through his chest, and she could hear the smile in his voice. "Keep talkin', woman. Flattery will get you just about anything you want. As long as it's not money or the ranch."

The ranch. Suddenly a chilly shiver went through her as she recalled their earlier conversation.

By the saints, what had she done? The man was out to take away the only place she had left in the world. By allowing him to make love to her, she had granted him power over her—over her body and her emotions. He might also get a notion to try controlling her in other ways.

She must be mad.

"So, shall we set a date?" he asked, settling his arms more firmly about her. "I think the sooner the better."

She blinked. "Date?"

"To get married."

The words whirled through her troubled mind like a North Sea storm. She froze. "Surely, you weren't serious," she said.

"Hell, yeah. It's the perfect solution to who gets the ranch. We both will. And being a couple obviously won't be too much of a hardship on either of us." His callused hand smoothed over her backside to curve intimately between her thighs.

His hand felt so good, and he made the idea sound so logical Rhiannon was almost tempted to go along with it. Almost. However, even if marriage were the most rational and reasonable answer to their situation—and to be sure, she wasn't convinced it was—there was one big difficulty.

"But, Hawk…"

Extracting herself carefully from his embrace, she sat up, knees bent. Which she quickly realized wasn't the brightest move. The feel of his hard, naked body beneath her made her nether regions tingle with delighted recollection of the past hour. The full moonlight shone off the burnished-copper skin of his broad chest, catching the red glow of the sandstone cliffs around them. He really was the most magnificent example of masculinity she'd ever encountered. She had to close her eyes against the overwhelming temptation of belonging to this man.

He sighed, and when she opened her eyes he was gazing at her with displeasure.

"But what?" he said, his voice cool.

"We hardly know each other." His brows rose and she grimaced. "Having sex doesn't count. I freely admit I'm attracted to you. More than attracted. But where I come from, marriage is forever. I want to be in love with the man I marry."

"Where I come from, when a woman makes love to a man who's just proposed marriage, it generally means yes."

"I honestly didn't think— Hawk, getting married just because it's convenient would be wrong. For both of us."

His mouth thinned. Grasping her hips, he sat up and set her away from him, on the other end of the trough. "In other words, you want the ranch all for yourself." He exhaled angrily, swung out of the water and onto the ground so quickly she had to shield herself from the splash.

"No, that's not—"

"Save it. I'm not interested in your philosophy of love and marriage. I get that you don't want to share. Anything." He leaned into her face. "But make no mistake. Irish Heaven is everything to me, and I've worked my ass off for it. Try to take it away, and you're in for one hell of a fight."

Her jaw dropped. How the man could be so tender and warm one moment, then cold as ice the next? He grabbed his clean clothes and stomped off, and she snapped her jaw shut. Rhiannon might be a newcomer to this land, but she was no stranger to hard work. And she was Fitz's flesh and blood. Irish Heaven was her second chance at a new beginning, and she didn't mean to lose it.

Fine. If it was a fight Mr. Redhawk Jackson wanted, then a fight was exactly what he'd get.

Stupid.

Really, really stupid.

What had *possessed* him to make love to that woman? Or worse, propose marriage?

Hawk zipped up his jeans, threw his boots onto the porch and slammed the screen door behind him. Marching to the middle of the kitchen floor—the annoyingly immaculate kitchen floor— he stopped and forced himself to take several deep breaths.

Easy, boy.

Going off half-cocked was not going to solve this one. He'd already done that once tonight—okay, twice—and look where that had landed him. He had to think. Hard. Somehow find a way to get rid of the woman. Fast.

Before the need to be inside her again overwhelmed what was left of his rapidly dwindling mental capacity.

Damn, she'd felt good. And the way she'd held him close, kissed him long and tender, it was almost as though…

He slashed a hand roughly through his hair. No. All that was lies. Any emotion he'd felt in her response to him had been in his own desperate imagination.

He took a final calming breath and realized it was spiced with salsa and refried beans. There was a note on the table, which had been set for two.

"Hawk and Rhiannon, dinner's on the stove when you finish your bath. I'm thinking I'll have an early night. Hugs, Fitz."

Hawk squeezed his temples between a thumb and forefinger.

So he'd seen them together. Great. Lord knew what conclusions he'd leaped to. Hell. Redhawk was no monk and Fitz knew it, but he'd always kept his affairs off the ranch. What would the old man think about his foreman seducing his innocent niece right under his nose?

He snorted. Innocent, nothing. She'd watched him undress, worn a practically transparent slip and joined him in his bath without blinking an eye. All that pointed to premeditation. *He* was the one who'd been seduced.

But why?

Did she think he'd trade the ranch for the use of her body?

He frowned, anger filling him. It was possible. She hadn't come across as that kind of woman, but... What other explanation was there? He had to find out.

The back door opened and Rhiannon walked in, her invisible dress clinging to her curves and dripping a trail of water on the floor as she beelined it to the laundry room. Belatedly, he realized she was carrying the dirty clothes he'd left hanging on the railing.

"I'll take care of those," he said, striding to catch up.

"That's quite all right," she said with her chin in the air.

He'd meant to protest further, but his attention snagged on her perfect bottom, perfectly visible through the drenched fabric as she bent over to put his things in the hamper. Before he was conscious of moving he was standing behind her, palms itching, battling not to flip up the thin see-through veil and take her again right there.

She turned, gasped at his nearness, and backed into the hamper so he had to reach out to catch her when she stumbled. Her eyes widened as he grasped her arm, pressing his fingers into her soft flesh. They stared silently at each other for an endless moment, sparks arcing between them. Her nipples peaked, swirling into tight, hard buds beneath the bodice she hadn't bothered to button back up.

"Are you on the Pill?" he asked harshly, reality suddenly smacking him in the gut.

Her eyes narrowed. "'Tis a little late to be asking now, wouldn't you say?" she retorted.

"At the time I didn't think it mattered. I'd just asked you to marry me."

Her mouth parted, surprise flitting across her face. After a slight hesitation she said, "No, I'm not on the Pill. But I counted days. We're fine."

"The rhythm method?" he asked, incredulous.

"I'm quite regular. Not that it will be an issue in future." She tried tugging her arm from his grasp, but again he found perverse pleasure in preventing her escape.

"Oh?" He held on to her and slid a deliberate finger down the edge of her bodice. He wanted to push her, to find out what she was up to. But mostly he wanted to touch her again. "What makes you say that?"

She sucked in her breath when he slowly scraped aside the wet fabric covering her breast, exposing her, and trailed his knuckles over the pebbled tip.

"We both—" Her voice cracked.

"Both what?"

She cleared her throat. "Agreed that making love was a mistake."

His mouth was watering so badly he barely resisted leaning down and sucking on her rosy nipple until she—

Damn.

He set his jaw and cupped her breast provokingly. "I believe what we did was have sex. And neither of us objected, so I noticed." He squeezed her nipple gently between his fingers, making her whimper softly. He wanted to do more, do it harder, make her cry his name in pleasure-pain, but he forced himself to drop his hand and let her go.

"I'll buy condoms," he said levelly, and handed her a towel from the shelf. "Meanwhile, supper's ready. Let's eat."

He turned and walked as calmly as he could back to the kitchen where he set about getting the food on the table. When she scurried past him to rush up the stairs, he called after her, "Five minutes. Don't make me wait."

He figured she'd disappear upstairs and try to hide out, but he wasn't about to let her. He wanted her across the table from him, having to meet his eyes. He wanted to push her until she broke, one way or another.

To his surprise she appeared two minutes early, dressed and her hair combed and pulled back into a neat ponytail.

"Mr. Jackson," she pronounced carefully.

He paused in dishing up the salad and nailed her with a bald look. If she was going to lecture him ten minutes after giving him the most intense sex of his life, she'd at least call him by his first name.

Her gaze flicked away momentarily, then returned to his face. "Redhawk," she started again, then licked her lips and gave up. "Look, there's something that needs saying here."

If he'd thought he intimidated her with his boldness in the laundry room, he was obviously mistaken. She didn't look the least bit intimidated.

"Yeah?" This ought to be interesting.

She sat up in her chair and straightened her silverware with long, tapered fingers. "I claim full responsibility for what happened out in the—" her hand fluttered "—outside tonight. I'm not proud of my behavior, but I fully acknowledge it."

"Nothin' wrong with your behavior," he muttered, and took his seat. "I enjoyed every minute of it."

She picked up her water glass and took a sip. He could see red-flagged reflections of her cheeks in the silvery liquid. "As I said, it would be wrong of us to marry simply because it's convenient. And it would also be wrong of us to continue…to continue to—"

He helpfully supplied a word that made her choke on her water and her cheeks turn scarlet.

"Exactly," she managed after coughing a moment. "Simply

because we are attracted to each other and find ourselves living under one roof doesn't mean we have to lower our standards."

"Thanks very much," he said, regarding her sardonically.

"Standards of *behavior*," she huffed. "I didn't mean— Oh, honestly." She picked up her fork and took a bite of salad. Her eyes widened and she took a quick gulp of water. "What *is* that?"

"Red-chili-pepper dressing. Too hot for you?"

She waved her napkin in front of her mouth. "Surprised me. I wasn't expecting salad to be spicy."

He tipped his head. "Everything's spicy in Arizona. Better get used to it. Now, about us—" she snapped him a glare and he held up his hands "—having sex."

"It won't happen again," she said succinctly.

He bet she even believed that. "Then why did you seduce me tonight?"

She did her best to look indignant. "I didn't."

He scraped up his last bite of salad and started to dish the steaming tamales onto their plates. "Bull."

Avoiding his eyes, she nibbled on her salad. Finally she murmured, "I didn't mean to. I just wanted to get your attention. Find out why you don't like me."

"I like you. And you had my full attention from the first moment I saw you with that steer."

"Because you thought I was a rustler."

He shrugged. "What difference does it make?"

She shrugged back. "None. This is good." She indicated the tamales.

"Not too spicy for you?"

She leveled him a look. "I like spicy."

"Then let me share your bed." It was out before he could stop it. Her lips parted in surprise, then closed. "No."

He shoved away his half-eaten meal. Feeling petulant. And unreasonably angry. He knew he had no right. None at all. He was being stupid and irrational. It was just…

Damn, he wanted her again. Wanted to feel her heat surrounding him. Her curves against him. Her soft moans in his ear.

Hell and damnation.

Of all the women to lust after, this was exactly the wrong one. He'd already realized what a huge mistake that marriage proposal had been. After that, she would never believe his wanting her had nothing to do with the ranch.

Hell, *he* didn't believe it.

How could this have *happened* to him in less than forty-eight hours?

He clenched his jaw.

Hormones, that's how. That had to be it. He refused to believe these strange feelings were anything more than a whopping case of raging hormones.

"Fine," he said, calmly and reasonably. Then he calmly and reasonably pulled his plate back and calmly and reasonably began eating again.

There. See? He could be calm and reasonable about this.

"Burton Grant seemed nice," she said. "What's Fitz—"

She looked up and halted in midsentence.

Or not.

He jumped to his feet and stalked to the door. Whirling, he pointed a warning finger at her. "Stay. Away. From Burton. Grant."

Chapter 5

Well!

If she didn't know better, she'd have thought Redhawk was jealous.

But she did know better.

Despite her clear refusal, that night and every night for the next week Rhiannon went to bed half expecting him to creep into her darkened room, slip between the sheets and have his jealous, passionate way with her.

Obviously, wishful thinking.

It had been a whole week since their encounter in the trough, and he'd made no attempt to change her mind about repeating it.

In fact, he'd been avoiding her.

He was doing so even now. After dinner he'd mumbled something about bills and buried himself in paperwork at the small, cluttered desk in the corner of the living room and hadn't looked up since. He didn't appear happy.

He could probably use a beer. Rhiannon fetched a bottle and twisted off the cap, setting it in front of him, then stood there, arms folded.

"How many of those do we have left?" he growled, eyeing the beer, a scowl darkening his handsome face.

"Most of a carton," she answered, somewhat surprised at the topic he chose to fuss over this time. He'd been fussing at her all week. And the nicer she'd tried to be, the more and longer he'd fussed.

He jetted out an irritated breath. "Great. Guess we'd better start rationing."

With a raised brow, she scanned the papers strewn in front of him, immediately recognizable as invoices and bank statements. "Is it that bad?"

"Worse." He grabbed the bottle and took a long draught. His old-fashioned wooden office chair creaked as he shifted his large frame to lean back in it. His eyes were tired and filled with worry and frustration. "We barely have enough money for food and propane through the winter. Thank God Fitz installed those solar-powered batteries way back when, or we wouldn't have electricity for lights and the water pump."

She glanced over at the woodstove in the middle of the room. "Guess I'd better add chopping wood to my list of chores."

"You know how to use an ax?"

"I can learn."

He looked none too happy over that prospect, either. He was still in a twist that she'd insisted on taking over several of his outdoor chores along with the house cleaning and laundry. It annoyed her to no end that he didn't believe her capable of doing these things.

She was about to tell him exactly where he could stuff his male chauvinism, when it suddenly struck her that the reaction she was seeing might go much deeper than mere masculine pride. Could Redhawk be the kind of man who wanted to take care of everyone and everything himself? That not being able to do so was making him angry?

She swallowed her retort and asked instead, "Can't you sell some of the cattle?"

"Not until spring, unless we want to take a real dive on the price. And even then, the rustlers have hit us so hard we have to make damned sure every last one of the herd survives the winter in good health. Otherwise we won't earn enough money even come springtime, and we won't have enough calves born to replace the steers we sell, so things will be even tighter next year."

He closed his eyes and swiped a hand over his forehead, pushing back the errant lock of raven-black hair that had fallen out of place. He looked so like a lost little boy trying desperately to find his way in the dark. Her heart went out to him. She wanted nothing more than to round the desk and take him in her arms. To comfort him, and assure him she'd help.

"What I'm really worried about," he said, yanking her back to the real world, "is Fitz's medication. It's so damned expensive. I've run the numbers over and over again, and there's just no way to squeeze it all in. It's either food or his medicine."

A sickening sense of dread washed over her. And déjà vu. She recalled vividly counting out dole pennies during the last year her mother was alive. Pennies to pay the rent, pennies to pay the butcher and the green grocer. There'd seldom been enough left over to pay for her mother's cancer medication. Certainly none to pay for the expensive treatments that might have saved her life.

Her heart sank. This was all her fault. If Fitz hadn't spent all their money on a plane ticket for her...

"Buy the medicine," she said, swallowing the bitter lump of guilt rising in her throat. "I'll find a way to get food."

Hawk's expression mocked. "How?"

"I'll plant a vegetable garden."

"Too late. It's September. It'll start snowing soon."

"I'll get a job."

"Where? Doing what? Besides, foreigners aren't allowed to work here without a work permit. Getting one can take years—unless you marry a U.S. citizen."

She ignored that last comment, delivered in a sardonic tone. "I'll find a way," she told him.

And she would. There wasn't a chance she would go through that torture again—having to choose between starving to death and watching someone you love waste away. She'd sell herself on a street corner before that happened again.

So the next morning, while Redhawk was out checking the cattle and Fitz was watching his favorite game shows on television, Rhiannon climbed in the Jeep and drove into town to find a job.

She started at one end of the few blocks that made up the not-so-sprawling metropolis of Windmill Junction and worked her way down the dusty line of shops, inquiring if they were looking for help.

Nobody asked about a work permit. But nobody was hiring, either.

"Have you tried Jake's?" the girl from the western-wear shop where she'd bought her jeans suggested.

"The saloon?"

"Yeah. I heard Josie up and lit out with a traveling art salesman from Wichita two weeks ago."

"Josie?"

"The barmaid."

She shouldn't ask, but couldn't resist. "Traveling art salesman?"

The salesgirl winked. "Most of his paintings were real ugly. But the guy was cute." She snapped her gum. "A real son of a gun."

Rhiannon smiled cluelessly and thanked her, heading for Jake's. What the heck was a son of a gun?

A barmaid, on the other hand, she knew. Could she do that? She thought about the pubs back home and decided they couldn't be much different here. Just other brands of beer. She'd never worked in a pub, but how hard could it be? The tricky part would be convincing Jake—or whoever owned Jake's—to hire a foreigner with no work permit.

By the time she went through the swinging doors she had her strategy set.

As it turned out, Jake wasn't all that worried about the technicalities of immigration law. But it made her very nervous that Deputy Sheriff Burton Grant was sitting on the next stool the whole time, listening to their conversation. He even nodded approvingly when she suggested Jake buy Fitz's medicine instead of giving her a paycheck.

"We can figure out how many hours I need to work to make it an even trade," she said.

"Smart," Burt remarked. "The old geezer is damned lucky to have you for a niece."

"Naturally, you can keep any tips you make," Jake told her. "Wear somethin' short 'n' tight and you can pull in a right tidy sum on the weekends." He grinned. "Can you start tonight? Bein' Friday night it'll be crazy busy. I could really use the help."

"Yes, indeed. Thank you, Mr—"

"Just Jake. See you at eight."

"Maybe I'll drop by," Burt Grant said with a broad smile.

"That would be lovely," she said, smiling back.

Too late she remembered Redhawk's warning.

Pleased with the progress he'd made in Crimson's training, Hawk rubbed the colt's neck and fed him his reward carrot for standing perfectly still as Hawk removed the saddle. Timing was everything in both cowboying and rodeoing, so a good mount knew to stand steady in all situations.

Now for something more fun. Well, dead serious, but it looked a bit like a parlor trick. Hawk always trained all his horses to "wake me up." You never knew when you'd be knocked unconscious in either line of work, so it was good to know your horse would automatically rouse you back to the world of the living.

In both the desert and the rodeo ring, that could mean the difference between life and death.

Hawk dropped down on the dusty ground of the corral and lay perfectly still. Sure enough, Crimson trotted up and started breathing in his face. It was tough not to laugh. The colt's stiff whiskers tickled his cheek, and his breath smelled like old hay. After a moment his soft muzzle began to prod at Hawk's ear and his breath came in hard bursts accompanied by several loud nickers. Yet he was careful not to jostle Hawk's head. There was always the risk of a spinal injury with unconsciousness, so he taught the horse not to move the person, just wake him up.

He was about to open his eyes and reward the colt when Crimson let out a big raspberry, spraying his face with horse spit.

"Hey! Cut that out!" Hawk sat up sputtering, and wiped his face with a sleeve. "No carrot for you, you smart-ass." The horse's eyes sparkled and he swore he heard a laugh under the whinny of protest.

"Very impressive," came an amused female voice from the fence rail.

"Nip it, O'Brannoch," he said, coming to his feet and batting the dust from the back of his jeans and shirt.

She smiled so genuinely, for a second he thought maybe she wasn't there to make fun of him.

"No, I'm serious. That last bit maybe needs work, but I saw the rest. I can't believe the progress you've made with him in the short time I've been here."

He wasn't sure what to say to that, so he swiped his Stetson from its fence post and mumbled, "Thanks."

She followed and watched him give the colt his rubdown. It made him uneasy to have her gaze on him every second. It seemed to register approval, but he couldn't help waiting for the other boot to hit the dirt. With her there was always something.

After several minutes she casually remarked, "I found work today. At Jake's."

Redhawk turned to stare at the woman in disbelief. "Work?" When had that happened? He hadn't even known she'd left the ranch. "At Jake's, the honky-tonk?" At her blank look, he said, "The bar?"

She nodded brightly. "Yes, I start tonight." She glanced at the ranch house. "At eight. Well, I guess I'd better start dinner so I can be ready on time." With that she began walking away before he could get his jaw up off the ground.

"What's that supposed to mean?" he managed, as she ducked under the rail. "How the hell— You'll be out till all hours!"

"I suppose weekends will be late," she agreed. "But I won't be working full-time. Just enough to pay for—" she halted and glanced around quickly "—Fitz's medicine. Jake and I have made an arrangement about my paycheck. To get around the work permit."

"Whatever it is, it can't be legal," Redhawk said, narrow-eyed.

"Well, if it's not, they'll no doubt send me back to Ireland, which would solve your problem neatly," she said, and gave him a tight smile. "Besides, that sheriff's deputy was sitting right there and heard the whole thing, so it can't be illegal."

"Burton Grant?"

Redhawk wasn't sure what Grant had done to Fitz in the past to earn his enmity, but the old man really had it in for the deputy. He was always calling the man a traitor or worse. Redhawk's own dislike had developed only recently—last week when he'd seen how the man had ogled Rhiannon in her shapely new jeans. At Jake's.

He clamped down on a sharp spurt of jealousy. "I don't like it," he stated, the words coming out growly and harsh from deep inside him.

Rhiannon drew herself up ruler-straight. "I'm a big girl now. I'll take care of myself."

Yeah. That was the whole damned problem.

* * *

From his second-floor bedroom window, Hawk stared down at the moonlit dirt track leading to town. The dust from Rhiannon's Jeep driving away had settled a good two hours ago, and he knew rationally she wouldn't be back for hours to come. But he couldn't help looking. Or wanting to run for his truck.

He would not go to Jake's.

First of all, they couldn't afford even the few dollars he'd have to spend on beers to rationalize his being there. And second… Second, he had no freaking business following her around like some lovesick puppy.

He was not lovesick. Not hardly. The woman drove him plumb loco. Poking her nose in everywhere and taking over like she already owned the place. Getting into bathtubs with him. Sleeping in his bed.

Sticking his hands in his pockets, he turned to peer at the rumpled covers and saggy mattress of the bed he'd slept on for over a decade. He should have gotten a new one years ago. But it had never really seemed to matter. He always fell asleep practically before his head hit the pillow, so he'd never noticed if it was saggy or uncomfortable.

It probably was. She probably tossed and turned every night up here because of that old mattress.

He frowned and took a step toward the bed. Maybe he should check it out. Just in case the couch was more comfortable, and he really should trade with her. He took another step.

Yeah. That's what he should do.

He checked his clothes in case they were dusty, but he'd already showered and changed, so he gingerly sat down on the bed, then stretched out. And immediately groaned.

He was assaulted by the scent of her. Sweet, unique and feminine. His body clenched painfully, remembering what it had been like to be surrounded by her, wrapped in her arms, enveloped by the smell of cool desert sage and warm female flesh. The sight of her wild red hair in the moonlight. The slap of water against metal as his body thrust into hers.

Damn and hellfire.

He sat up and ground his palms into his eyes. He had to get a grip. Making love with her had been a mistake. Still lusting after her was an even bigger one. And starting to like her was probably the biggest mistake of all.

Where had that thought come from?

But it was true. He'd been fighting it tooth and nail, but in the ten days since she'd arrived, he'd honestly grown to like and admire her. Just look at today. All he'd done was sit around and whine about their rotten financial situation. She'd actually gone out and done something about it. Things would still be tight, but now they'd be able to eat and get Fitz his meds, too. Thanks to Rhiannon.

But that didn't mean he had to like the idea of her fighting off drunks and rhinestone Romeos at Jake's. The very thought made his teeth clench. Unfortunately, beggars couldn't be choosers.

He lay back on the bed again and closed his eyes, imagining what it might have been like if he hadn't had such a miserable start in life. Hell, even if he hadn't had that bull riding accident that'd left him with a trick knee. Maybe then he could have worked harder and the ranch would have prospered, and Fitz would be raising his Thoroughbreds and Redhawk'd have his string of rodeo ponies and maybe even a place of his own. Something to show for a lifetime of busting his butt. More than broken dreams.

Something to offer a woman like Rhiannon. She shouldn't have to work like a slave just to have enough to eat. She deserved more. She deserved better than a broken-down ex-rodeo cowboy and a broken-down ranch teetering on the verge of bankruptcy.

So he'd best just go on staying out of her way, keeping to himself and barking at her when she came close, making sure she didn't care to spend any more time with him than necessary.

Because if she ever started wanting him the way he wanted her, they'd both be in a world of hurt.

Hawk eddied gently toward consciousness as the ebb and flow of rushing water sounded somewhere nearby. A storm maybe? *Nah.* He must be floating on the river, maybe on an air mattress. He drifted back into an easy sleep, pulling the pillow close to his nose. Damn, it smelled good. Like…something he couldn't quite put his finger on. Spring flowers or something.

The boat he was drifting in dipped, and someone said, "Oh!"

He knew that voice. He'd dreamed about it. Except it had been whispering in his ear.

"Hawk?" it whispered.

Yeah…just like that.

"Mmm," he mumbled, and reached for it. "Float with me," he murmured, pulling the voice close, so it vibrated softly against his neck. There was that great smell again. Stronger now. "Mmm," he purred, and slipped back off to sleep.

Rhiannon blinked, captured in Hawk's slumberous but immovable embrace. He was obviously not going anywhere, and neither was she. He'd shocked her, waiting here in bed for her in the dark. Or maybe he hadn't actually been waiting for her. Maybe he'd just come in for some clean clothes and collapsed from sheer exhaustion as he did every night, and just not made it back to the sofa first.

She moved, tried untangling herself. But his grip was as tenacious as that of a Galway Bay limpet.

Thank goodness she'd put on her shift.

She blinked again and resigned herself to spending the night in his arms. The *remainder* of the night, she reminded herself, glancing at the luminous dial of the digital clock, which read 3:28 a.m.

Letting out a sigh, she snuggled closer to the man who held her. *Her lover.*

She tested the two words in her mind, turning them over, examining them, dancing around them, savoring them.

But he wasn't her lover. Not really. They'd had sex. He'd made that clear—right after she'd turned down his marriage proposal, and ever since. He didn't want to be her lover. He wanted the ranch, and was simply willing to take her in the bargain, if he must.

But Rhiannon O'Brannoch would be no part of a bargain. When she married, it would be forever. Marriage was sacred. There would be no deals or bargains or secrets between her and the man she married. And there *would* be love.

In his sleep Redhawk pulled her tighter to his torso, banding an arm over her bottom so their legs wound up in a tangle all the way down to their toes. It felt so good. She felt so safe and secure she forgot all about loneliness and betrayal, money woes and her aching feet, and just enjoyed the rare moment of peaceful bliss.

Too bad it couldn't go on forever....

When she woke, he was gone.

Had she dreamed it all? She might have thought so, except the scent of him lingered on her skin and in her bed, and she had to brace herself against a wave of powerful longing. She wanted to call out to him, to seek his warmth and bury herself in his sheltering embrace once more.

No.

Flipping onto her stomach, she pulled the blankets up over her head and fought the urge to despair. It would be all right. *She* would be all right. She didn't need Redhawk Jackson or his disquieting effect on her. She didn't need anyone. She only needed to *belong* somewhere, and she'd found her place in the world.

Irish Heaven. The place she'd make her own, come hell or high water.

Rhiannon finally bounded downstairs well into the morning. She was excited because she'd counted her tips from the night before and found they added up to a whopping $47.65. It had been worth having to memorize twelve kinds of beer and seventeen hard liquor brands, dodging countless cowboy come-ons and smiling till her cheeks hurt. She was rich! And she couldn't wait to tell Fitz and Hawk.

Hearing voices, she made for the kitchen, and stopped in her tracks when she came through the door and found Burton Grant sitting at the table, along with Redhawk and an unknown woman. Fitz was nowhere to be seen.

Burt immediately got to his feet with a smile. "Rhiannon. Good morning."

She answered his greeting, including everyone at the table.

Hawk glanced up, his scowl deeper than usual. "There you are. This is Dr. Kenner from the university." He indicated the woman, who offered her hand as he introduced Rhiannon. "Dr. Kenner's the archaeologist."

"Ah, the Indian burial we found by the road," Rhiannon said, her interest piquing. She walked over to the coffeepot and grabbed a mug. "Did you take a look, then?"

Dr. Kenner nodded soberly. "Not an Indian burial, unfortunately."

Rhiannon paused in adding milk to her coffee. "No? What was it then, an animal after all?"

Burt's smile dimmed as he strolled over to the counter close to where she was standing. "It was human, all right."

"Dr. Kenner thinks it's recent," Redhawk said. "That's why we called the Sheriff's Office."

Rhiannon felt her eyes widen. "Recent? How recent?"

"I'd guess within the past couple of years," Dr. Kenner said. "We'll have to call in a police forensics team to know for sure." She shook her head. "Kind of creepy. I've never found anything like this before." She actually looked a little green.

"I can imagine," Rhiannon said, still stunned by the news. Then it struck her. "Oh! Do you know who it is?" She glanced between Hawk and Burt, who both shook their heads. "Thank

God for that," she murmured. Her original nervousness over being in this wild country returned in full force. "Is this sort of thing normal here?"

Hawk looked insulted, but Burt gave her an indulgent smile. "Not usually. This isn't the Wild West anymore."

She wasn't so sure, but politely refrained from saying so. "What happens now?"

Hawk opened his mouth to speak, but Burt cut him off. "The medical examiner will take charge of the body and a state team will come in and process the scene," he explained.

Hawk glared at him. "Don't you have some phone calls to make, Grant?"

Dr. Kenner rose. "Well, I sure do. Thanks for the coffee, Mr. Jackson."

Irritation skidded across Burt's face, but he set his cup in the sink and ambled after Dr. Kenner, turning to Rhiannon at the door. "See you tonight at Jake's?"

"I start work at eight." She started to follow them to the front door but suddenly Hawk's hand was around her arm.

"Let them find their own way out," he muttered, low and angry. His gaze bored through her. "I thought I told you to stay away from him."

Shock whipped through her. "I—"

"Fitz hates Grant, and it would upset him if he thought you had anything to do with the man."

"I don't. I can't help who comes into Jake's while I'm working," she whispered fervidly, listening for the front door to close and trying to yank her arm loose.

He pinned her against the counter, his large frame looming over her. The front door slammed and her heartbeat thundered into double time.

"I should make you quit," he said roughly.

"Just try it," she dared, her limbs turning to jelly as his familiar scent swirled around her, teasing her. Taunting her. She reached into her jeans pocket as she met the challenge in his eyes. And pressed thirty dollars of her tips into his palm. "We need the money."

He stared down at the green bills for a long second. When he looked up his eyes were shuttered. Then he was gone and stalking out the back door, leaving her hot and limp and thoroughly ashamed.

"Hawk!" she called, but she was talking to the slamming screen. "Stubborn, stubborn man," she muttered. "What am I to do with you?"

They needed the money desperately. But it was obvious Redhawk was having a hard time accepting her help. Or maybe he resented it, thinking the only reason for her doing it was to save the ranch so she could inherit. Which, of course, was partly true. But she'd do it, anyway, even if Fitz showed her his will and it stated there in bold letters that Irish Heaven would go to Hawk. She prayed that wasn't the case, but she'd still help if it were. Because she cared about Fitz. And him.

But how to convince him of that?

She glanced out the window and caught a flash of bare, bronze shoulders bent over the water pump next to the trough. He was filling it with water.

A rush of conflicting emotions burst through her. Memories of the last time, exactly a week ago, saturated her body with an acute yearning to feel him again inside her. Fear also avalanched through her, of what would happen if she did. To her, to her willpower, to her heart. For she was beginning to realize that Hawk was a man who could claim her totally and mercilessly, and leave her completely devastated if he then tossed her aside. Which, chances were, he would. Once he'd gotten what he wanted.

She'd have to guard her heart carefully. But she must find a way to get through to him. To make peace. And if it took climbing into that trough again to do it, well, she'd just have to do that.

And pray her poor heart survived the ordeal.

Chapter 6

Tired and sore from being in the saddle all day checking fences and counting cattle, then putting in a long training session with Crimson after supper, Redhawk put his hands on his hips and contemplated his warm, inviting private Jacuzzi. Then he lifted his eyes to Rhiannon's Jeep bouncing away from the ranch toward town.

Decisions, decisions.

The thirty dollars she'd given him this morning was burning a hole in the pocket of his working jeans, urging him to clean up in the house and head out after her. Not like a puppy, y'understand. More like a junkyard dog on the trail of a thief.

He didn't like spending a single dime on anything that wasn't necessary—not that he'd probably need the money, knowing his friends. But for some reason, watching Rhiannon work the cowboys at Jake's seemed like an absolute necessity at this particular moment.

And then there was Burton Grant. The man was definitely up

to no good. Hawk aimed to find out what it was. It would kill
Fitz if Rhiannon got involved with him, especially if she got the
ranch and Grant ended up—

Nope. Not goin' there.

He shook his head to clear it, then limped back to the house.
Fitz was in the living room watching TV, something he did more
and more lately. Hawk didn't have the heart to ask the old guy
to pitch in with the heavy work, and Rhiannon was taking care
of the light stuff, so there was no real reason to object. But it made
him sad that the once lively, vibrant man had been reduced to this.
He was looking older by the minute.

"Hawk, how'd it go today?" Fitz called to him with a happy
smile.

"Good," he said, putting on his best face. "The cows are gettin' fatter and the horses gettin' faster."

"That's what I like to hear." Fitz started to rise. "There's a plate
for you in the oven. I'll get it—"

Redhawk waved him off. "That's okay. I'm going to wash up
first anyway. Thought about takin' a trip into town tonight. Want
to come?"

Fitz sat back down, a sad-dreamy look coming over him.
"Nah, I'm t'inking I'll stay home. Expecting a phone call."

"Okay, old man." Redhawk sighed, knowing Fitz hadn't gotten a call past 6:00 p.m. in years. "If you're sure."

"Give my love to Janet," Fitz said, picking up the remote.
"Treat her right, Jamie lad, or I'll steal her for meself."

Jake's was packed and rockin' by the time Hawk strolled in
through the swinging doors wearing his newest blue jeans and
best white western shirt. His hair was wet-combed, and he'd
even polished his black boots.

God knew why. Not like he had anyone to impress.

A chorus of howdy's and hey pard's greeted him as he pushed

through the crowd and past the pallet stage where a four-piece local band was whining out an off-key country tune.

"Lookin' good, cowboy," said a sultry voice above the din. "Long time no see."

"Teresa," he said, turning to accept a hug from his ex-girl-friend. "How you been, darlin'?"

"Missing you, baby. Buy me a beer?"

He calculated the wisdom of such a move, and decided it would not be wise at all. Teresa was a knockout, and way too high maintenance for him. Besides, their short but intense relationship had been over a long time ago, even if he'd occasionally re-lapsed since. She was a hard woman to say no to. But looking into her dark, heavily made up eyes, suddenly he wondered what he'd ever seen in her.

"Sorry, darlin'," he said, pulling the five-dollar bill he'd al-lowed himself for this fool's errand out of his pocket and snapped it between his fingers. "This has to last me all night."

She pouted prettily. "Damn, sugar. Those rustlers must have done a real number on you. Guess I'll just have to buy *you* one." She looped her wrist through his arm and led him to a table packed with several of their rowdier friends and a couple of men he didn't recognize.

"Make room, guys," Teresa ordered, and tugged him down on the bench next to her.

"Can I get you something?"

He looked up at the familiar lilt and found an unfamiliar chill in Rhiannon's eyes as they met his.

"Rhee," Teresa said before he could open his mouth. "My friend here will have a longneck and I'll have another draft. Put them both on my tab."

"Yes, ma'am," Rhiannon answered sweetly and strode off without looking at him again.

Hawk hid a wince. Calling Teresa "ma'am" was a surefire way of making an enemy for life.

"Say," Teresa said after a few minutes of amusing the men with bawdy stories about her latest ex-boyfriend, with whom everyone at the table was well acquainted, "isn't that Irish waitress the one who's living with you? Some kind of relative of your boss?"

"Fitz's niece," he supplied casually. "Yeah. She's sleeping in my bed."

The conversation came to an abrupt halt. At that exact moment Rhiannon returned with the beers and smacked them down in front of him and Teresa. The men at the table grinned at her with sudden open interest and the women giggled, except for Teresa, who looked like she was contemplating homicide. Rhiannon glanced around in confusion, her face flushing at the stark assessment in the men's eyes. She pinned him with a scowl and stomped off.

"'Course," he added then, "I'm sleeping on the couch."

"Oh, you!" Teresa exclaimed, hitting him in the arm.

"Then you won't care if I ask her out," said one of the men he didn't know, leaning into the aisle to watch Rhiannon in her tight jeans weave in and out among the patrons, carrying her round tray filled with drinks. Jake must have given her one of the official bar T-shirts which she'd cut off at the arms and midriff into a kind of crop-top muscle shirt. Damn, she looked sexy.

Hawk took a long sip from his bottle before facing his challenger. "Don't believe I know you," he said. The guy looked a few years older than Hawk's thirty-six, with a passable appearance but a bit weasly.

"Name's Jeremy Lloyd." No smile.

Lloyd. Sounded vaguely familiar. "You from around here, Lloyd?"

"Four generations."

Hawk dredged out a distant memory. "From down on the Lost Man Ranch?"

"That's me." Lloyd's lips finally moved upward, but Hawk wouldn't exactly call it a smile. "What about you, Jackson?"

Hawk lifted his beer in a salute. "Nobody from nowhere. Just a hired hand."

Jeremy Lloyd's gaze slid back to Rhiannon, who was laughing with some cowboy trying to buy her a drink. "Mighty pretty gal," he said. "Wouldn't blame you if you got lost on the way to the couch one night."

"I think you better shut up," Hawk said, grinding his teeth together.

"Now, baby, she's not worth a fight. Let's go dance, okay, sugar?" Teresa pushed at him until he got up from the bench, and she hopped to her feet after him. "Oh, good! I love this song."

He balked at putting his arms around Teresa in a slow dance. "Darlin', I'm not really in the mood. Thanks for the beer."

He gave her a peck on the cheek, turned decisively for the bar where he'd seen one of his good buddies shooting the breeze with Jake, and left her standing there with her forehead scrunched and her toe tapping. Aw, she'd get over it. She could have any man here. Any man but him. Tonight he only had eyes for a certain red-haired Irish sprite with a fiery temper and a touch to match.

Hell, was he ever in trouble.

He squeezed in at the very corner where the bar met the wall and tried to look invisible. Naturally she spotted him right off. And proceeded to ignore him all night. Except when she seemed to take extra delight in flirting with all the best-looking cowboys in the place, then she'd flash him a triumphant glare. The little witch.

He ignored her right back, talking to his buddies, and casually observing every man in the room, trying to figure out who could be involved in the rustling ring. He'd decided it had to be locals running it. The hits seemed a little too well timed to be random. And that meant inside information.

Unfortunately, scrutinizing all the men also meant Rhiannon was constantly waltzing through his field of vision bringing them drinks and joking with them. So between thinking about one of his neighbors ripping him off and watching his woman flirt with every guy in pants, he just got angrier and angrier.

Wait just a second. *His* woman? No way.

Clearly it'd been hugely stupid coming here tonight. By half an hour to closing, he knew he had to get out or risk making an ass of himself.

He thanked his friends, who'd heard about the latest rustling incident and seen to it he never had an empty bottle in his hand, waved to Jake and headed for the door.

"Leaving so soon?"

Rhiannon appeared in front of him, tray lifted and jaw jutted.

"You care?"

"Heavens, no. It'll be a relief to be out from under your black scowl." She pretended to look around. "Where's your pretty little brunette friend? I'm sure she'll be disappointed. *Baby,*" she added in a perfect imitation of Teresa's desert drawl.

His lips twitched with satisfaction. He had to admit, Teresa had done her worst, swinging back to hang off his arm every time she thought Rhiannon was looking. He'd tried to discourage her. Really he had. But the woman was mule stubborn.

"Jealous?"

"In your dreams." She turned on the toe of her silly pink boot and started to walk off.

Sure. "Rhiannon."

She stopped but didn't turn back. "What is it, then?"

It was all he could do to stop himself from grabbing her and dragging her out with him. "I'll expect you home in an hour."

Her spine straightened a fraction just before she strode off without comment. He forced himself to stride with equal determination through the swinging doors and out to his truck, the effect being spoiled only marginally by his tired, uneven gait.

Wrenching open the truck door, he cursed inwardly. This was not working. He had to get hold of himself. There were too many real problems to deal with on the ranch to spend this kind of energy on a libido gone haywire.

One way or another he would have to put this uneasy thing between him and Rhiannon to rest. Too bad the only way he could think of required her being naked and him on top of her. And for that to happen he'd probably have to hog-tie her to the bed.

He swore roundly and gunned the truck to life, grateful for the long drive home to cool off. *That* was an altogether too potent image to dwell on.

One thing was for damned hellfire certain. This had to stop or he'd go stark raving mad.

Tonight he'd confront her. Though he didn't have a clue what he'd say.

Maybe he wouldn't say anything at all. Maybe he'd just haul her to him and kiss her until she gave in to what they both wanted.

Yeah. That sounded good.

He drilled his hand through his hair. Or maybe he should just grow up and stop acting like a horny teenager.

Probably the better choice.

But his traitorous mind was suddenly flooded with memories of sleeping with her last night—just sleeping. He wasn't exactly sure how he'd gotten there, but in the middle of the night he'd woken up to find himself in his own bed with his arms wrapped around Rhiannon, who was snuggled up to his chest slumbering peacefully. It'd been…nice. Real nice. Of course, he'd had to get up at dawn, before he started getting ideas. But he hadn't slept so well in…well, frankly ever.

Maybe that's what they could do. Just sleep together. Share the bed and the warmth. No sex. Just closeness.

Yeah. That sounded good, too. And more likely to happen.

That's what he'd suggest to her. Just as soon as she got home from work, he'd ask her.

"Rhiannon," he'd say. "Will you please, for pity's sake just sleep with me?"

* * *

Rhiannon pulled the Jeep up to the ranch house, switched off the engine and stretched her aching body before getting out.

What a night. She could barely stay up to speed and keep the drinks straight, let alone with Redhawk-bleeding-Jackson watching her every move from the shadows. By the saints!

But again it had been worth the hard work and frustration. Tonight over sixty dollars in tips filled her jeans pocket with its comforting bulk. Sixty dollars! She might even be able to buy herself a new blouse to wear to work. The cut-up T-shirt had been Jake's idea, and it was slightly embarrassing to appear in public wearing something hacked off with a pair of blunt scissors. Though, she had to concede, the customers seemed to like it.

But this time Redhawk wouldn't get a single penny of the money. She was furious over him spending her hard-earned tips buying beers at Jake's just so he could spy on her. What did he think she'd do? Pick out a new man for every week?

She grabbed her sweater and boots from the seat and walked to the house in her new flip-flops—her big purchase for the day—tiptoeing when she got inside. She needn't have bothered. Fitz's door was closed as always this time of night—and Hawk was not fast asleep on the sofa as she'd expected—or rather, hoped.

She glanced nervously up the stairs. Could he be up in her bed again? A shiver sifted through her body. After the way he'd watched her in the bar tonight, he probably wouldn't be content with just sleeping this time.

A sudden, sickening thought jolted through her. Unless…unless he was with someone else, and that's why he wasn't on the sofa. That petite, beautiful brunette might be holding him in her arms at this very moment.

Rhiannon felt like someone had smacked her hard.

Then she took a deep breath. Well, fine. If that's what he wanted, it was just fine and dandy with her. Who needed the beastly man anyway? Certainly not her. He had the disposition of a badger and the manners of a hungry wolf.

She'd be far better off with him distracted by some other hapless female. Let someone else contend with his bloody moods.

She marched up the stairs, her new flip-flops snapping against the oak risers, each snap louder than the last. She flung open the bedroom door. When she saw the empty bed, her heart constricted. But only for the merest second. Then she breathed a sigh of relief.

"Good," she said firmly. "And good riddance."

She flung down her things and marched to the window to let in some fresh air. She raised the sill—

And saw him. Lounging in the water trough. Alone.

The noise must have alerted him, for he looked up and saluted her with the bottle in his hand. A beer bottle.

That's it. This was the last straw.

It took her about ten seconds to steam downstairs and out to the trough, glower down at him and demand, "What do you think you're doing?"

"Havin' a soak and waiting for you. Here, have a beer." He twisted off the cap and offered her the bottle.

She exploded. "How *dare* you spend the money I gave you on beers all night and then come home and drink the ones you told me to ration?" She'd wanted to scream the words, but was proud that they came out only as a low, intense hiss.

A muscle below his left eye twitched, the only outward sign that he'd heard her. "Do you see any other bottles sittin' around? Empty or not?" he asked, still holding the bottle aloft for her.

She faltered, and glanced around. "No," she had to admit.

"I've had enough to drink tonight. This was for you. I thought you'd be thirsty after working so hard. Take it."

"Oh." Embarrassed, she did as he asked.

Meanwhile he'd dug something out of the pocket of the white shirt that was hanging on the fence post and handed it to her. She looked down and realized it was the thirty dollars she'd given him earlier.

"But—"

"Where I come from, friends take care of each other when they're down on their luck. I didn't spend a dime tonight."

Shame heated her face and neck. "I'm sorry. I thought…"

The muscle twitched again. "Well, don't. You don't know anything about me, so don't try to second-guess my behavior."

"No," she said, thoroughly chastised.

"Now," he said in a low growl. "Take off your clothes and get in the damn water."

Shock blazed a trail through Rhiannon's insides, burning away all traces of the shame she'd been feeling. And replaced it with an unwelcome mix of anger and…searing physical need.

"What's the matter?" he asked. "Shy?"

"No," she gasped, focusing on the anger. Ignoring the temptation of his beckoning hand. "But if you think—"

He wagged a finger at her. "There you go again, second-guessing my motives."

She drew herself up. "Your *motives,* Mr. Jackson, are clearly visible to anyone looking."

She tried valiantly but couldn't prevent her gaze from dipping south. Just as she thought. Plain as day, even in the murky moonlight. And growing. *Oh, mercy.*

"Get in, Miz O'Brannoch, and I'll show you you're wrong."

She swallowed. *She doubted it.* "About what?"

"Everything."

She doubted that, too. "I'm tired. I need to get some sleep."

"I won't touch you," he said.

She regarded him skeptically.

"I promise I won't. Even if you beg."

"I don't beg."

But she blushed and turned away, because they both knew it

wasn't true. She'd begged him last week in this very place, as they were joined together, for things she hadn't even known she wanted.

"Then *I'll* beg," he said, his voice gravelly like the landscape around them.

"No," she whispered quietly. Almost desperately. "You mustn't. Because if you do, I might give in. And we shouldn't."

"Why?"

She shook her head. Unwilling to discuss it. She turned to leave.

His hand shot out and grabbed her calf. "Why shouldn't we?"

"Because you don't really want me. You only want the ranch."

With that, she handed him back the beer and hurried across the pasture to the house. To escape.

Because she couldn't believe how much the truth of that hurt.

Sunday morning Rhiannon was awakened by the sound of tires crunching on the gravel driveway below. It was late again, after ten, but she felt as though she hadn't gotten more than a few seconds of sleep. Thinking about Redhawk and his tempting bedroom eyes. Tossing and turning. Wishing he were there with her.

Had she been wrong to turn him down last night? Did it matter so much that he had an ulterior motive for making love to her? They were both adults. As long as she clung tightly to her heart and didn't let him steal that along with her inheritance, maybe taking him for a lover wouldn't be such a bad thing.

The night he'd spent in her bed had been so nice. It had felt so good to sleep tucked securely into his warm embrace, the dusky smell of him dancing through her senses, the rhythm of his deep, even breaths soothing her like a lullaby. It would be heaven to have him there every night....

She groaned in frustration, then heard voices below and flung off the covers. *Enough.* Mooning over the man would solve nothing. She'd decide about him later. After she found out what all the fuss was about downstairs.

It turned out to be Burton Grant, again.

"The M.E. identified the body found on your property," Burt announced, taking a seat at the kitchen table across from Hawk while Rhiannon poured three mugs of coffee.

"Who was it?" Hawk asked.

"Itinerant ranch hand named Rudy Balboa," Burt said, watching him closely.

Hawk shook his head. "Don't know him. Who'd he work for?"

Burt took a sip of coffee and consulted a small notebook from his pocket. "The past few years he's been at the Bar-T, the Sanderson place, up at Lost Man Ranch, and he spent a few months at a big spread down in Yavapai County."

Hawk's head shot up as she handed him his mug. "The Lost Man?"

"Know it?"

"Met the owner, or maybe his son, last night at Jake's." He glanced at her. "Didn't like him much."

"How did this Rudy Balboa die?" she asked, squirming under Hawk's frown as she sat down next to him. She didn't know why he was looking at her like that. She hadn't done anything at Jake's last night other than work. Unlike him.

"The findings are still preliminary, but it appears he died from a crushed skull. Trampled by a bovine type animal, judging by the bone indentations."

That whipped Hawk's attention back to Burt. "Damn!" he said, vaulting to his feet. "Balboa must have been one of the rustlers!"

"You sure he never worked for you or Fitz?"

"Positive. Not in the last eleven years, anyway."

The deputy slowly closed his notebook. "Any idea why he was killed on Irish Heaven property? You didn't happen to run into him before he died, did you?"

Hawk's eyes narrowed in anger. "What are you trying to say, Grant?"

"Nothing. Just keep yourself available in case we have more

questions for you. Meanwhile, we'll look into the rustling angle. The Cattlemen's Association is putting big-time pressure on us to find these guys."

"I understand they've offered a sizable reward for the arrest of the cattle thieves," Rhiannon said to break the mounting tension.

Burt rose and tugged on his Smokey hat. "That's right." He gave Hawk a sideways glance. "Enough to start a man off with his own place."

"Or woman," she said, and both men turned to stare at her. "Well, a woman could be involved," she stated defensively.

"I suppose," Burt said with a shade of indulgence. "In any case, it might tempt one of the gang to turn in the others."

"Let's hope so," Hawk said. "Keep me informed, all right?"

"You'll be the first to know." He turned to her. "Walk me out, Rhiannon?"

She didn't dare look at Hawk. She could feel his reaction in the sudden negative electricity charging the atmosphere, which had already been taut. "Of course."

She slipped on her boots and went out into the bright, late-summer day, walking with Burt to his sheriff's cruiser. Her hair flew around in the hot wind and her skin felt instantly sucked dry of moisture. It was going to be a scorcher, as they said here.

"I was wondering if you'd have dinner with me sometime this week." Burt leaned against the cruiser, his eyes in the shadow of his hat brim. "Some evening you're not working."

Rhiannon studied her boots and toed a sparkly bit in the sand. "Um, I appreciate the offer, but, it might be, um, difficult," she hedged. She liked Burt, but not in that way. And she didn't want to lead him on.

He studied her with a small frown. "You and Jackson?"

She turned toward the towering cliffs so the hot air hit her face. She closed her eyes, acutely aware of the unfamiliar sensation of heat and wind together buffeting over her body. In Ireland, breezes were always chilly and laden with cold mist. This felt strangely exciting, though she knew it would ruin her complexion.

"No," she answered finally. "Not exactly. It's just…complicated. What happened with you and Fitz?" she asked, to deflect the conversation from the subject of Redhawk. "To make him dislike you?"

He gave a shrug. "Hell if I know. I figure it's because my people are Irish Protestant. But it might also have something to do with my dad. I gather there was a bit of controversy when Fitz first arrived and bought up this land all those years ago. Not sure what the story was, though."

He opened the cruiser door and slid in.

"Sorry about dinner," she said, watching him buckle up.

"I hope to change your mind. Listen," he said, face inscrutable. "I want you to be careful around Jackson. Let me know if he does anything suspicious."

"Hawk? You really think he had something to do with this murder?" She made a face. "That's madness."

"So I guess you know about his cousin." It wasn't a question, but he waited, as though he fully expected her to say no.

"I know he's not close with any of his family."

Burt chuckled humorlessly. "No. I s'pose not. That would be tough. Since the man is in jail."

She knew better than to react. Or read anything into that fact. Her own father had died in prison, for pity's sake. But she couldn't help asking. "For what?"

"He got eight to fifteen years," Burt said. The cruiser's tires started crunching gravel and his mouth thinned. "For attempted murder."

Chapter 7

Attempted murder. Well, now. It seemed to Rhiannon she had more in common with Redhawk than she'd imagined.

As she walked back to the house, she could feel his gaze follow her from the living room window. It had undoubtedly been Burt's intent to make her feel more nervous around Hawk. But instead she felt...closer to him. She, too, had born the brunt of public opinion—for better or worse—through no fault of her own.

"I hear your cousin is in prison," she remarked, trailing him back to the kitchen.

"That's what Grant wanted to tell you?" he said disgustedly as he refilled their coffee mugs.

"Among other things." She sat down across from him. "Attempted murder. That's what my da was convicted of by the British, you know. Seven counts." Her father had been lucky none of those seven people died, or he'd have been six feet under long before he succumbed to complications from pneumonia. "That and domestic terrorism, of course."

"IRA?"

She nodded. But that no more made her a murderer than Hawk's cousin made one of him.

"Tough break. I wondered why you reacted so strongly when Fitz admitted to being in the IRA."

"I was brought up to abhor the violence. My mother hated what it did to my family. She never forgave Da. Ever."

"Or Fitz, either, I'm guessing. Since she didn't come to Arizona like she promised."

"Jamie, lad!" Fitz appeared suddenly in the doorway in his pajamas. "Should we be runnin' to warn t'others?"

"It's Hawk, Fitz. And no, I think we're safe for now." Hawk walked over to put his hand gently on her uncle's shoulder. "Why don't you get dressed, old man, and I'll make you some breakfast."

Fitz searched Hawk's face uncertainly, then glanced over at her. Shock registered in his eyes and he looked quickly back to Hawk. "Hawk," he said, his voice strained by confusion.

"Redhawk, your foreman. And that's your niece, Rhiannon. She looks a lot like her mother, Janet, doesn't she?"

Rhiannon felt the sting of tears as she watched her uncle grapple with not knowing who they were. Would the fog be there for a minute, or an hour, this time?

He was getting worse, she thought with despair. Even in the short time she'd been at Irish Heaven, she could see the downward spiral of his disease.

With a breaking heart, she watched Hawk soothingly squeeze Fitz's shoulder and lead him back to his room to help him dress. He followed along docilely. Even in his dementia, her uncle knew instinctively to trust Hawk. Poor Hawk; she could see in his eyes this was killing him. What would he do when he lost his mentor and best friend permanently to the darkness?

What would he do when he lost the ranch to her?

Blinking to clear her watery vision, she went to the stove to start some oatmeal cooking, which was Fitz's favorite. And made a silent pledge to herself.

They were going to make it. The three of them. Together. They would stay on Irish Heaven and no one and nothing would ever make any of them leave. Not disease. Not rustlers. Not well-meaning sheriffs. Not a will.

This was her home now, and she'd do everything in her power to make sure it stayed a home to the others, too. During the day she'd do the ranch chores and Hawk would take care of the cattle and horses. At night she'd work at Jake's to see they had money for essentials and Fitz's medicine while Hawk did the books and rested his knee for the next day.

Romance had no place in her scheme. It didn't matter if she and Hawk were attracted to each other. It didn't matter if she yearned to take him to her bed and let him make long, slow love to her. That's not the kind of relationship he was interested in anyway, slow and loving. Besides, they'd be too busy. They would both have to focus in order to make the ranch prosper.

And prosper it would, she vowed, if it took every last ounce of strength she had to make it happen.

Something had changed in her.

Redhawk lay quietly on the couch listening to Rhiannon's soft footsteps as she tiptoed past him to the stairs. She was always so considerate of his sleep when she returned late from work, silent as a wisp of cloud drifting by in the night.

Little did she know he was never asleep. Not until he knew she was safely home.

After that first Saturday night, he hadn't gone back to Jake's. She was just doing her job; he knew that. But he hated watching her laugh and talk with other men. Watching them flirt with her and ask her out. Burton Grant hadn't stopped asking her out since that day six weeks ago when he'd practically accused Hawk of murder. He knew because Teresa kept calling every week to give him bitchy little updates, hoping to rile him into going out with her again, now that she was between boyfriends. Not that it had worked.

Jeremy Lloyd had also tried his hand with Rhiannon, asking her to a meal before work one day just last week. She'd gone, too. *That* he knew because Rhiannon actually told him. She'd said it was only to find out any information she could about Rudy Balboa, since the cops had hit a dead end in their investigation. Unfortunately, Lloyd had told her nothing. But strangely enough, Hawk believed her about the reason.

Probably because she'd been working like a prairie fire, relentlessly consuming every task in her path, living on air and adrenaline. Making sure Hawk had time to concentrate on the herd, Crimson's training and on doing the ten-page list of overdue repairs that had piled up all over Irish Heaven since the last ranch hand had been let go. She had no energy left for anything else, she'd say to Fitz on his good days over breakfast when they chatted about how her shift went at the bar the night before.

That was for damned sure. In the six weeks since Hawk's last encounter with her out at the water trough, she'd barely been in the same room as him, unless Fitz was there, too.

He missed her.

"Rhiannon?" he called softly when the staircase creaked as she went upstairs to her room. He heard her almost silent halt.

"Yes?"

"Good night, darlin'."

After a moment, she murmured, "Good night, Hawk," and continued up the stairs.

Six weeks of loneliness and frustration, catching glimpses of her only in passing.

Six weeks of torture, wanting her so much his throat ached.

He let out a deep sigh. How he wished he could join her!

But it was better this way. Best not to get close to her. Because when the will was eventually read and the worst happened, he wanted to be able to limp away with at least his heart in tow.

He wasn't right for her. She knew it. He knew it. He had nothing to offer her except the shirt off his back, and even that was getting a bit tattered.

The only thing he could do was keep on doing what he was doing. Help get Irish Heaven back to the profitable million-dollar estate it should be, and bide his time to see which one of them would be able to hold on to their dreams.

More than that just wasn't in the stars.

Hell and damnation.

The next day the weather was beautiful. Mid-November, it had already been chilly for weeks, but today the sun was hot, and a warm breeze blew up from the south instead of whipping over the northern plateau as usual.

Before riding out, Redhawk decided to fill the trough for probably his last soak of the season. He'd sorely miss lying back in the water gazing up at the vast, starry canopy of the universe above, wondering if tonight might be the night Rhiannon would come home early from Jake's, strip off her clothes and join him.

Never happened. But a man could fantasize, couldn't he?

After filling the trough to the brim, he went to the barn and grabbed a snub-nose shovel, tucking it next to the saddle holster where he routinely carried Fitz's old Winchester. Today he'd spend making sure the natural springs on the property were running well and the catch pools clear of debris for winter. There were three springs, all located deep within the crenulated walls of the stone cliffs that formed the canyonlands north of the ranch house. The shelter of the maze of box canyons and arroyos was where the cattle would take refuge from the storms that ravaged the landscape every winter. During the worst times, Hawk would haul bales of hay up to sustain the animals when the snow was too deep to get to the grass.

Though, God knew how he was going to accomplish that this year without Fitz's help. One more damn thing to worry about.

But not today. The weather was too glorious to worry about anything but basking in it. Cleaning springs wasn't the worst job to be doing on a beautiful day, and he planned to enjoy every minute of it. He even brought a blanket, thinking he might catch some rays after he ate his lunch al fresco.

In fact, he fell asleep all afternoon. Not that that was such a big shock. But by the time he got back to the ranch late that evening, it had been dark for a long time.

To his surprise, Rhiannon's Jeep was parked out front. She didn't work at Jake's full-time, but except for Friday and Saturday, she liked to go in for a few hours, spreading them out over the whole week. Must have taken today off.

A single light burned in the kitchen.

Mounting the porch, he realized his knee didn't bother him near as much as usual. Must have been the long nap. It had also improved his disposition considerably. He'd actually been singing on the ride home, belting out an old James Taylor tune about midnight ladies, to the amusement and accompaniment of coyotes from all four directions.

Toeing off his muddy boots, he went into the laundry room and tossed his shirt and socks in the hamper. He had his pants zipper down when he heard Rhiannon's lilting voice singing a mournful ballad in a strange, haunting language.

Padding to the kitchen door, he leaned against the jamb and listened. She had her back to him, finishing up the dishes in the sink. Her hair was pinned back in some kind of barrette, but redblond tendrils escaped every which way, surrounding her head in a halo of delicate curls. She had on the pink spaghetti tank top which she'd taken to wearing under the cut-up T-shirt Jake liked her in at work. With the last echoes of her song, she turned to put away the final plate and almost dropped it.

"Hawk!" A look of relief blazed across her face. "You're back!"

"Yeah. Sorry. I got a little delayed out there."

A mouthwateringly short jeans skirt and bare feet completed her outfit. Her legs looked long as the Colorado, and just as curvy.

"I was worried when you didn't come home."

"Yeah?"

"It's so late." When he just looked at her, she set down the plate with a clatter and smoothed her hands down her skirt.

That's when he noticed she wasn't wearing a bra. The soft, natural mounds of her breasts topped by beaded nipples were accentuated by the thin, clingy fabric of her top.

She looked gorgeous. Good enough to eat.

"Hungry?" she asked.

"Oh, yeah." He took a few steps into the room.

She nibbled on her lip. "There's some chile stew left from dinner."

He took another couple of steps, bringing him within range of her. Her unique woman's scent, the scent that had dogged him for six long weeks, played havoc with his senses. "Darlin', I'm not really interested in stew."

Her eyes widened. "Hawk—"

No sense beating around the bush. She knew exactly what he was thinking, and it wasn't because he'd forgotten to zip up.

"Baby," he said, and reached for her. He put his hands on her hips and tugged her closer.

She didn't throw her arms around him, but she didn't back away, either. "We shouldn't," she murmured.

"I keep hearing you say that, but it's not happening for me. I still want you just as bad as the first time."

Lifting his hand, he drew his fingers along her cheek, sifting through the soft tendrils at her temples. "And you want me, too."

She closed her eyes and shook her head, a look of torment suddenly on her face. He hated seeing that.

"Look at me, darlin'."

She swallowed and hesitantly gazed up at him.

"I know you want me. I can see it in your eyes. Hear it in your voice. I can even smell it on your skin. Say it, Rhiannon. Say you want me."

He pulled her closer, felt her tremble. "Yes," she whispered. "I want you."

Sliding his fingers into her hair, he cupped the back of her head and banded his other arm around her waist. He held her there for a moment, waiting for her to protest. But she didn't. So he lowered his lips to hers and kissed her.

She opened to him, and the taste of her soaked into him like a summer rain on the desert sand. He absorbed it, letting it slowly saturate his senses, filling him with its life-giving essence and healing succor, banishing the dust of loneliness and nurturing the fragile seeds of possibility.

She moaned softly and wound her arms around his neck, clinging to him like a windflower fluttering high on a cliff.

"I won't let you fall, baby. I swear. I know there are a million other things going on here, but this is real."

"Is it?"

"Absolutely."

He wanted to believe that. And he did, regarding himself—he'd never felt this way about any other woman—it was her he was unsure of.

But right now none of that mattered.

He deepened the kiss, spreading his hand over her bottom, pressing her to him, center to center. She undulated, catching her ankle around his leg. And kissed him back.

He groaned, aroused as hell. Damn, she was hot. He backed her up against the counter and stepped between her legs, spreading her feet apart to get as close as possible. She made a hum of excitement, sliding her hand down to toy with the open edge of his zipper. Dangerous territory.

"Don't even think about it," he murmured. "I've waited almost two months for this, and I aim to make it last."

Instead she slid her flat hand up his bare abdomen and torso, making him crazy when she reached his nipple and rubbed over it. His erection flared and thickened. Wanting equal time with her, he grabbed the hem of her top and whipped it over her head.

She gasped in surprise, a throaty, sultry sound, and he had to grab her arms so she wouldn't cover herself.

"Hawk," she murmured, but only half objecting.

He took her in—the full, sensual swells of her breasts, peaking in tight, rosy-spiraled tips. His tongue longed to curve around them and linger there for hours. Unable to resist, he lifted her onto the counter and bent to take one into his mouth, cupping her in his eager hands.

She moaned on an exhale and raked her fingers through his hair, holding him to her, inflaming him with her passionate response. He loved that this usually steady-as-a-rock woman lit up like a desert sunrise throwing sunbeams when they came together.

He switched to the other, wishing he'd picked somewhere more romantic than the kitchen counter to do this. Too late. He didn't plan to let her go for a single second.

He reveled in her breasts, losing himself for ages in their soft fullness, in the taste and scent of them. He tongued the pebbled tips, licking and biting, eliciting moans of pleasure, taking his time, drawing out the bliss for both of them. He'd been lost for hours it seemed when she squirmed and he realized he'd unconsciously worked her skirt up to her waist and yanked her panties off.

He moved back up to her mouth and kissed her deeply, sending his fingers to seek her moist folds. Making her squirm and moan even more. He thrust his tongue into her, mimicking what he was doing below, and felt her body clench.

"That's right, baby. Show me how you like it," he roughly whispered in her mouth. "Come to me now."

He was relentless, needing her surrender in a primal, visceral way he'd never experienced before. With each stroke she made a desperate groan of pleasure. Her nails dug into his shoulder and back. Then her body bowed, and she cried out his name. *His name.*

At the sound of it on her lips, the thrill of possession shuddered through him. He took her over the edge. With a primitive satisfaction he watched and felt her give herself over to him completely, her body coming apart in his arms.

"Hang on," he said as the tremors subsided, and from his back pocket plucked out the protection he'd been carrying since the day after the first time.

Ten impatient seconds later he thrust into her. Pulling her to the edge of the counter, wrapping her legs around his waist. Groaning with ecstasy.

"Damn, woman," he moaned, holding her tight, battling not to lose it. He was dizzy with need, throbbing with the knowledge that he was exactly where he wanted to be. He wanted to stay like this forever, never moving. Perfect. So perfect.

She pushed against him, drawing him in deeper, and he couldn't help himself. Responding to her needy sounds, he let himself go and pounded into her, holding her tight, sharing the same panting breaths, sharing the same space as they plunged over the precipice into exquisite oblivion.

"I have something to show you," Rhiannon said to Hawk a couple of hours later as they were stretched out on her bed upstairs, recovering from making love again.

She didn't think she'd ever felt as content in her life as she did right now.

After the first time in the kitchen, they'd gone out and had a long soak in the trough, then come back inside and made love again. They hadn't done much talking, just a lot of body tangling and cuddling. Somehow, words hadn't seemed necessary. Or perhaps, both were worried that words might spoil the peace they'd finally found together in each others' bodies.

"Yeah?" he said sleepily. "What is it?"

She took his hand and tugged him to get out of bed. "I have to show you."

He groaned. "I don't think I can move, darlin'"

"It'll just take a minute. Come on, lazybones."

Reluctantly, he followed along as she took him out into the hallway. But instead of turning left to the stairs, she turned right, to the door leading into the unfinished area of the second floor, and to her special project. Holding her breath in anticipation of his reaction, she pulled the chain of the single overhead bulb.

"What the—"

Obviously shocked, he looked around as it illuminated what should have been an unfinished attic. Big, dirty and empty.

Instead he saw what she'd been painstakingly working on for the past two months. A bedroom for him. Well, at the moment it was just a skeleton of studs framing out the shape of the room and closet within the gaping space. But eventually it would be his room—or hers if he preferred. So they'd both have their own and he wouldn't have to sleep on the sofa anymore.

And they'd be right next door.

"Who the hell did this?" he demanded.

"I did."

He stabbed his stunned gaze at her, then back at the orderly framing, carefully measured and painstakingly hammered into place.

"You?" He spotted her secondhand do-it-yourself home-repair book lying open on a sawhorse and his jaw dropped. "You're kidding, right?"

She shrugged, inordinately proud of her accomplishment. She'd never done anything like this before. Sewing a dress was the most difficult construction she'd tried until now.

"Framing's not that difficult. I'm more worried about the

electrical. That's why I decided to tell you now, instead of surprising you with the finished room. I could use your help."

He still looked gobsmacked. "But the lumber… How did I not know you were doing this?"

She smiled and wrapped her arms around his naked body from behind, loving the warmth and the strength it exuded. "I bought one or two studs at a time from my tip money and hammered them up the next day while you were out with the cattle. Everyone at Jake's heard about it eventually, so every once in a while I'd find a few studs in the Jeep that I didn't buy. People here are really nice."

He turned his gaze on her, his eyes showing awestruck disbelief. "You're a pretty amazing woman, Rhiannon O'Brannoch." He looked around at the room. "You put me to shame."

"Don't." She folded herself into his arms and hugged him tight. "You work harder than any man I know. Hitting a few nails is nothing compared to what you do around here."

"Still. I should have thought of this."

"Well, I'm glad you didn't." She grinned up at him, trying to tease him into a smile. "You wouldn't believe how satisfying it's been to whack those nails as hard as I could. A great tension reliever."

It worked. His lips curved up and his eyes sparkled from the moonlight beaming through the newly polished window in the outside wall. "I'm sure it was. But I'll bet I know an even better way."

Then he swung her up into his arms and carried her back to bed.

Rhiannon didn't think it was possible to be so happy. The next day she sang through her morning chores, thinking about the previous night and the long, tender kiss Hawk had given her before climbing onto his horse and riding off for the day.

Nothing had been solved between them, but it felt so good to ignore all that and just bask in the sunshine of infatuation.

Oh, yes. She was falling for him, all right. Hard. She knew

that was asking for a real bit of trouble, but today she couldn't make herself care. She'd deal with the consequences another day when she wasn't feeling so fine.

Suddenly she heard a string of Gaelic curses such as she'd seldom heard, coming from outside. Fitz!

She rushed to the door and flung it open. She couldn't believe what she saw. Fitz was out in the meadow behind the corral, lasso in hand, chasing after the Christmas pig!

She slapped a hand to her mouth, stifling a burst of laughter. Poor Fitz looked mad as a bee in a bonnet. The muddy pig easily stayed two lengths ahead of him, darting and turning, evading every toss of the rope and every running dive her uncle made at him. Little hooves trotted gleefully through the large mud puddle under the cottonwood tree that had been created when Rhiannon drained the Jacuzzi trough earlier that morning. Wet, muddy goo splashed everywhere. Including all over Fitz.

She giggled behind her hand.

"Don't just stand there gawpin', girl," he shouted at her. "Help me corner d'blasted t'ing!"

She put her hands to her hips and harrumphed to hide her grin. "Me? You won't be catching me frolicking in the mud. I've better things to do," she called.

"Aye, such as figurin' out how to tell Redhawk you lost his Christmas dinner cuz you didn't want to get durty."

She let out a scandalized huff. "Now that's just plain blackmail!" Aside from which her cotton shirtwaist dress wasn't exactly designed for pig chasing. "And it's weeks till Christmas!"

"'Tisn't! It's tomorrow, it is!"

That explained why Fitz was fussing with the pig now. Nevertheless, she ran out to help, approaching the meadow so the pig couldn't see her coming. Maybe she could surprise the beast before it knew she'd joined the fray. Naturally he spotted her, and to her surprise trotted right toward her, ears flapping and a silly smile on his little piggy face. But when she reached out and made a grab for him he veered at the very last second, making her trip on her skirts. And sending her headlong into the mud.

Fitz snorted, dangling the rope in his hand. "I t'ought you came out to *help*."

She lifted her gooey chin and silently counted to ten. Since her front was covered in clay mud from head to toe, anyway, it didn't much matter if it got worse. She rolled over to sit up.

And was greeted by the sight of Redhawk strolling across the meadow toward them from the barn. Brilliant.

When he reached them, he pursed his lips and looked from her to Fitz and back again. "So. Mud baths are all the rage now, huh?"

She opened her mouth to retort, but just then the Christmas pig trotted up and plopped down at his feet like a faithful dog, its pugnacious little snout snuffling up at him as though the vexing creature expected a treat for being so clever.

He reached down and scratched between its ears, took the rope from Fitz and wound it around its fat middle, handing the end back to her uncle.

With head high Fitz wordlessly stomped off, dripping reddish-brown slime from every body part, the pig prancing along beside him like a show dog. In his pen, Lucky Charm, the stud bull, watched the parade with interest.

"So," Redhawk said conversationally, turning back to her. "This fondness for rolling in the mud—that something I should be aware of?" His lips curved up ever so slightly.

In the wet dirt under the edge of her sodden skirt, which had flared artistically out to one side, Rhiannon drummed her fingers. Fondness, indeed.

"Perhaps," she said sweetly.

There was one person in that meadow who was too clean by half, she decided.

"Maybe we can talk about it in bed tonight," he said suggestively.

She gave him a coy smile. Oh, sooner than that, she thought as he stuck out his hand to help her up. *Much sooner.*

"Not too messy for you?" she asked, all innocence.

"Hell, no," he answered, curling his fingers around hers with a lascivious grin. "I like getting dirty as much as the next guy."

"I'm so glad," she said, batting her eyelashes.

And yanked on his hand with all her might.

Chapter 8

"H_{ey!"} Hawk yelped as he plummeted to the ground next to Rhiannon. She had a firm grip on his hand, so it was impossible to break his fall with more than his good knee, which plowed into the wet clay along with his free hand. Then she grinned and tugged again, going backward with him, rolling so she ended up on top, straddling his splayed-out body.

Surprise and shock made him gape up at her like a fool, warm muck oozing wetly through his hair and clothes.

"What the *hell* are you doing?" He wasn't quite sure if he should erupt in anger or laughter.

She cocked her head. "I thought you said you liked getting dirty."

"I had something a bit different in mind."

She grabbed hold of his other hand and lifted them both above his head, pressing them into the soft mud. "Did you now?"

His body stirred. Memories of last night spun through him, egged on by their position and the mischievous sparkle in her eyes.

"Yeah, I did," he said, definitely deciding on laughter. He abruptly bent his knees up and slid her bottom right where he wanted her. Then he spun them again so she was the one lying in the muck.

"Oh!" Laughing with him, she shoved him off and started to scamper away on hands and knees. "No!" she screeched when he grabbed her ankle and started dragging her back, and giggled, "Don't you dare!"

Grinning, he hauled her back. He was covered in mud, so why not go with it? To his delight, for every inch he pulled her, her skirt rode further and further up her thighs. Laughing and screaming in protest, she vainly tried to prevent it from bunching at her waist, and batted at his hands as he turned her and grabbed for the row of buttons on the front of her dress.

He had a sudden powerful urge to see her with nothing on but mud.

Figuring turnabout was fair play, he captured her wrists and held them above her head. Then one by one he undid her buttons as she continued to wriggle and giggle.

"Stop!" she cried, but her laughing eyes were telling him something else altogether.

Her flaming hair was caked in thick, red-brown strands, and her face was splotched with dark patches, but she'd never looked so beautiful. He dipped his head for a kiss, thankful her lips were still pink and fresh. She pulled to get her wrists free, but he wasn't willing to give up his dominance just yet. Holding her firmly, he slid his other hand inside her dress and ran it over her breasts.

She arched under him, responsive as always. He deepened the kiss.

"Hawk," she whispered when he pulled up for air. "Anyone can see us."

The only one around was the bull. The pig pen was on the other side of the barn, and Fitz with it, but she was right. Another minute and he'd be undressing her completely.

Reluctantly, he struggled to get his rampaging desire under control. It wasn't easy. Her buttons were undone to her waist, her pretty bare thighs were cradling him between them, and a small square packet was tucked in his jeans pocket.

Aw, hell.

He let her wrists go and took a deep breath. But she didn't move. She gazed up at him, arms reposing above her head, the picture of willingness and submission, as though she awaited his next command. He knew it was an illusion. She was anything but a submissive woman. But the sensation made him feel powerful. Like at least this small part of his life he could control.

Needing to explore that feeling, he gathered a small glob of silky mud in his fingers and began to spread it over the swells of her breasts like war paint. After a gasp of surprise, her shallow breaths pushed her chest rhythmically up and down under his fingers. As the cool clay covered her flesh, she broke out in goose bumps and her nipples hardened under the thin fabric of her bra. Swiftly he pulled the two scraps aside, exposing both beautiful breasts to him.

Her breathing quickened, but still she didn't move.

Gathering up more, he smoothed it over her ivory skin.

Her eyes drifted closed. "That feels so good."

He swallowed. "Darlin', you're probably right. This is not something I should be doing out here."

Her lips curved up. "Mmm. Probably not." She didn't lower her arms, though. Her eyes opened innocently. "Don't suppose we have any chocolate syrup in the pantry?"

He groaned and covered her body with his, pasting them together from laced fingers to the tips of their boots like a sticky sandwich. "Buy some," he ordered roughly. "Next time you're in town. I don't care what it costs."

Her sultry laughter rumbled through his chest. "I will." She tightened her fingers in his, seeking his mouth for a kiss.

He knew he had to stop. Fitz was wandering around. It was

the middle of the day, for Pete's sake. But all he could think about was being inside her again. It was all he'd been thinking about all morning. And why he'd come all the way back from the far canyon pasture for lunch. Now that he'd finally gotten her where he wanted her, he was having a difficult time letting her up. He wanted to spend the rest of the day like this. The rest of the week. Hell, the rest of his life.

"Marry me," he said without thinking. "Marry me so we can stop this stupid fighting about who gets the ranch. So we can just work together and be together. Like this. Like we both want."

Under him, her body stilled.

His heart sank. *Damn and hellfire.* How could he have been so dumb as to bring *that* up again? He must really thrive on rejection.

"Hawk—"

He put a finger to her lips. "I know. Forget I said that. Let's just go back to the part about the chocolate syrup."

Unfortunately the mood had evaporated.

"Hawk—"

But not his want of her. He cut her off with a bruising kiss. Part desperation, part wanting to show her how wrong she was. Yeah, maybe he was all about the ranch, and maybe he didn't love her. But he could. He was falling for her; with every day that passed he found it tougher to imagine his life without her in it. And he wanted her like no woman before.

Wasn't that enough? To build on?

She kissed him back like she wanted him, too. At least that was something.

"I'll share," she whispered when their lips parted. "I'll share everything with you. The work. My body. Irish Heaven, if I get it. You'll always have a home here, Redhawk. Nothing will change that. Ever."

And just like that, white-hot fury seared through him. More empty promises. Did *everyone* think he was an idiot?

Well, maybe he had been in the past. But no more.

"That's very noble of you, Miz O'Brannoch, but you can keep your damn promises. I don't accept charity, *ever*, and I sure as hell don't need yours."

He reeled to his feet and stalked off toward the house to clean up. Leaving her there. Ignoring the wounded look in her eyes.

Hell, he'd had plenty of promises in his lifetime. Too many. From his mother, his teachers, the cops, his rodeo career, from Fitz. But he'd recently stopped believing in them. Promises were like tumbleweeds, here today, tomorrow gone and forgotten. Time to start remembering that. From now on he wanted everything on paper, nice and legal.

It was time to take the reins of his life firmly in hand. He'd earned his place on this ranch with his own sweat and blood. If Rhiannon wanted to share anything with him, great. But she'd have to earn her place with *him*. As his wife.

He stopped halfway across the meadow and turned. "You were right about another thing," he called to her angrily. "I'm ready to ask Fitz about his will. We'll find out tonight."

At least that way he'd know one way or another. And could make some long-overdue decisions. Like what he'd do with the rest of his life if Rhiannon inherited Irish Heaven.

Or how to make her marry him if *he* did.

Rhiannon put her trembling hands to her face and battled hard not to cry. Mature women didn't cry. And she didn't. Not since her mother'd died had she shed a single tear about anything. She wasn't about to start now.

By the saints, but she wanted to badly. How could things have gone wrong so quickly? One minute she and Hawk were practically making love, the next her broody lover was stalking off—after she'd offered him everything she had in this world, herself included.

But everything she had was not good enough for him. He wanted more. He wanted her fate linked with his for all eternity, in marriage. To a man who didn't love her.

She couldn't believe he'd proposed a second time. A marriage of *convenience*. And here she'd thought such a thing only existed in the pages of lurid nineteenth-century Gothic novels.

But she was not willing to compromise on such an important decision. Temptations of the flesh would be forgiven. But marriage was sacred. She'd only marry a man who loved her with all his heart.

Hawk was not that man.

With a deep sigh, she buttoned up her cotton dress, rose and made her way to the water pump to rinse off.

At least one good thing had come of it all. Tonight she'd know the worst. Tonight she'd know if she had a home of her own, or if, once again, her dream of belonging would be shattered.

"God damn it!"

The back door slammed hard, startling Rhiannon so badly she dropped the pan of cornbread muffins she was taking out of the oven. She added her own choice word to Redhawk's diatribe blasting in from the laundry room.

"They've hit us again," he announced, slamming his hands against the door frame as he stormed into the kitchen.

"What?" she asked in dismay, swiping the pan up and turning off the oven before facing him. "The rustlers?"

He drilled a hand through his hair. "Four more steers are gone. Four!"

Fitz looked up narrow-eyed from the table where he sat slicing vegetables. "It's that Grant fella, I tell you. He arrested two of the boyos on the last raid an' turned 'em over to that British colonel. Ye can't trust him, Jamie lad. It'll be you next, I tell ya."

Rhiannon blinked, and met Hawk's gaze. He gave his head a brief shake. "I'll be careful, Fitz."

"Are you sure the animals are gone?" she asked.

"I followed the trail to the chute next to the highway. There were three men on horseback herding them fast. Tracks looked fresh. Probably last night."

She swallowed a prick of guilt. *While they were making love.* Could the rustlers have known?

No, how could they? And what difference would it have made if they had? That far away, Hawk couldn't have heard anything anyway.

"What does this mean for us?"

"It means we're screwed. We only have twenty-three steers left in the herd. At $500 a head profit—if we're lucky—it'll be impossible for three people to live on that next year. Especially…" He took a sidelong glance at Fitz before shaking his head.

"I have my job," she said. "That'll help."

He gave her a level look, then sat down opposite Fitz. Gently, he set the knife aside and took the older man's hands in his.

"Fitz. I know we've always vowed we'll never sell a single acre of Irish Heaven. Not even if it meant living under the stars and eating cactus. But with you being sick, things are different. We need to be able to take care of you. What happens if you get worse?"

"What are you saying, lad?" Fitz asked, a heartbreakingly puzzled look coming over his face. "You want to sell our home?"

At his use of the word "our," a stab of misery sliced through Rhiannon.

"No, I—"

"I'll never sell Irish Heaven," Fitz said emphatically.

"I don't want to, either," Hawk said. "But we may have to consider it. Just a few acres of the land, if we can find a buyer. You remember that offer you had a couple years back? Maybe the lawyer can contact the party and ask if they're still interested."

"I won't," he repeated, crossing his arms.

"The thing is…" Hawk went on as though he hadn't seen Fitz's determination. "The situation has changed now, what with Rhiannon being here and all."

"Rhiannon?" Fitz glanced over at her and started, as though he hadn't realized she was standing there. "Janet!"

"Rhiannon. Your niece. Janet's daughter," Hawk patiently repeated for at least the hundredth time since she'd arrived at the ranch. "Fitz, you're going to need help making some important decisions soon. And we were wondering…that is, Rhiannon and I felt it would be most fair if that person is the one who'll be inheriting Irish Heaven from you."

Fitz stared at him, apparently not comprehending the words.

"Fitz, we need to know. Who are you leaving your ranch to, in your will?"

His mouth dropped open, and Rhiannon's heart literally stopped in her chest. She wanted to cover her ears, or scream "No!" and run from the room. But she made herself stand perfectly still. And take the worst, if it should come.

The old man gaped at Hawk in surprise. And said, "Why, you, of course, Jamie! Who else but me own brother?" He nodded at her. "And your Janet, when ye wed."

She squeezed her eyes shut and took the breath her lungs were starving for. *Nothing.* He'd told them nothing.

"Fitz." Hawk bent in closer. "Jamie's gone now. And Janet, too. You have to tell us. Is it me or Rhiannon?"

Her uncle jumped to his feet, visibly agitated. "I'll not be selling Irish Heaven! And that's that." Then he hurried from the kitchen, leaving an awkward, awful silence in his wake.

After a moment Hawk leaned back in his chair and let out a long breath. "That went well."

"The poor man," she whispered. "He's so confused."

"At least we got our answer," Hawk muttered, and hauled to his feet.

"What answer?"

He approached her and pinned her with a slow, penetrating look. "That he's leaving the ranch to me."

"You think—"

"What else could he have meant?"

"That he really did leave it to my da, in which case it'll be *mine.*"

Hawk parked his fists on his hips and glared down at her. "If

I recall correctly, your *aunt and uncle* were your daddy's heirs, not you."

She gasped, and reeled back as if slapped. "They won't want this place!"

"Don't be so damn sure. Not when they can turn around and sell it for over a cool million in cash." He backed her up against the counter and put his face in hers. "So you better start praying he *did* mean me."

His breath on her forehead was hot and swift, smelling of sage and piñon nuts, like the scorching wind off the cliffs. And yet she shivered.

He put his hands to her waist and held her fast, bending his lips to her ear.

"I'll make you the same offer as you made me," he growled. "To *share*. My land, my home, my work, my bed. But I have one stipulation." He grasped her chin and jerked it up so she was forced to look into his eyes. "If you accept, you'll do so as my *wife* or not at all."

He let her go, turned and walked away, not a hint of limp in his powerful stride.

With a quiet sob of anguish, she wrapped her arms around her middle, swung and leaned over the sink.

He'd won. Now she really had nothing, and belonged nowhere.

Pain razored through her insides, and she had to clamp her jaw against crying out.

What would she do? Where would she go? She couldn't stay here and marry him. She *wouldn't*. A loveless marriage would be condemning herself to being no one and having nothing of her own for the rest of her life.

No.

She was better than that.

She took a steadying breath. She had her pink boots. They were hers. She'd bought them with her own earned money. And her new clothes. And the room upstairs she was building.

That would be hers, too, she decided. Not Redhawk's. She'd build it with her own hands and move into it just as soon as possible. It would be all new, and wouldn't remind her of *him*. Of the night they'd spent together in his bed, and the things they'd done together there.

She didn't want to think about that. Because if she did, she might consciously have to acknowledge that she really *wanted* to marry him. In a *true* marriage.

Because she'd already fallen in love with Redhawk Jackson, and nothing would make her happier than to share the rest of her life with him, along with everything in it.

But that was even more of an impossible dream than owning a million-dollar ranch in Arizona.

Because he didn't *want* her love.

Thanksgiving was subdued.

Hawk remembered not too long ago when it had been a big, noisy affair at the ranch, all the hands bringing their gals or wives and families, Fitz helping Estella, their former cook, whip up a real dandy feast in the kitchen. That was back when they had money. And ranch hands. And a cook. And plenty of reasons to be thankful.

Rhiannon did her best with the dinner, but he supposed they didn't get much call for turkey in Ireland. Fitz tried to help, but just muddled things up more and more the later in the day it got. For some reason he always seemed a lot worse in the afternoons and evenings than he did in the morning.

Hawk figured it was about time for another trip to the doctor. Expensive as it was, the old man's medication didn't appear to be helping much anymore. Maybe there was something stronger they could give him.

Anyway, Hawk decided to rescue the poor Thanksgiving bird and slow roast it on a spit over the grill. Barbecue was about the only kind of cooking he was any good at. Hell, it was the only kind of cooking he'd ever tried.

It wasn't so bad. In fact, it was downright tasty after he'd spread on the last few drops of Fitz's famous red chile-chocolate oil that he'd put up last fall. With a batch of Rhiannon's perfected cornbread muffins, a few roasted veggies and a homemade apple pie for dessert, it was more than a passable meal.

Too bad no one was talking.

He and Rhiannon hadn't done a whole lot of that in the week or so since they asked Fitz about his will.

For the life of him, he couldn't figure why that woman was so damn blasted stubborn. It's not like he'd seduced her, then dumped her. He'd asked her to *marry* him for chrissakes.

But he wasn't going to think about that. Because every time he did, he just got mad. The woman was going to be the death of him. He still wanted her with a physical ache that kept him awake long into the night. First waiting for her to come home from her job at Jake's, then imagining what it would be like to follow her upstairs and climb into bed with her. Demand she share with him, as she'd promised. The bed, and her.

He took a long swig of his one allotted beer and stabbed another slice of turkey.

"You can sleep in your own bed tonight," she said, breaking the silence and jerking his attention—and his body—like a puppet on a string.

"What?" He had to have heard wrong.

"You can move back upstairs," she calmly said, dishing another helping of vegetables onto Fitz's plate, who was busily eating, oblivious to the tension between them or the lack of conversation.

"All right," Hawk said slowly, wondering if she'd gotten a little mixed up about what Thanksgiving actually entailed. Not that he intended to set her straight. If she wanted to thank him in that way, he was all for—

"I finished roughing out the other room. Jeremy helped me with the electrical earlier this week and—"

"Excuse me?" he interrupted, his fork halfway to his mouth. "Jeremy Lloyd? Was in this house?"

"You were off doing something or other. Fences, I believe. And—"

"And so you decided to ask Jeremy for help. Instead of me."

He did his best to control his temper. He did. But he could feel the muscle below his left eye begin to tick. A dead giveaway he was set to explode. He tamped down on it, hard.

"Would you have?" she asked, brow raised skeptically. "Helped?"

Probably not. He hadn't been in the mood to do anything but snap at her all week. Or kiss her to within an inch of her life. He gritted his teeth.

She harrumphed. "I thought not. In any case, it's nearly done. Uncle Fitz's friend, Otis, is an electrician. He promised to come inspect and make the final connection at the breaker. The only thing left is sinking a register into the heat duct, and then the drywall."

Breaker? Roughing out? Drywall? Where had she picked up all this construction lingo? She'd obviously been talking to folks about this project.

So everybody knew about their sleeping arrangements.

The muscle ticked wildly.

What the hell did *that* matter? He'd told them all himself at Jake's two months ago that he was sleeping on the couch.

So why did it suddenly feel shaming that everyone knew he and Rhiannon weren't sharing a bunk?

Because he *wanted* to be, that's why. And he wanted everyone to think they were. Correction: to *know* they were.

"What about a bed?" he asked, proud of how he wasn't jumping up from his chair, throwing her over his shoulder and dragging her upstairs to show her exactly where she belonged, and with whom.

"I bought one of those blow-up mattresses. That'll do until I can get a proper bed. It'll be easier to move around, anyway. For the work that's left."

He carefully put his fork and knife down and wiped his mouth with his napkin, folding it neatly in his lap. Then he pinioned her in his sights.

The blood drained from her face and she licked her lips. But she didn't look away. Feisty to the end.

"There's no lock on that hall door," he said, his voice low and suggestive. "Aren't you worried?"

She swallowed but she wasn't eating. "No," she answered.

He cocked his head. "No? And why's that, Rhiannon?"

"Because—" Her voice cracked and she suddenly shot up from the table and headed straight out the back door. The screen door smacked closed, startling Fitz.

Hawk tossed his napkin on the table. "I'll go see if she's all right," he told him, and followed her outside, where he found her standing at the porch rail, staring up at the cliffs, arms tight over her midriff.

"Because why?" he said, coming up behind her. He planted himself so they were nearly touching. So he could smell her shampoo and the lingering scent of cranberry and the apple pie she'd baked earlier. He couldn't stand not touching her, so he grasped her arm and turned her, making her face him.

"Why?" he repeated, keeping his hold on her.

"Because, I've never locked your bedroom door, Hawk. Ever. You could have walked in anytime. But you never bothered to try."

He regarded her for a long moment. "Is that an invitation?"

"No," she whispered. "Why would I want a man in my bed who all he can do is scowl at me? You know how I feel about you, Hawk. But sex is not enough. Once in a while a woman likes a man to make love to her. Cherish her."

"Baby—" He tried to step closer, to take her in his arms, but she slipped away and walked back to the door.

"I'm sorry. I won't marry you. Not even for the ranch. So maybe I'd better try to find a lock for that door."

Then she went back inside, taking his aching heart with her. And closed the door firmly behind.

She left him standing out there alone, suddenly an empty shell of a man. Wondering why the hell he'd even want the ranch, without her by his side to share it?

Chapter 9

The next day Otis came over with Fitz's pals Pete and Jim, to finish up the electrical connection on Rhiannon's "project."

Hawk refused to call it her "bedroom." Even after the guys had gone and had left Fitz most of the case of beer they'd come with, along with a promise to Rhiannon to scrounge up some cheap leftover drywall from the job sites Otis was currently working on. Even when she announced after supper that she had moved out of Hawk's old room and he should plan to sleep there tonight. Even then he refused to call it her bedroom.

"Baby, there's no furniture, no carpet, not even any walls. You can't be serious."

She frowned at him. He wasn't sure if it was his endearment or his incredulity that irked her more. He'd taken to calling her baby all the time now, refusing to let her withdraw from what intimacy they had together. At least verbally.

He was also working on scowling less. It wasn't easy.

"I have a mattress and the closet has a pole to hang my clothes on. That's all I need."

"You stay in my bed. I'll move in there," he insisted.

"No!" She set down the sponge she was using to wash a pan. "I mean, no, thanks, that won't be necessary. I want to be in my own space tonight. It'll be fine."

Sometimes she could be so stubborn. "All right," he said, making a sudden decision. He stacked up the dirty plates on the counter for her. "Doesn't matter either way. I don't plan on sleeping here tonight, anyway."

"Oh?" she said in a cool tone, turning her back to him. After a slight hesitation, she added, "Going for a sleepover? Teresa maybe?"

He set his jaw. He wanted to spin the woman around and shake her. "I'm not interested in Teresa, Rhiannon. You're the only woman I want to sleep with."

She didn't respond, but he saw her grip the edge of the counter. He had to resist the urge to peel her hands off the tiles and make her squeeze *him* that tight. Except she'd probably just go for his throat.

"It's been a week since the rustlers hit. I'm worried they'll be back. Maybe if I watch the herd I'll get lucky and catch those sons of bitches in the act."

She finally turned to face him. "What brought this on?"

"The Cattlemen's Association has doubled the reward for their capture. I want that money. It's enough to put Irish Heaven back on its feet." Maybe even start his string of rodeo ponies. Like he'd always dreamed of raising, instead of cattle.

He could see the defiance in her eyes. The refusal to believe his supposition that Irish Heaven was as good as his. Of course, he wasn't sure he believed it himself. Fitz hadn't told them anything concrete, and every time Hawk'd brought up his will since, he'd become agitated and started talking about the old country and his brother.

Still, it was the only straw Hawk had, so he'd grasp it.

But there was a silent, private battle going on between him and Rhiannon, neither of them giving an inch, conducted through looks and stances, hard work, and her ignoring the deliberate brushes of his hand over her skin whenever he got close enough to touch her.

He liked her defiance, her gritty unwillingness to give up. It showed character. But sooner or later she'd come around to him. She had no choice.

He was hunting her, like a wolf stalking a lone doe, tiring her out, wearing her down, until the day she'd finally surrender. To him.

Hawk didn't care anymore that he currently had nothing to offer her but his name. With the reward, things would change. Then he'd be worthy of her. He just had to make damn sure he was the one who caught those rustlers.

Because he wanted her.

And one day soon he intended to have her.

Permanently.

Rhiannon gazed out the window of her new room onto the vast moonlit landscape of sand, chaparral and piñon that stretched endlessly from the silent ranch house to the distant black horizon. Murky shadows stirred in fits and spurts, prompted by soft gusts of desert wind. She pulled up the window sash and shivered in the blast of cold, sage-scented air.

Peering into the darkness, she listened carefully. Wind whispered through dry branches; far away a pair of coyotes howled back and forth in mournful yips and yowls.

There was no sign of Redhawk. Neither sight nor sound.

She wrapped her arms around herself uneasily. He'd been gone when she got home from work tonight, just as he'd said he'd be. Glancing down at her makeshift bed, she tried to make herself get back in it and close her eyes. But she knew sleep would elude her, as it had until now.

She didn't like sleeping without Hawk close by.

In fact, she was miserable. She hadn't realized how safe and secure his mere presence in the house made her feel. Not that she was afraid of anything specific. Other than a vague disquiet caused by the overwhelming loneliness and emptiness of the miles and miles of the foreign desert terrain surrounding the house. She'd gotten over her fear of wild animals, and so far the rustlers hadn't hurt anyone in their raids. Unless you counted the wounded steer—and Rudy Balboa—but those appeared to be accidents. There was nothing to be afraid of, she told herself.

Rubbing the goose bumps on her arms, she slid the window closed. And looked around for something to do for the rest of the night. Or at least until he came home.

"Darlin'?"

A gentle hand shook Rhiannon's shoulder as Hawk's voice softly called her name. She lifted her head and blinked, disoriented. She was lying curled up on the living room floor. For the life of her she couldn't remember why.

"What on earth are you doing?"

Peering around, bleary-eyed, at the stacks of cartons and piles of papers surrounding her, she suddenly remembered. Filling time until he came home. "Cleaning out closets."

"What the— Why?"

Good question. She realized she was holding something against her chest, and glanced down. A flood of sad consternation filled her as she recalled the thick bundle of ribbon-bound letters clutched in her hands.

"Rhiannon? Baby, what's going on?"

Sitting up, she cradled the letters in one arm and rubbed her eyes. "I couldn't sleep. And the closets were all so cluttered I could never fit—" She halted at his dubious look. "I guess I fell asleep on the floor."

He jerked his chin at her arm. "What have you got there?"

She hesitated before answering. It wasn't that she didn't want him to know. It was just…she felt a little guilty. The letters were, after all, private. And Fitz was right in the next room.

Hawk reached for the bundle, and she let him take them.

"It's letters. To Fitz." He squinted at the return address. "From your mother?"

Eyes suddenly stinging, Rhiannon nodded. "Oh, Hawk, I never should have read them."

He tossed the letters aside. "Come here."

Pulling her to her feet, he enfolded her in his strong embrace. His rough ankle-length duster was still stiff and cold from being outside, and he smelled of horses and dust and masculine sweat. But she'd never felt so comforted, or wanted to be anywhere so badly as she wanted to be right where she was.

"They were in love," she murmured threadily. "My mother was in love with her husband's brother."

Hawk sighed. "Yeah. I figured as much."

Her heart squeezed. Was she the only one who hadn't known? What about Aunt Bridget and Uncle Patrick? Had they—

She gasped. Her father! Was that why he'd given the farm to them? Because maybe he thought—

"Shh," Hawk soothed, running his hand up and down her back. "Leave it be, darlin'. This tired, you're apt to come to all sorts of wild conclusions."

"Too late," she whispered.

He kissed her forehead. "Let's go upstairs," he whispered back. "I'll help you forget."

Wrapped in his calm, powerful arms, she was, oh, so tempted. She looked up and saw sympathy radiating from his warm chocolate eyes, but she also saw weariness. The sharp planes and angles of his handsome face were softened by fatigue, the sensual curve of his mouth bracketed by deep furrows. No need to ask if he'd caught the rustlers.

Time to think of someone else besides herself. "Did you get any sleep out there?"

"A little."

Probably about as much as she had. "You go up," she said. "Get some sleep."

"What about you?"

"I better clean up this mess."

"Rhiannon—"

She put a finger to his lips. "You're about to fall over. Go on." Then she kissed him. A sweet, tender kiss. He went to deepen it, but she pulled away.

He didn't let her go. "I'll sleep better if you're with me."

It was their usual ritual. Him pushing, her pulling back. She kissed him on the jaw and shook her head. "Sun's coming up. Chores to do."

He sighed and loosened his hold, letting his hands slide down her arms. "You'll break down eventually and come to me," he said. "You're mine. You know damn well you're mine."

With that he turned and slowly walked away. Leaving her standing there, her whole world tilting on its axis. His claiming words thrilled her to the core. But also made her dizzy with panic. Because he was right, on both counts. She *was* his, heart and soul. And if he kept up his pursuit, she *would* break down, sooner or later, and let him take what he wanted.

Swallowing, she watched him drop his duster onto a chair and climb the stairs, the yellow light of dawn painting the dusky skin of his face a glowing bronze. She wanted him so badly, it would be easy to give in.

But if she did, where would that leave her? And her heart?

She would have to think carefully about that. Especially after this last blow. Her own mother had married the wrong man and paid for it by living a life of loneliness, five thousand miles from the man she truly loved.

Would it be better to be with Hawk, even if he didn't return her feelings, than to spend a lifetime filled with regret?

The answer frightened her as nothing else ever had.

Because either way, she would lose.

And that was the loneliest feeling of all.

The next night, Hawk again spent out in the canyons watching the cattle. And the night after that. And the night after that.

Rhiannon was worried about him. The weather had turned chilly during the day, dipping down close to freezing at night. He claimed he had an arctic-weight goose-down sleeping bag, but she saw how drawn and ragged he looked when he dragged in just after dawn each morning.

"You have to stop this nonsense," she told him sternly on the fourth day. "You'll make yourself ill. Or freeze to death."

"Guess you'd get the ranch then," he said with a tired, wry smile, warming his hands over the woodstove. She'd taken to lighting a blaze in it when she spotted his silhouette galloping over a rise about five miles away, coming home.

"Don't be morbid," she snapped. "That's not funny."

He leveled her a look. "I won't stop until I catch them. I can't. You know that."

"At least light a fire to sleep next to," she pleaded.

"Yeah. And alert everyone within a hundred miles I'm there. No, Rhiannon. I'm fine."

She huffed out a breath and stomped into the kitchen to fetch him a cup of coffee. And he called *her* stubborn. She'd met donkeys less obstinate than that man.

"But if you're so worried," he said, accepting the mug, "come upstairs and warm my bed for me."

The man was also relentless.

She allowed him to pull her into his arms and kiss her. "Don't spill your coffee," she warned when the kiss threatened to go too far. She'd found it impossible to deny him when he kissed her, but she was always careful not to let it go beyond the point of danger.

"Woman, if the frost don't kill me, you will," he muttered when she slid from his embrace.

She helped him off with his long duster and went to hang it on the peg in the laundry room, along with the jacket he wore under it. He usually left the duster in the barn, so she called, "Do I need to rub down Tonopah?" thinking he must have come right in without tending to his horse.

"No. I got him. It was just so freaking cold I had to put my coat back on to walk to the house." He downed his coffee and set the cup on an end table. "Sure would like a warm body to snuggle up with, falling asleep. Take the chill off." He sent her a lazy smile.

"Falling asleep, eh?"

He winked. "Eventually."

"Take an extra-hot shower. Or maybe a cold one. That should do the trick."

He let out a long, mock-aggrieved sigh. "Like I said, killin' me." Shaking his head, he started up the stairs.

He was limping badly. His knee must be hurting like the dickens from sleeping outside in the harsh, frigid weather. This really had to stop, she decided. It didn't matter about the reward. His health was far more important than any amount of money could ever be. Rhiannon knew that with bitter certainty. Tonight she would have a talk with him.

A half hour later she suddenly heard a loud crash from upstairs.

"By the saints!" She bounded up the stairs two at a time, calling, "Hawk! Are you all right?"

When she reached his bedroom, she found him sitting on the floor, wincing in pain and holding his knee in both hands.

"My God!" She dropped to his side and hovered, not knowing whether to hug him or call the hospital. "What happened?"

"I'm fine," he said gruffly, adding a few curses under his breath. "Go away."

"You are not fine, and I will not go away. Here, let me help you into bed." She got up and tried to lift him, but it was like trying to raise a two-ton anchor. She also realized with a start that he was wearing nothing but a bath towel; his body was warm and steaming, fresh from the shower. How could she have missed that?

He slanted her a glance from under his lashes. "Oh, sure. Now that I'm crippled you'll get into bed with me."

With a cough, she dropped her hands from under his bare, muscular biceps. "Who said anything about *me* getting into bed? Honestly, Hawk. You really are shameless."

"And *you* are heartless." He leaned over and grabbed a pillow from the bed. She was pretty sure she still had a heart because it fluttered wildly when the bath towel threatened to come loose from his waist. "Don't worry about me," he said. "I'll sleep right here on the floor. Hand me a blanket, will you?"

Her jaw dropped as he lay back on the carpet, propped the pillow under his head, folded his arms over his broad chest and gazed up accusingly at her.

"You get into that bed right this minute, Redhawk Jackson."

His bottom lip jutted out. "I'd like a couple of aspirin, too, while you're at it."

Her jaw dropped even further. She put her hands to her hips. "Stop acting like a two-year-old!"

"Or you'll do what, Miz O'Brannoch? Spank me?"

"I just might, at that!" she declared.

The twinkle in his eyes should have warned her. "So wait," he said, "are you saying you'll spank me if I stay on the floor, or if I get into bed?" The corner of his lip twitched.

She finally twigged. "Oh!" she cried, scandalized, and grabbed the pillow to whack him with it.

He burst out laughing, caught her around the waist and tried to pull her down onto the floor with him. Against her will, she started to giggle. It was impossible to fight him, convulsing with mirth.

"Ow!" he growled, when he rolled toward her. "Damn knee!" He let her go to grab it.

"Oh, love," she murmured, and put her arms around him.

"I'm so sorry! Please let me help you into bed. This hard floor will kill that knee."

Reluctantly he nodded, and together they got him sitting up on the mattress, his long leg stretched out gingerly.

"I'll get an ice pack," she said, studiously ignoring the fact that the bath towel had been left on the floor.

He grasped her hand before she could leave. "You'll come back?" She nodded. "And you'll lie down with me?" She hesitated. "I really want to hold you."

Her stomach zinged at the thought. Of its own volition, her head nodded again. How could she deny a wounded man? "All right, then. But just for a little while."

When she returned with the ice pack and carefully placed it over his swollen knee, his breath hissed in. "Damn, that smarts. Must have banged it good to hurt this bad."

"You don't remember?" She propped a pillow under it to ease the muscle tension.

"Always knocking into something or other during the course of the day. Nothing jumps out."

She sat on the edge of the bed and moved the ice gently back and forth over his knee. "Better?" He nodded. "You can't keep sleeping nights on the hard, cold ground, Hawk. That'll just make it worse."

He regarded her. "What's worse is sleeping in the room next to you and not being able to touch you."

"Hawk—"

"I thought you were going to lie down with me." She must have looked uncertain, because he added wryly, "Baby, I can't move my leg without screaming in agony. You're safe enough tonight."

A slight exaggeration, but she got the point. She started to climb over him to the empty part of the bed, but he grabbed her arms, shaking his head. "No. Take off your clothes first."

Her lips parted in consternation. "I don't think that would be a good idea."

"I swear, the way I'm hurtin', any hanky-panky's gonna have to be your doing. But I need to feel my lover skin to skin."

She sat back down and gazed at him in misery. "We're not lovers, Hawk."

"You can't change what's happened between us, Rhiannon. We're lovers, and always will be, whether you want to acknowledge it or not."

He grasped her sweatshirt and pulled it over her head. After searching his exhausted, guileless face, she relented, hesitantly unbuttoning her cotton blouse and unhooking her bra.

"So proper," he murmured, watching with half-lidded eyes. "Next time just wear the sweatshirt."

She shivered in the chilly dawn air, her nipples tight and hard.

"Keep goin'," he encouraged, flicking open the snap of her jeans. "Hurry so we can get under the blankets."

Without giving herself time to think about the folly of her actions, she stripped out of her jeans and panties and climbed into bed with him.

He caught her when she was halfway over and pulled her down on top of him. Her breasts pillowed softly onto his solid chest, and her leg slipped between his thighs. She couldn't help herself, a choking moan of need slipped from her throat as their bodies made contact, meshed and settled together in a perfect fit of male and female puzzle pieces.

He was aroused. Blatantly, wonderfully, long and hard. But he made no overtly sexual move. Just drew his arms around her and held her close, after flipping the covers over both of them.

She tipped her head up for a kiss, knowing she was already lost.

His mouth was warm and persuasive, the bed a musky cocoon of bare limbs and heated skin. He held her there, his hands brushing lightly over her naked body.

She trailed her lips over his cheek and down his throat, dipping under the covers to spread kisses over his shoulders and chest. But when she went to move lower still, he stopped her with firm hands and lifted her back up to his face.

"No, baby. I said I'd just hold you, and I aim to keep that promise."

"You didn't promise," she countered huskily. "You said any hanky-panky was up to me." She wriggled to escape his grasp and continue her journey down his luscious body.

He held fast and smiled weakly. "I never thought you'd actually do anything. You've been pretty adamant about not."

She pushed out a breath. "What are you saying? You don't want to make love?"

"Darlin'," he said with a sardonic snort, "I think you can feel just how much I want to. The thing is, if I let you do this, next time I say I just want to hold you, you won't believe me."

"Hawk, I didn't believe you *this* time."

He groaned. "Which is exactly why I can't let you do what you're doin'." His smile faded, and he reached to cup her cheek in his hand. "Rhiannon, when we make love I don't want it to be an accident or because we got swept up in the moment. I want it to be because you want me."

"I do want you," she insisted.

"Ten minutes ago you didn't. I want you to come to me, to my bed, knowing exactly what you're coming for."

"Ten minutes ago that's not what you were saying."

"I know." He sighed deeply, gathered her closer and whispered, "But when I felt your body next to mine, tasted your sweet kisses, I realized pressuring you into having sex will never give me what I want."

"And what's that?"

He gave her a sad smile. "More," he said, leaving her more confused than ever.

A couple of hours later Hawk awoke to a reality better than all his dreams. A soft bed under him, a warm woman over him, and a feeling of peace in his heart.

Then he tried to move his leg.

"Son of a—"

He swallowed the rest of his curses, not wanting to wake Rhiannon. Gritting his teeth, he eased out from under her and staggered to his feet. His knee hurt like the fires of hell, but he had work to do. The animals needed tending and then he had to—

Nope. He wouldn't be doing any range work today. He couldn't even imagine getting on a horse, let alone riding out more than two yards. So much for his rustler watch. Maybe he could get in some extra training time with Crimson, if he could figure out how to stay standing without hanging on to the damn fence post.

Inwardly he swore again. This was the last thing he needed to deal with.

Rhiannon stirred in her sleep, her hand searching the spot where he had slept. After a tiny moan, her eyes fluttered open.

"Hawk?" she said sleepily.

"You go back to sleep. I'll do the stalls today."

"Come back to bed," she whispered, the hint of a smile on her lips.

He almost groaned. Why today, of all days? He went to lean over and give her a kiss, and almost stumbled.

She sat up. "Are you okay? Is your knee worse?"

"Nah," he lied. "Just a bit tender."

She gazed at him assessingly, and he knew that she saw right through him. "You are going to the doctor. I'll hear no arguments. You can take Fitz and talk about his medication while you're at it."

There was no percentage in arguing. He'd seen that mulish expression before. He'd lose. "Fine."

"I'll call and make the appointment," she said, sliding out of bed.

The sight of her nude body had him catching his breath.

"Come here," he murmured, opening his arms to her. She slid into his embrace, for once willingly and without hesitation. If nothing else, their pillow talk had convinced her to trust him, physically. His heart gladdened. It was a step. An important one.

Her curves pressed into him, and despite his honorable intentions, he had to battle the desire that welled up within him. There was nothing he'd rather do than ease between her legs and plunge up into her, staking his claim, making her his again.

Instead he kissed her. And breathed in the intoxicating scent of her hair. And relished the tenderness in her green eyes as she helped him dress and limp downstairs.

While she was on the phone, he hobbled into Fitz's room to let him know about the trip to the doctor's.

He wasn't there. Strange, he hadn't been in his favorite spot on the couch watching TV, either.

"Appointment's for 2:30 p.m.," she told him when he went into the kitchen after having searched the whole downstairs.

"Have you seen Fitz?" he asked.

"Why, no." She glanced up. "Is he not in his room?"

He shook his head. "He's not in the house. I checked everywhere."

"Oh, dear," she said, biting her lip. "I'd better check outside. Lord knows where he's gotten to this time."

Hawk frowned. "This has happened before?"

"A few times," she said with a concerned glance out the window. "He's never wandered far, though. I generally find him in the barn or out in the meadow."

"Lost?" Hawk asked, worry increasing by the second.

"He usually thinks he's back home in Ireland. He says he has to meet someone, urgently."

"Why didn't you tell me?"

She looked at him apologetically. "I— You have enough to worry about. As long as I found him, I didn't want you to fret over this, too."

He understood her logic. But if he was in charge here, he needed to know everything that happened on the ranch.

Of course, she would debate that he was in charge. To her, this was her family and her business.

And here he'd thought they'd made so much progress.

"We'll talk about this later. Right now we better find Fitz."

Afterwards he'd put an end to this tug-of-war, once and for all. And then they could figure out what to do about their relationship.

Because one thing was for damn certain. After holding her in his arms all morning, there was no way in hell they were going back to sleeping in separate beds.

Chapter 10

"Be careful."

Hawk gave a final tug on Jasper's cinch and placed the toe of Rhiannon's pink boot into the stirrup. Jasper was Hawk's other saddle horse, the gentler of the two.

She gave him a tight smile. "Oh, I will."

"And don't go too far. If you don't find him, come back and we'll call Pete to round up some of the boys to help."

"I'll find him. How far could he have gotten?"

"God knows. But I don't want you both out there lost in the desert. The wind's up. I'm afraid we're going to get some weather."

Hawk was beside himself with apprehension and annoyance. They hadn't found Fitz anywhere in the area around the house or outbuildings. None of the vehicles or mounts were missing. And Hawk was in no condition to climb into a saddle and look for him.

It's not like Rhiannon hadn't ridden before. She'd occasionally taken Jasper out alone for short exercise rides, and longer ones when Hawk was with her. She'd do fine, or he wouldn't be letting her out of his sight.

But he still worried. The desert was a big, formidable place if you weren't used to it. It could swallow you up in a minute and not spit you out again for years. Especially if it started snowing.

For the tenth time he shook the canteens hanging from the saddle horn and patted the first-aid kit tucked in the saddlebag. "Maybe I should get you a blanket. Just in case."

"Hawk, don't fuss," she admonished. "I must go now, before he gets any further." She leaned down and gave him a quick kiss. "Don't worry. I'll be right as rain."

With that she spurred Jasper and was gone in a puff of dust.

Instantly Hawk regretted letting her go. He should just have downed half a dozen aspirin and gritted through the pain, regardless of what she said. He'd hurt far worse back in his rodeo days.

Okay, maybe not. But it went against everything he believed to let his woman carry the weight meant for him. It was his job to take care of her. He'd failed his mother when he was young. It made him crazy to think he was failing Rhiannon in the same way.

It seemed like hours before he spotted Jasper trotting back over the rise with Fitz bouncing behind Rhiannon, but in fact it was only forty minutes.

Meanwhile Hawk had downed some painkillers, fed the animals and made coffee. With a sigh of relief, he trudged to the barn to meet them.

Helping Fitz down from the horse, he asked, "What were you doing, old man, running off like that? You had us real worried."

"Gettin' a Christmas tree," Fitz declared. "Only three weeks till Christmas, y'know. Gotta find a good one."

Hawk could only stare. He flicked a glance to Rhiannon, who lifted a shoulder along with her brows.

"There's only junipers and piñon grow around here, Fitz. We need to go farther up in the mountains for pines."

"Where d'ya think I was headed?" he answered calmly.

"Next time take one of us with you when you go hiking," Hawk said, struggling to keep his voice mild. "In fact, we can all go. We'll bring a picnic. How would that be?"

Fitz beamed. "Brilliant." He started walking back toward the ranch house. "Don't forget, we need to slaughter that pig in time for Christmas dinner," he called over his shoulder. "He's a nice fat one, he is."

Hawk sighed and turned to Rhiannon, whose face had gone a few shades paler. "What?" he asked.

"I quite like the little beast. I'm not sure I can bring myself to eat him."

Hawk didn't usually get sentimental about stock raised for food, but he had to admit he'd also grown fond of the Christmas pig this year. With cheerful snorts and grunts, it had always trotted out to greet Hawk each morning when he'd come with the bucket of slops and feed, gazing up at him like a faithful puppy. He missed owning dogs, and had taken to giving it a scratch between the ears whenever he walked by. They were pals. How could you eat a pal?

He shook his head of nonsense and said, "It's either that or another turkey. We can't afford much more."

"Maybe we can sell him to a child looking for a pet," she suggested. "And use the money to buy a ham at the store."

He gave a bark of laugher, then saw he'd offended her. "Maybe," he said with as straight a face as he could muster. "Why don't you ask around at Jake's?"

"I'll do that," she said with a nod.

He took Jasper's reins from her and put his other arm around her shoulders as they walked to the barn together. "You have Christmas trees in Ireland?"

"Of course. And presents and carols and figgy pudding. What else do you do to celebrate here?"

"Not much," he admitted. "In the past, Fitz would drag us to midnight mass every few years. We weren't big on exchanging gifts, being mostly bachelors on the ranch. Back when there were a few families with kids, we'd have a little party on Christmas Eve for them. The Christmas Day pig roast was always the highlight, of course."

Oops. He checked her reaction, and when their eyes met, she made a choking noise. Then they both laughed.

"Sorry. We'll skip that part this year. Don't worry, Fitz will probably forget, anyway."

"It's silly, I know. It's just…"

"I understand. Once you start caring for someone, you don't want to see them hurt, even if it messes up your plans."

She nodded. Their gazes met again and held for a long moment. And suddenly they weren't talking about pigs.

"Rhiannon—"

"Please, Hawk," she interrupted in a beseeching voice.

"You know I care about you."

"Don't," she said. "If you really don't want to hurt me, don't ask me to marry you again." She shook her head sadly. "Besides, you don't have to, now that we know Irish Heaven is going to you."

He stopped dead in his tracks. It was the first time he'd heard her concede the inheritance. He didn't know what to make of her sudden change of heart.

"You're wrong," he said. "That's exactly why I have to keep asking until you say yes. You deserve to share this land, and Fitz is never going to allow it to be divided. It's the only way."

She wouldn't look at him, damn it.

He threw up his hands, startling Jasper. "I don't understand you! You seem to like me, we have great sex together, and I'm offering you over a million dollars' worth of property. If it doesn't work there's always divorce. Is there a down side to this I'm not seeing?"

Stroking the horse's nose to gentle him, she still wouldn't meet Hawk's eyes. "I don't believe in divorce," she said quietly.

"And even if I did, we'd be right back where we started. One of us losing. Better to get it over with now."

"You're assuming our marriage won't work. Don't you think I can make you happy?" He held up his palms, warding off a reply. "Never mind. I guess I know the answer to that."

Hurt cascaded through his body, worse than the pain in his knee could ever be. He clenched his jaw and turned away so she wouldn't see.

He didn't know why her rejection should hurt him so bad. He didn't love her. He hadn't loved his mother, either, when she'd kicked his butt out at fifteen. Hadn't loved the rodeo when that big bull had bucked him off and stomped his leg to bits, ending his career. He didn't love anything in this life other than the land he was standing on. And that land was going to be his. He didn't need anything else. Certainly not Rhiannon O'Brannoch.

He'd been generous, but if she didn't want him, fine.

Because he didn't love her.

Honest to God he didn't.

That afternoon steel-gray clouds crept down from the north, shrouding the high plateau in a dark, biting chill. While Hawk and Fitz drove to their doctor's appointment, Rhiannon prepared the ranch for the snow she could smell coming. It would be a bad one, she thought, lifting her nose to the angry, roiling skies.

Almost as angry and roiling as Hawk's mien had been after their conversation that morning.

She didn't know why *he* was so upset. *She* was the one who stood to lose everything. She'd even admitted as much aloud for the first time ever, much to her own consternation. She hadn't meant to admit defeat. Indeed, she was still unconvinced he would inherit from Uncle Fitz. If she truly believed that, she'd be making plans to return to Ireland as soon as she had enough tip money scraped together. Though no longer her birthright, the family farm was generations ago bought and paid for, and money not a source of strife. Life there was comfortable—if depressingly meaningless.

With a sigh she battened down the barn for the coming storm, bringing in Lucky Charm and the horses, making sure the animals would be cozy and safe inside. Then she carried an extra pile of logs for the woodstove into the house, so the humans would be, too. At least physically.

If only it were that easy to make two people emotionally comfortable with each other.

She had a feeling it was going to be a very, very long winter.

The first snowflakes were already falling when Hawk pulled the truck into the driveway just before suppertime. Rhiannon went out on the porch to meet them.

"How did it go?" she asked.

"Good."

"Janet, me love!" Fitz sang out, disgorging from the passenger seat with a flourish. Obviously they'd made a stop at Jake's before coming home. The grin on his face and the scent of beer clinging to his day-old whiskers gave them away.

She gave him a hug, and he swung her around in an impromptu jig. It was wonderful to see him this cheerful.

"We got you a tree, we did," he said, urging her down the steps to the back of the truck, where Redhawk was opening the tailgate to reveal a compact little pine tree. He hauled it out and held it up straight for her approval. A bit taller than him, it was lush and green.

She clapped her hands. "Oh, it's perfect! The shape is exactly right!" She stepped in closer and ran her fingers up the soft-stiff needles of its branches, inhaling deeply of their spicy, tangy scent. "It smells divine."

Hawk watched her wordlessly the whole time, an unreadable expression on his sculpted face. Snowflakes danced around him like mischievous fairies, settling on his broad shoulders and coal-black hair, his long, thick eyelashes and the coppery slashes of his cheekbones and nose.

Her breath caught in her throat. He was so beautiful. Enhanced by tight, worn jeans and an old jade-colored flannel shirt, his tall, athletic body would make any red-blooded woman feel the tingle of desire. She was no exception. But it was no mere tingle she felt, it was an avalanche.

Too much. She had to turn away.

"Where shall we put it?" she asked, to mask her dismay at how deeply under his spell she found herself.

"Next to the front window," Fitz said, taking the top while Hawk lifted the heavier bottom. "That's where it always goes."

She noticed Hawk wasn't limping nearly as badly as before. "What did the doctor say about your knee?" she asked, following them up the steps.

"Inflammation of the ligaments. He gave me a couple cortisone shots and a prescription, and told me to stay off it for a few days. Feels better already."

"I'm glad," she said. "You look better. What about Fitz?"

Easing the tree through the door, he murmured, "We'll talk about it later, okay?"

She nodded bleakly. That couldn't be good news.

But for the rest of the afternoon and evening, she put it determinedly out of her mind as together they fetched a large, ragged box of ornaments from the attic and decorated the tree and living room. Fitz had insisted Hawk buy eggnog for the occasion, and produced a bottle of twelve-year-old Irish whiskey to sweeten the mix. He even dug up an old Bing Crosby Christmas album and played it endlessly on the ancient stereo.

By the end of the evening they were all having a fine time, tensions forgotten, joking and laughing over Fitz's outrageous renditions of bawdy Irish Christmas carols. It didn't matter that he called them Jamie and Janet and chatted on as though he were as young as they, and his long-ago friends were just down the road waiting to be well met for a holiday pint.

Rhiannon had never felt more at home. Like she belonged. As though they were all a family, three people who truly liked and cherished each other.

The glow of the holiday magic, the soft fall of snow on the windowpanes, the mellowing effect of the Christmas grog, how she wished it would go on forever.

She didn't notice when Fitz yawned and Hawk took him in to get ready for bed, and was startled when she glanced up from watching the crackling fire in the woodstove and saw Hawk gazing down at her, a determined look on his face.

"Shall we go up?" he said. It wasn't a question.

Instead of answering, she lay back on the thick Indian rug she was sitting on next to the warm stove and stacked her hands under her head.

"Tell me what the doctor said about Fitz," she said.

Hawk's mouth turned down, and for a moment she didn't think he'd answer but pull her to her feet and march her up the stairs to an uncertain fate.

But then he said, "The bad news is there's nothing much we can do about his downward progression, no other medication. The doc says it's unpredictable how fast or slow it'll go. The good news is he's healthy as a horse and as long as he's happy and there are no complications we should be fine."

She pressed her eyes closed. "Thank God. I can deal with answering to 'Janet' as long as he's all right."

"Yeah," Hawk agreed. When she opened her eyes again he had moved to her side. "Let's go upstairs," he repeated.

"Relax," she said, feeling a teasing smile steal back over her lips. "What's the hurry?" She waved a hand at the steady snowfall outside. "Looks like we're not going anywhere anytime soon. We have all night and probably tomorrow, too, to talk."

His brow hiked.

Such a man. So gruff and serious. She almost giggled, but managed to hold it in.

"Or whatever," she added with another sweeping gesture, just so he'd smile again. She loved when he smiled. His eyes lit up, and fan-shaped crinkles appeared next to them, his cheeks hollowed, and he looked so deadly sexy she could hardly stand it.

Except he didn't smile. "How many eggnogs did you have tonight?" he asked, his lovely forehead creasing into a frown.

"Not nearly enough," she pronounced succinctly. "But clearly more than you."

His frown deepened. The man was obviously conflicted. He wanted her. Oh, yes, she could see it in the tension of his muscles, barely restrained. But if he thought she was drunk, his sense of honor would never let him take what he'd consider advantage of her.

Too bad. Tonight she felt like being taken advantage of.

The warmth and happiness of the evening filled her with a sense of infinite possibility. As though nothing they could do together would be wrong. As though everything would turn out right and well, and they would never have another bad day again.

She realized with a start that he'd gone to the kitchen and was returning with a cup of coffee in his hand.

"Here, drink this," he ordered, holding it out to her.

She didn't move. "Why? So I'll be sober when you seduce me?"

He scowled. "I'm not going to seduce you. I told you that this morning."

"Hmmm," she hummed. "Such a shame."

Setting the cup aside, he stepped over her, planting his feet on either side of her legs. "What are you saying, woman?"

"I'm saying I want to go to your bed, and I know exactly why, and what we'll be doing there," she said, shocking herself with her boldness. And honesty.

His nostrils flared. "Would you still want to even if you'd drunk your eggnog straight up, no whiskey?"

She let her gaze slide slowly up his long, lean legs and slim hips, over his flat abs and broad chest, up to his meltingly sensual mouth and expressive black eyes. "Oh, yes," she whispered. "That I would."

He continued to stare down at her, a myriad of emotions parading across his face. "I don't understand you," he said at last. "But I'd be a damn fool to turn you away."

He helped her up, and she kissed him. To her surprise she sensed hesitancy in his touch.

"I'm not drunk," she said softly, stroking her fingers over his tight jaw. "I'm happy. It's been a wonderful evening and I can't think of a better way to end it than with you."

He nodded, his expression gentling just a little. "I agree," he said, and for a brief moment she wondered if she wasn't making a mistake. She wouldn't marry him because he didn't love her. But was this the way to make him fall in love? Or would sleeping with him without his emotional commitment simply make him take her for granted?

Too late now. And to be honest, she didn't care at the moment. All she wanted was to be in his arms and feel his body moving in perfect harmony with hers. To have his powerful strength all around her, to feel it within her.

She wrapped her arms around his neck and kissed him deeply, unable to stop the emotions pouring from her lips, her tongue, to his.

She despaired. How could he not sense her feelings for him? The love she carried in her heart for this amazing man who gave everything he had, and much more, to keep those who depended on him safe?

What would he do if he knew her true feelings?

He urged her up the stairs and she forgot her qualms as he undressed them and eased her onto the mattress below him, slid between her legs and entered her with a single fierce thrust.

"I'm a fool for you, Rhiannon," he murmured, pounding into her again.

"And I for you," she sighed, clinging to him, wrapping her legs about his waist, pulling him deeper inside her with every hard thrust.

He groaned, and she threw her head back, opening herself to him completely.

It was different this time. The sensations more vivid. The actions more violent. The emotions more desperate.

And when it was over, the touches were more achingly sweet. The kisses more lingering. And the knowledge in her heart more certain... More certain that if this ended badly and she was forced to walk away from him, that she would never recover. That she would end her days, wherever she was, alone and dreaming of this man, just as Fitz still dreamed of her mother.

"Darlin'?" he whispered into her hair, rubbing her back with long, loving strokes. "You okay?"

No, she'd never be okay again. Not until he loved her.

"Yes," she said, snuggling closer, smoothing her hand over his heaving, sweat-slicked chest. She could feel his heart hammering like the drumbeat at an Indian powwow he'd taken her to a few months back. *Tha-thump, tha-thump, tha-thump.* Loud and insistent. Steady and sure. The source and the drive and the foundation of all around, the singers and the dancers following its solid, unyielding lead. Just as she followed Hawk's. And would follow, until her heart told her it was no longer any use. That she was wasting her time.

Until then she would stay right where she was, sharing his bed, sharing his burdens. And hoping.

Praying that one day he'd ask her to marry him for the *right* reason:

Because he loved her.

Chapter 11

It was still snowing two days before Christmas.

After finishing breakfast, Hawk went to the kitchen window and stared morosely toward the distant cliffs and canyons where he knew his remaining cattle were huddled, taking shelter from the unseasonable weather. When he'd ridden up there a few days ago, it had taken hours battling the wind and sleet and snow to reach the herd. They'd still been able to eat, pawing through the shallow layer of white to get to the grass growing deep in the sheltered canyons. But after three more days of snow, Hawk knew they'd be hurting for food by now.

"I've got to go to town," he told Rhiannon. "Pick up a load of hay for the cattle. They must be getting hungry."

"Do you want me to come?" She looked up from a button she was sewing on a shirt. He did a double take. It was one of *his* shirts.

He couldn't believe she was sewing on his shirt. Nobody had ever fixed anything of his. Ever. He'd always done his own mending, from the day he could thread a needle. He'd always fixed *everything* himself.

"Hawk?"

"Uh, no. Thanks. I, uh— What are you doing?"

"You had a button missing. I found one in the kit that matches pretty well." His disbelief must have shown, because she bit her lip and said, "Why? Was that your lucky missing button or something?"

"Lucky…? No. It's—" He shook off the impulse to explain that nobody had ever thought enough of him to bother with doing a little kindness like that.

Right. She was probably just going stir-crazy being snowed in with nothing to do for days on end. He shouldn't take it personally.

"Never mind. If I'm not back by lunchtime, ride out and see if I got stuck on the road, okay?"

"Sure."

Before he left, he brought in a stack of wood so she'd have plenty. Then he gave her a kiss, revved up the truck, lowered the snowplow blade and took off for town. The going wasn't too bad, since he'd plowed the ranch road every day so Rhiannon could get the Jeep out to go to work. Today he did a few extra passes here and there so when he returned with the heavy bales of hay he wouldn't get mired in any deep drifts.

When he got to the feed store, he counted out a stack of one-dollar bills from his wallet to pay for his purchase, acutely aware of whose money he was using. He'd carefully recorded every contribution Rhiannon had made to the household from her tips, and he meant to pay her back every cent. Meanwhile, he was grateful that so far he hadn't had to dip into their painfully slim bank account to pay for anything. They might make it through this winter yet.

"Those rustlers been leaving you alone lately?" the feed store guy asked as he was ringing Hawk up.

"Yeah, thank goodness. Guess the snow is keeping them indoors like everyone else."

"Heard the sheriff got a possible lead on them."

"Yeah?"

"A restaurant down in Flagstaff got caught serving black-market beef. Owner claims he got it from a guy from up hereabouts. Sheriff figures it might be our outlaws. He's tracking it down."

Hawk nodded, torn between relief that the crooks might soon be behind bars and frustration that he hadn't put them there himself. He really wanted that reward. He needed it.

As he loaded up the hay, he suddenly stopped in midtoss.

He might yet have a chance to bring them in.

Because they were going to hit again.

On Christmas.

He couldn't believe he hadn't realized it before. They'd all felt safe because no one in their right mind would go out at night in this kind of weather, even criminals, and they'd always struck at night, just before dawn. But in two days they wouldn't have to. While normal people were busy celebrating the holiday, the rustlers would swoop across the plateau and take what they wanted. *In broad daylight.*

Rhiannon had tried to convince him they wouldn't hit Irish Heaven again, that it was too risky and there were plenty of other herds for them to rustle. But Hawk thought otherwise.

It felt too personal. Like the rustling was directed right at him, or Fitz. That the times the gang had stolen from other ranches were just decoys. Hawk hadn't confessed his theory to Rhiannon or anyone else. But it was there in his head, gnawing at him, growing bigger with each passing day.

What if someone was targeting Irish Heaven?

And *why?*

It made no sense. Which is why he'd kept his theory to himself.

If he caught them, he'd know.

So that's what he had to do.

Slamming the truck's tailgate, he walked determinedly to the cab and slid in. *Hell and damnation.*

Rhiannon wasn't going to be happy about him missing Christmas.

* * *

"Surely you can't be serious!"

Rhiannon's words pierced Redhawk's heart, but he held firm. "I have to, darlin'. I know they're going to hit us again, and what better time than a holiday everyone spends indoors with their family? The rustlers won't be expecting anyone to be on guard."

The three of them had spent the afternoon carting hay bales up to the cattle. After supper an exhausted Fitz had crawled into bed, and that's what they'd done, too. Now they were snuggled up together under a huge pile of covers in Hawk's bed.

Her face fell as she gazed up at him. "But it's Christmas. You can't spend it out there all alone."

"I'll have the cows," he said lightly, though inside he was ripped up at the thought of missing the holiday with her and Fitz. "When I get the reward for bringing in those bastards, I'll take you out to the fanciest restaurant in Arizona, that's a promise."

She let out a long breath. "I suppose we could move it back a couple of days. Pretend it's Christmas on the twenty-seventh."

He hugged her close. "I have a better idea."

"And what would that be?"

"We can celebrate right now."

"Now?" Her eyes widened when he reached behind her to the nightstand and pulled a beribboned package from the drawer. "What's this?"

"Your present." At her sudden wary look, he chuckled. "Don't worry, it's not an engagement ring."

His determination to marry her was just as strong as ever, but he had yet to convince her. The fact that he'd succeeded in romancing her permanently into his bed gave him hope. But a ring would be premature, and he knew it. *One day.*

"You're sure?"

"Positive. Go on. Open it."

She took a deep breath and tore apart the paper, then opened the box, revealing the antique silver and turquoise necklace he'd managed to talk Pete into paying him with for mending a giant pile of used leather goods and tack that came in to Pete's Gem and Mineral Emporium and Indian Trading Post.

"Oh, my stars! It's absolutely beautiful!"

"This is a bear paw," he said, fingering the centerpiece of the necklace. "Signifies courage. For the bravest woman I've ever known. Merry Christmas, baby."

He kissed her and she melted under him, clutching him with one hand and the necklace with the other.

"Oh, Hawk, it's lovely. I'll treasure it forever." She gave him another long kiss, then said, "I haven't wrapped yours, but I want to give it to you now, too."

"Darlin', you didn't have to…"

"What kind of a woman wouldn't give her lover a Christmas present?"

He smiled. *At last.* Hearing her admit they were lovers was the only gift he needed. "What is it?" he asked as she slid out of bed to fetch a bag from her sewing drawer.

She handed it to him. "Look and see."

He pulled out a sky-blue long-sleeved shirt that was made of cotton that felt like silk. On the front yoke she'd sewn four long narrow ribbons in different colors. He recognized it immediately as the kind of fancy shirt Indian people wore to powwows and other festive occasions.

"Baby, it's beautiful." He held it up, amazed that she'd picked up on that detail at the one powwow he'd taken her to a few months back on a rare day off.

"Turn it over," she said, her beaming eyes giving away that there was more.

He did, and sucked in a breath of astonished delight. A large red hawk was embroidered on the back, with claws extended and wings spread, their tips reaching to the shoulders of the shirt, where more ribbons fluttered.

"Holy— Rhiannon! Did you do this? Embroider it?" He met her eyes in wonder.

She nodded, her face wreathed in a big smile. "Do you like it?"

"Like it? Are you kidding? I love it. I've never— Jeezus, Rhiannon." He crushed her to his chest and rocked her in his arms. "You never cease to amaze me, woman."

He covered her lips with his and held her close, absorbing the warmth of her body and her love. For surely she must love him, just a little, to have created this incredible gift for him. He basked in the heat of that tiny ray of hope.

To know that she loved him, that would be the greatest gift of all.

He hung the shirt over the headboard so he could see the intricate embroidery, and clasped the necklace he'd given her around her neck. With a finger he traced the beautiful curves of the dark silver and lustrous turquoise, forged and polished by caring hands many years ago. Hands like his own. The colors of the necklace stood out in stark relief against the creamy, fair skin of his chosen woman, as did the copper of his own tanned, work-roughened fingers.

She deserved so much more than him, so much more than he could give her. But he refused to give her up. He would keep her. Somehow he'd find a way.

He dropped his hand to her breast, caressing its pale fullness, enjoying the contrasts of silken to callused, white to bronze, female to male. Somehow it all fit. Better than he ever thought possible.

"Love me," she whispered.

He eased her down beneath him, sliding into her with the half growl, half sigh of a man who knew just how lucky he was to be there. Love her? Yeah. He could do that.

And suddenly he thought, maybe, just maybe, he already did.

Determinedly, Rhiannon refused to look at the date on the calendar or the clock on the wall. She hated, hated, hated that it was

Christmas Day, and she hadn't seen Hawk for over forty-eight hours. She hated even more thinking about him out there in the bitter cold and snow, possibly freezing to death while she paced the cozy kitchen.

Nearly 5:00 p.m., and no sign of him. She'd had her fingers crossed the rustlers would show up today, so Hawk wouldn't have to spend another night out there.

"Only two days till Christmas!" Fitz declared for the third day in a row after peering at the dates crossed out with big *X*s on the page for December. She had decided not to draw *X*s for the past two days, so they could celebrate the holiday when Hawk got back and Fitz wouldn't be disappointed. So far he hadn't caught on. "It'll be a fine feast."

"That it will, indeed," she agreed, surveying their handiwork. While Hawk was gone, she and her uncle had stayed busy cooking and baking up a storm. Luckily most winter vegetables were inexpensive, so they'd tried every recipe for squash, yams, cabbage and potatoes they could find in the few cookbooks Fitz owned. They'd also baked three pies: apple, pumpkin and berry.

And then there was the honey-glazed ham, of course. Bought with the thirty-five dollars Jake had given her for the Christmas pig, which he'd dressed up in a big green and red bow and taken home to his 4-H enthusiast niece, who he was sure would groom the creature to within an inch of its life and win a dozen blue ribbons at the county fair next fall, then retire it to a life of leisure siring future blue ribbon generations. Rhiannon missed the silly swine with its cheerful face. But she knew it was in a better— and much safer—home now.

"We should go into town and do a bit o' shoppin'," Fitz said eagerly after they'd cleaned up the dirty baking dishes and put plastic wrap over all the food so it would be ready to heat and serve whenever Hawk came home.

"Oh, now, look at the weather outside, Uncle Fitz." Rhiannon pointed to the light but steady snowfall swirling outside the windowpanes. "Hawk wouldn't like us to drive today. Why don't we just have a nice cup of tea and chat instead?"

"I expect you're right," he said. "I'll just put on the kettle."

As they sipped their tea, their eyes met over the rims of their cups and she smiled at her uncle, glad for the good day they'd spent together. He'd seemed content for the past few weeks. As though when she and Hawk had finally made peace with each other, he'd felt it, and taken on the same serenity. His memory even seemed to have improved.

"What about Christmas presents?" he asked. "It looks a bit sparse this year under the tree."

"It doesn't matter. Just being with those who love you is enough, don't you think?"

The old man nodded happily. "Aye, it is."

Despite the hardships, December had been a good month for all of them. But their conversation led her to thoughts of her mother, and being with the one you love.

"Uncle Fitz?"

"Aye?"

"I was wondering if I could ask you about something."

"Of course, love."

"Why did my mother marry my father and not you?"

His teacup rocked in his saucer as he set it down. She held her breath, certain she would lose him, that his memory would make a left turn back into the past and away from her question. If it weren't so important to her, she would never have asked it and risked spoiling their day. But she had to know. Before it was too late.

Amazingly, he looked up from the steaming tea and met her gaze, his eyes clear and comprehending. "How did you know?" he asked.

She swallowed. "You keep mixing me up with her. Some of the things you've said… And then I found her letters."

His head bowed. "Her letters. Ah, how could I have forgotten?"

She reached out and covered his hand with hers. "Uncle Fitz, if you don't want to talk about this, I'll understand."

"No. You deserve to know. Though in truth, there isn't much to tell. Your ma came up from County Kerry to work in Belfast with her big sister, Bridget, when she was seventeen. They moved into the attic flat in the building my family lived in. Ah, they were a lovely pair. All the fellas on the street had their eyes on 'em."

"But Bridget was older."

"By eight years, same as me. Janet was of an age with Jamie. Which is why it was natural for them to fall in together."

"But you and she were attracted?"

"We shared a few kisses, I'll own up. But Jamie was mad for the lass. And then there was Bridget."

"Bridget?" What part had her aunt played in all this?

"She fell for me, y'see. I didn't love her, but didn't want to hurt her. Or Jamie. So I mostly kept my feelings to m'self."

"And so did Janet."

"Aye. It wasn't until—" He stopped abruptly, jumped to his feet and looked sharply at the window. "Where is he?"

She blinked at the sudden change. "Who?"

"Jamie! He's out there, isn't he? What's he doing?" Fitz started to pace agitatedly. "We have to find him!" he said without giving her a chance to answer. "He's been betrayed! While we were lingering here safe and sound, he's—"

"Uncle Fitz!" she interrupted his panic attack, running over to steady him with firm hands on his shoulders. "You're not in Ireland any more. We're in Arizona now." At times like this Hawk always reminded him his brother was dead, but she had a feeling that news would only agitate Fitz more.

"But Jamie…someone…there's someone else…"

"You mean Redhawk. Your foreman. Hawk is just fine. He's out in the canyons checking the herd."

"How long has he been gone?"

"It's all right. He said he might camp out tonight. You remember the rustlers?"

"Rustlers…" Fitz glanced away, and it was clear he didn't.

"Never mind, Uncle Fitz. Why don't you go and rest for a while? I'll watch for Hawk."

He still looked troubled, but nonetheless he nodded, gave her a kiss on the cheek and padded off to his room.

Releasing a long breath, she walked over to the window and stood gazing out at the pristine snow-covered desert for a long time, thinking about the small glimpse he had given her of his and her mother's relationship. It sounded typical enough. Unrequited love for the wrong brother, the wrong sister. But there was more. She knew there had to be. Otherwise her mother would never have written such intimate letters to Fitz for so many years.

And what had he meant at the end? It wasn't until…until what? What had happened to change their relationship? And why had the memory catapulted him into a blind panic over her father's safety?

Another day she would try to ask him about it. But for now, she had another relationship on her mind. And another man.

Feeling edgy and nervous, she glanced at the clock, wishing Hawk would walk through the back door, kicking snow off his boots, demanding hot coffee and a hotter kiss.

Yes, things had been going well this month so far at Irish Heaven. Almost *too* well. The other shoe was bound to drop sooner or later.

She just prayed it would be later.

Much later.

Redhawk pulled his goose down sleeping bag tighter around his face and blew out a breath laden with vapor. Damn, he was freezing. And it wasn't even dark yet. It had stopped snowing, but with the cloud cover dissipating, the cold had become merciless.

Where *were* they? He'd been certain the rustlers would show up today. He'd have bet his life on it. Hell, he might *be* betting his life on it. After two days of shivering like an aspen, it would be a pure damned miracle if he didn't catch pneumonia and die.

Which he wouldn't mind nearly as much if he could see those bastard rustlers put in jail first.

Zipped from head to toe in his green mummy bag, it was tough to stand up, but somehow he managed. He'd forced himself to stand every hour, partly to get his blood circulating again, partly to get a longer perspective on the uneven terrain leading up to the canyonlands where the cattle were grouped together, munching on the hay he'd brought up two days ago.

Camouflaged by a stand of junipers at the top of the center canyon, from his vantage point he could see around two hundred degrees in three directions—

And suddenly he saw them. Three dark dots moving over the sparkling white carpet of fresh snow.

Attacking the zipper and drawstring with near-numb fingers, Hawk struggled out of the sleeping bag, whistling for Tonopah. By the time he was free of the puffy fabric, his horse had trotted over. He whipped the thick Indian blanket off his mount and jumped into the saddle, heading for the trail off the plateau. Pulling the Winchester from its holster, he checked it for action. Better to be ready for anything.

Chafing with impatience, he held his pace sure and steady on the downward trail, so as not to injure Tonopah, who was as cold and cramped as he was. He had plenty of time, he told himself.

Nevertheless when they hit the bottom of the cliffs, he urged Tonopah into a slow lope through the snow, aiming toward the rustlers' trail. He wanted to backtrack to their waiting truck and get the license plate number before doing anything else. Too bad he didn't have a cell phone. That would sure have come in handy to call the sheriff. But he was on his own for this one.

He found the triple grooves left in the four-foot snow by the rustlers' horses and reined Tonopah into one of them, turning him away from the canyons. Riding hard, it took him a good hour to get to the last rise before the property fence; just beyond that lay the highway.

Dismounting, he crept cautiously up the hill, keeping his head below the level of the snow. At the crest, he peeked over. And there was the truck, just where he expected. It was an unmarked eighteen-wheeler cattle transport, big enough to fit eight or ten animals. He swore violently under his breath. There was no way this was not personal. These guys meant to wipe him out completely and drive Irish Heaven into bankruptcy.

But why? The question kept pounding in his brain. Who hated him—or Fitz—that much?

Well, he'd soon find out.

He hadn't spotted anyone around the truck, so he topped the rise and started down the other side. He'd almost made it to the back, to check the plate, when the calm, silent air was suddenly shattered by a deafening bang.

A terrible pain ripped through his arm and he looked down, horrified to see the snow below him turning crimson.

Aw, hell. The bastards had—

But the thought evaporated in another flash of blinding pain in the back of his head, then everything around him, the glittering snow, the robin's-egg sky, the white lines on the highway, all went black.

Chapter 12

Slowly Redhawk clawed his way to consciousness. Was he alive?

He wasn't rightly sure. He was colder than he'd ever been in his life. Which made no sense at all if he was in Hell. But surely Heaven had central heating?

He tried to laugh at the absurdity of his thoughts, but a heavy pressure prevented him from expanding his chest more than a fraction. Damn. It felt like he was...

He pried open his eyes. All he saw was black.

Damn, he *was* buried! In something incredibly cold and—

Snow! How the *hell...*?

Desperately he tried to get his brain to work despite the mind-numbing cold. His head pounded and his arm throbbed, but he forced the pain away and cleared the cobwebs.

Then he remembered. He'd been shot. *Shot for crissakes.* Then...then someone must have whacked him over the head with a two-by-four or a crowbar or something. And buried him in a snowdrift.

The snowpack couldn't prevent a groan from rumbling through his chest.

He was so dead.

Maybe it was the cold, but for some reason the thought didn't panic him all that much. All he could think was, it was a hell of a way to go, after everything he'd been through in life. To survive all that other crap and end up dying frozen in a snowdrift, well that was just plain typical.

Experimentally, he tried to move his good arm and found he could bring it up past his chest, so he scraped the snow from around his face, packing it over to the side so he had a few inches of air to breathe. He was feeling a little warmer already.

Of course, dying now when for the first time in his life he had everything to live for, yeah, that was also typical of his damn bad luck.

What would Rhiannon think when they found his body? Would she be happy, because she got the ranch all to herself?

He hoped she would be sad. Yeah, she'd be sad. She didn't love him, didn't want to marry him…but she did like him. She liked being with him, liked talking with him, liked sleeping with him.

Yeah, she especially liked sleeping with him.

He liked sleeping with her, too.

The thought of never sleeping with Rhiannon again, of never seeing her again, finally had the panic rising in his chest.

Damn. He had to get out of there!

But how?

Suddenly, he heard a distant whinny and a nicker. Or maybe— No, it was right above him!

"Tonopah!" he called, his voice coming out scratchy and woozy. "Is that you, boy?"

The horse whinnied again, and Hawk heard the sound of something scraping in the snow. The horse's muzzle? Or his hoof? Hell, he'd take either. What was another contusion? He heard more scraping.

"Wake me up, boy!" he croaked, never more grateful for his horse's cleverness and his own training regime.

Was it his imagination, or was the pressure getting lighter on his chest?

He moved his good arm again, making a fist and forcing it up through the snow as hard as he could. To his surprise, the pack wasn't too difficult to push through. Probably because of the cold weather and light, steady snowfall that hadn't had a chance either to settle or to melt.

Thank God.

Scraping away crazily, all at once he felt a warm, velvety muzzle in his hand, blowing and mouthing his palm.

"Man, am I glad to see you," he said metaphorically, his eyes stinging from the icy snow dripping into them. He grasped the bridle and felt for the reins. Winding them around his wrist, he gave the tongue click command for Tonopah to back up. Which he did, dragging Hawk up from the snow as he went.

And suddenly he was free.

It was dark out, but at least it had stopped snowing. Bracing himself on Tonopah's flank, he staggered to his feet, gasping at the pain in both his arm and knee. He was one useless cowboy.

Standing patiently, his faithful horse waited as Hawk lay across the saddle then awkwardly hoisted his good leg up and over, hanging on to the saddle horn as best he could with numb hands and a bleeding gunshot wound. His head was spinning like a midway ride at the county fair. Breathing heavily, he wondered how on earth he'd ever make it home.

At his signal, Tonopah started to walk. Hawk clung to his neck, letting the horse take charge. Not that he had a lot of choice. But he trusted his friend. They'd been through a lot together.

"Take me home, boy," he whispered as he started to slip from consciousness once again. "Take me home to Rhiannon…."

"Oh, my God!"

Rhiannon bolted from the door and down the front steps to

where Hawk's horse stood whinnying, the man on his back lying there still as death.

Blood was everywhere.

"Oh, my God," she cried again, putting her hands to Hawk's deathly cold face, testing for a pulse in his neck while a sickening sense of terror crawled through her body. "Fitz!" she screamed, hoping he'd hear her and wake up.

Hawk moaned, a slight, nearly inaudible sound.

With a silent prayer of thanks, she grasped the folds of his duster and tried to tug him off the horse. He clung to the saddle horn like a limpet.

"Hawk, you need to let go," she urged, fighting to get a better grip on his coat.

"What's going on—" Fitz appeared in the doorway and halted with a spill of curses. "Jamie!" he cried, and ran to her side. "Ah, Lord, what have they done with ye, lad?"

"Help me get him down, Uncle," she said desperately. "Then fetch the keys to the truck and my purse. He needs a doctor."

Together they managed to lift him off Tonopah, whom Fitz attended to after running for the truck keys. A few minutes later she was driving as fast as she dared over the icy roads toward Windmill Junction.

The warmth in the cab finally brought Hawk around. "Damn, I'm freezing," he muttered, swallowing thickly. "Or maybe burning up. Can't decide." He cracked an eyelid and peered glassy-eyed over at her. "You found me."

"Actually you found us. You rode all the way back to the ranch from— Hawk, what happened? It looks like you're—"

"Some bastard shot me," he said, shifting with a low groan. "Aw, hell."

"Are you okay?" she asked, alarmed at his desolate tone.

"It was the rustlers again. God knows how many steers they made off with this time."

"*Steers!* Hawk, do you have any idea how lucky you are to be alive? This is attempted murder!"

"Who did this to you, lad?" demanded Fitz from the back bench. "Why, I'll slit his quisling throat meself." He continued to mutter agitatedly to himself, but Rhiannon didn't have time to worry about Fitz right now.

"Did you get a look at them?" she asked Hawk.

He winced at a jostle. "No. But I saw their truck."

"Hopefully the sheriff can trace it from your description."

He closed his eyes and didn't answer.

"Hawk?"

His tipped head and slack jaw told her he'd slipped back into unconsciousness.

Tears stung the back of her eyes as she pressed harder on the gas pedal. She had to hurry! What would she do if—

No, she refused to go there. Hawk would be all right. And Fitz, too, she added mentally as he continued to talk gibberish to himself behind her.

Stark fear and a sense of inadequacy swamped over her with sudden vehemence. The same feelings she'd had as a child, over not being able to help her ill mother. With a deep breath she battled back against the constrictions in her heart. She would not give in to despair.

Gritting her teeth, she clenched the steering wheel and made the turn onto the highway.

Fitz would be fine.

And Hawk would not die.

Nobody died from being shot in the arm. Not in this day and age.

And nobody thought any of this was her fault.

That's what she kept telling herself all the way to the small emergency-care clinic on the outskirts of Windmill Junction. And the whole time Hawk was with the doctor getting prepped and sewn up. And even when the nurse led a badly stammering Fitz into an exam room to give him a sedative.

She'd survived the past and she'd survive this, too. After all, what else could go wrong?

Looking up, she saw Burton Grant stroll through the clinic door.

She couldn't help it. She had to laugh. It was either that or cry.

Okay, so it could get worse.

"Hello, Rhiannon," he said, walking up to her. "I hear Jackson got himself shot."

She kept her grim smile firmly in place. "Doing *your* job, deputy. The rustlers hit us again."

He took a seat next to her. "On Christmas? That's cold."

"They tried to kill Hawk. You really need to catch them, Burt." She glared at him. "That's *murder,* in case you need it spelled out."

"We're doing our best, Rhiannon. The sheriff has three men on this case. Now, what's all this about murder? Surely it was an accident?"

She shook her head adamantly. "No." She related what Hawk had told her.

Burt frowned. "Those are serious allegations. Does he have any proof of this?"

"I imagine a forensics team could confirm it."

He slashed a hand through his hair. "I can't believe they're resorting to murder. He must have surprised them or something."

"Are you making *excuses* for these wankers?" she asked incredulously.

He got to his feet and stood for a moment, hands on hips, staring at the door leading to the surgery. Finally he said, "Have Jackson call me. I'll need a description of the vehicle, and the location of the incident so we can send a team." And then he walked off without even saying goodbye.

That was odd.

"Miss O'Brannoch?" It was the nurse who had taken care of Fitz.

"Yes? How is my uncle?" Rhiannon asked.

The nurse sat beside her in the chair vacated by Burton. "I'm afraid it's not good. For some reason the trauma of seeing Mr. Jackson's injury seems to have caused a turn for the worse in your uncle's condition. He should see his regular doctor as soon as possible. Sometimes shocks like this can lead to a permanent decline."

Rhiannon's hand went to her mouth. "Oh, that would be too cruel."

"Unfortunately, there's nothing to be done now. Just be sure not to leave him alone until you see how this is going to affect him. You should take careful note of any new symptoms, especially changes in his personality or long-term memory."

"Long-term? I thought it was just the short-term memory that's affected."

"In the beginning. But by the end, the old memories are lost, too, and even language itself."

Rhiannon felt her hand tremble. She didn't know which was worse, seeing her mother's body waste away while her mind remained sharp and conscious of every horrible detail, or now Fitz, whose body was hale and healthy but whose mind was slowly shutting down.

She buried her face in her hands.

She didn't think she could take this.

How could she go through all of it again? The fear, the suffering, the helplessness? It was too much to ask. And on top of everything else having to deal with the ranch and the rustlers— and Redhawk Jackson's stubborn pride.

For the first time in her life she considered giving up.

She should just swallow her own pride and write her aunt and uncle for a ticket home. She wasn't cut out for a life in this savage country.

"Baby?" Hawk was standing in front of her, pale as a ghost, worry creasing his brow as he gazed down at her.

"Hawk!" She sprang to her feet and threw her arms about him, mindful of his bandaged arm.

"Darlin', are you all right?"

She hugged him tighter, refusing to let the tears fall that she felt threaten. "I'm fine. Are you?"

"I'll live. Let's get Fitz and go home."

She managed to keep it together on the way home. And while she tucked each of them into bed. And as she ate her solitary Christmas dinner. But when she pulled out stationery and pen and started writing a letter to her aunt and uncle, it all poured out of her. By the time she wrote "Love, Rhiannon," her cheeks were streaked with moisture, and small, round droplets stained the paper.

With a deep sigh she folded the letter and slipped it in the envelope she'd already addressed, setting it behind a vase on the mantel.

Mailing it would mean admitting defeat. But she honestly didn't know what else to do.

They'd have to sell the ranch now. Hawk had clearly said if any more of the cattle were stolen they'd be unable to survive next year. They'd have no choice but to sell.

And with the ranch gone, there'd be no reason for her to stay. Even if she might want to.

Boxing Day, the day after Christmas, dawned cold and gray, but at least the snow had stopped for good.

Rhiannon trudged out to the barn to take care of the animals, opening the big double doors and the stall Dutch doors to let in some fresh air and sunshine. After feeding the chickens, she put the bull Lucky Charm in his outdoor pen, then threw blankets over the three horses and led them out into the corral. Except for the past few days, Hawk had kept it snowplowed so he had a clear place for training Crimson and so the other horses could run around a bit.

She was sitting on the rail watching them play when she heard Hawk come up behind her. She smiled as he slid his arm around her waist and stood so her back was resting against his chest.

Closing her eyes, she painted a mental picture, trying to memorize it all so she'd never forget what this one moment in time felt like. The crisp, snow-scented air, the dazzlingly beautiful red cliffs and tall green trees, the warmth of Hawk's body pressed into hers, the smell of his soap-scrubbed skin, the taste of his mouth kissing her good morning.

"You should be in bed," she whispered.

"Got lonely," he whispered back, and kissed her again.

"How's your arm?"

"Lonely."

"What about your knee?"

"Lonelier."

Her smile widened. "Hawk, be serious."

"I am."

She turned to give him a fierce hug. "Don't ever do that again. You scared me to death."

"You weren't the only one," he murmured, pulling her close with his uninjured arm

"What are we going to do?"

"Go on. There's nothing else we can do."

"But how? The herd…"

He shrugged. "We'll find a way."

She looked up into his dark, confident eyes. "How can you be so sure?"

"Because," he said with a kiss on her nose, "we have to."

She heard a car, and they turned to see Burton's sheriff's cruiser drive up.

"Sorry, I forgot. He wanted you to call," she told Hawk.

His eyes narrowed. "He was at the clinic? News travels fast."

"I'm pretty sure gunshot wounds have to be reported."

She hopped off the rail and they walked over to the cruiser as Burt was getting out.

He flipped open his notebook. "I'll need your statement, Jackson."

"Let's go inside. I'll make coffee," she suggested.

As Hawk described for Burt exactly what had happened, Rhiannon kept in the background. But she couldn't help being horrified once again at what she heard. At how close she'd come to losing him.

"How many did they get this time?" Burt asked.

Redhawk shook his head. "Don't know yet. Six or eight if they filled the truck."

Burt pursed his lips. "Sounds like you're pretty much wiped out."

Hawk rose and slowly limped over to the counter to refill his cup. "We'll see about that."

"What did you mean?" Rhiannon asked later, after Burton had left. "Is there some option I don't know about?"

"No." He rubbed the back of his neck with deliberate fingers. "But now they've made me mad. No way I'm letting them win."

She shivered. There was something cold and formidable in his voice when he said it, and a very hard gleam in his eyes. "Hawk, please tell me you're not thinking of going back out there."

"Thinking? No," he said, and she knew with dead certainty that he'd already made up his mind. *Dead* being the operative word, with a greater possibility than she wanted to contemplate.

"You can't," she told him. "What will happen to Fitz if you're hurt? If you're not here to take care of him?"

Hawk turned away. "He'll have you."

She opened her mouth to tell him…tell him what? That she'd decided it would be best for all of them if she went back to Ireland? One less mouth to feed, one less contender for the ranch, one less love affair to end….

But for some reason the words got stuck in her throat.

No. Best to wait. Just a while. Until they knew about Fitz. Until spring, maybe, when the calves were born and the final count made on the herd and they knew where they stood financially. They, meaning the ranch. Fitz and Hawk. Because she wasn't part of that "they."

She looked up and he was standing in the laundry room door,

holding his duster and staring at her. "You did it again. You mended my duster."

She bit her lip, recalling the horror of seeing the water turn to crimson when she'd rinsed out the sleeve, and the way her fingers had shaken so badly she'd pricked herself a hundred times with the needle before the gaping hole had been patched.

"I, um, I got bored last night," she managed. "Nothing but Christmas carols and *It's a Wonderful Life* on the telly. I've seen it," she added. "About a hundred times."

She saw his Adam's apple bob, then his gaze fell to the duster. "I'm sorry," he said softly. "That I'm so useless. I'll make it up to you, I swear."

"Oh, Hawk." She went to him and wrapped her arms around him. "Don't say that. You do more than any man I've ever known. I'm the one who's useless."

He kissed her hair. "You're so wrong. When this is over—" He shook his head. "Baby, you know I have to keep going out there until I catch these bastards. You know that, right? It's the only way."

"But they tried to kill you!"

"Don't you see, they're killing us either way. Six feet under or being forced to sell the ranch, the effect's the same."

"Not quite," she murmured, feeling his warm, muscular shoulder beneath her cheek, so vibrant and alive she could feel the power radiate from it, leashed but ready to strike at anything attempting to hurt those he loved.

He might be wounded, but he was so far from useless it made her knees weak just being close to him.

"I don't want to lose you," she whispered, clutching him bleakly.

"You won't," he said, and tipped her chin up. He ran the rough pad of his thumb over her bottom lip, gazing deep into her eyes. "I'll be here for you, as long as you need me."

She had to close her eyes for fear he'd read in them just how desperately she did need him. Would always need him. His lips came down on hers, softly, quietly, and her mouth quavered beneath them. His fingers slid up her nape and into her hair, and he held her there for the most exquisitely tender, achingly gentle kiss she'd ever received.

She wanted to break down. To tell him she loved him, that she would need him forever. That the hunger in her soul to be his, to stay in his embrace, would never go away.

But she stopped herself just short of blurting it all out. That wasn't what he needed from her. He needed her to be strong. Independent. So he could do what he had to do to save the ranch without worrying about her getting wrong ideas about him and their relationship. It was all about the ranch. She had to remember that.

"Rhiannon," he whispered, and kissed her again. "Rhiannon, I—"

Suddenly, the doorbell rang, startling them apart.

"Who could that be?" she said with a nervous laugh, pressing her damp palms onto her skirt.

"Whoever it is I'm going to kill them," he muttered, heading for the front door. "Can't a man be left in peace to—" He flung open the door. "You lost or what?" he asked gruffly of whoever was standing there.

She went back to the kitchen. She was in no shape to see anyone right now. Her knees were still shaking.

When Redhawk walked back into the room, he was carrying one of those cardboard, overnight-type envelopes.

Rhiannon looked up from the table. "What's that?"

"Registered letter. Special delivery."

"Strange. What does it say?"

He zipped open the top of the cardboard, took out an official-looking document and quickly scanned the top page.

"Well?" she asked anxiously.

His gaze lifted with a curse. "It's a purchase offer."

"Purchase? For what?"

His mouth thinned. "The ranch. It's an offer to buy Irish Heaven."

Chapter 13

Furious, Redhawk flung the papers on the table. "Now, that's what I call impeccable timing," he growled.

"You think they know about yesterday?" Rhiannon asked. "Who's it from?"

"Don't know. Don't care," he spat out. "There is no way I'm going to be pressured into selling Irish Heaven just because—" Suddenly it hit him. "My God!" He grabbed up the papers from the table again. "That's it! That's why this is happening!"

She looked puzzled. "Why?"

"Someone wants Irish Heaven bad enough to put us out of business to get it. Maybe even—"

Her mouth dropped open. "*Murder?* By the saints, Redhawk, that can't be true. Can it?" Her expression filled with horror.

At the moment he would bet his life on it. But she looked so scared he backed off. "Well, maybe not murder. It's possible Grant's right and I just caught them by surprise. But I'd be willing to bet whoever sent this—" he waved the papers in his hand "—is behind the rustling."

"So who did send it?"

He flipped through the pages to find the signature. Just as he suspected, the name of an attorney proxy was scrawled on the line for the buyer. "The lawyer is acting on their behalf. My guess is it'll be impossible to find out who the real client is."

"Because of attorney-client privilege."

He nodded grimly. "But they can't hide forever. If they want the ranch it's for a reason. They'll have to show themselves eventually."

"But by then it'll be too late. Especially…"

She didn't have to complete the sentence. He knew exactly what she meant. "Yeah. Especially if I'm dead and Fitz is declared incompetent."

The next day the attorney called for Fitz's answer, and Hawk barely resisted the urge to hang up on the man. Instead he minded his manners, and pumped him for all the information he could. Which amounted to exactly nothing. If the guy knew who he was working for, he was a world-champion liar. He insisted the offer had all been presented through another lawyer on behalf of a shadow company. Hawk knew the more filters in place, the more impossible it would be to break through to the real people behind it.

"I'd like to speak with Mr. O'Brannoch himself, if you don't mind," the attorney said when Hawk told him to take his offer and stuff it.

"I'm afraid he's indisposed," Hawk replied. "Indefinitely." And hung up.

After which, he called to report everything to the sheriff, making sure to bypass Burton Grant while doing so. He didn't care if the deputy was in charge of the case. He didn't like the man, didn't want him coming out to the ranch asking stupid questions and making moon eyes at Rhiannon.

Rhiannon was *his*.

"Can I come with you this afternoon?" she asked, interrupting his inner tirade.

He was taking Fitz to the doctor, as the nurse at the emergency-care clinic had advised.

"I'd like that," he said, his anger swiftly turning to sadness at the prospect of what they might find out. "I'm not looking forward to it."

Bad things were happening too quickly on all fronts. But the one that tore his guts out more than anything was the change in Fitz.

When they got to the doctor's, the news was not what they wanted to hear.

"I'm sorry to say Fitz has entered the advanced stages of the disease," the doctor told them after completing his tests and examination. "I very much doubt he'll bounce back from this recent setback."

Depressed, Hawk tried to wrap his mind around the fact that Fitz was not getting better. "Are you sure?"

"It's always possible he'll have some days that are more lucid than others."

"But he won't get even worse, will he?" he asked, taking Rhiannon's hand. He needed something to hang on to.

"Right away, you mean?" The doctor pursed his lips. "Hard to say. My guess is you'll start seeing more compulsive behaviors, like the muttering he's already started exhibiting, and maybe some personality changes, as well. Sometimes it all happens quickly, sometimes it takes years to run the full course."

"He can stay home, can't he?" Rhiannon asked worriedly.

"If someone is there with him at all times. As his long-term memory goes, he'll need more and more help with orientation and everyday tasks. He can easily get lost or hurt himself. Tell me. Have you thought about taking him back to Ireland?"

Hawk was stunned by the suggestion. "Why?"

The doctor steepled his fingers. "He seems to be living there in his mind now, more and more, would you agree?"

Rhiannon nodded. "He's forgotten nearly everything about his life in Arizona, except his close friends. He talks almost solely about his younger days in Ireland."

"Sometimes it can be a comfort for a patient to return to live in a familiar place from childhood, if it's possible. It won't slow the disease, but can ease the panic over memory loss."

They were both subdued as they walked out of the office with Fitz, who didn't seem to understand exactly what was going on.

"Want to stop for a pint at Jake's?" Hawk suggested. "Maybe the guys are there." This might be the old man's last chance to see them and possibly know them....

Fitz nodded eagerly, then started mumbling excitedly. Hawk knew it was probably not a good idea to give him alcohol, though the doctor hadn't expressly forbidden it, and it was definitely a bad idea for himself to indulge because of the pain medication and anti-inflammatories he was on for the hole in his arm. But at the moment he didn't give a damn.

He needed a drink bad.

While Rhiannon settled Fitz in at his friends' usual table and spoke a few quiet words in Pete's ear, Hawk grabbed the two of them a private booth toward the back and waved at Jake to bring them a couple of beers.

He eased onto the seat and leaned his head back on the padded vinyl. The reassuringly familiar cocoon of the booth enveloped him as did the whine of the jukebox playing softly in the background. The smell of peanuts, stale beer and horses and the sound of Jake's smoker's laugh as he pulled their drafts were comforting in their sameness. This was the way Jake's had been for as long as he could remember.

What would it be like if suddenly all that turned foreign, unknown, and scary?

That's exactly what was happening to his best friend, and

there wasn't a damn thing Hawk could do about it. The thought ate at him like acid in his stomach. He wished he had the means to take Fitz back to Ireland, as the doc had suggested. But unless he robbed a bank, it wasn't going to happen.

Why was he never able to help those he loved?

Rhiannon slid in next to him and he let out a sigh. How he needed her right now. How glad he was that she'd come to Irish Heaven. How much he wanted her to stay. For him.

"You okay?" she asked.

He rolled his head and gazed at her with a wan smile. "Hell, no. You?"

"Me, neither." She shook her head. "Suppose I'll have to quit my job."

He digested that. "Gonna make things hard. No more filet mignon for supper."

She smiled dryly. "Or champagne to wash it down."

"That sucks," he said, taking a sip of his beer.

"Yeah," she agreed, and laid her head on his shoulder.

He slid his arm around her. "We'll be okay. As long as we're together." He gave her a kiss.

"Hawk," she started, but was interrupted when a commotion rose at Fitz's table. "What's going on?"

"It's Grant," he muttered, watching carefully while Fitz was turned away and calmed down by his friends. Hawk switched his attention back to the deputy, who walked up to his and Rhiannon's booth.

"Been looking for you two," Grant said, ignoring the stir he'd caused on the other side of the room. He frowned at Hawk's arm around Rhiannon.

Hawk pulled her closer. "Yeah? The sheriff find out who made that offer on Irish Heaven?"

The deputy slid into the opposite side of the booth. "No. But I thought you'd like to know, forensics confirmed your story about the incident yesterday."

"I told you they would."

"Yes, well, we also think we located the truck you described. Abandoned at a shopping mall up in Kaibab."

Hawk sat up. "And?"

"If it's the same one, it was reported stolen last week. Belongs to the Lost Man outfit up the road."

"You mean Jeremy Lloyd's ranch?" Rhiannon asked in surprise. "Where the dead guy, Rudy Balboa, worked?"

"Believe so."

"That's a bit of a coincidence, don't you think?" Hawk remarked, his mind churning.

"I thought so, too. Unfortunately, there's no way to connect any of this to Lloyd. No trace of the cattle, and no witnesses. Everyone there seems to have an alibi. We're still working on it, though."

"Great," Hawk said, slumping down again. Damn. Every time they got close, the slippery bastards slid through their fingers. Rather, the cops' fingers. Maybe he'd have to start doing his own investigating.

"Oh, I almost forgot," Grant said as he got up to leave. "We also received a heads-up from Social Services. Someone has filed a petition with the county probate court regarding Fitz."

"What about?" Hawk asked indignantly. "If they're saying his care—"

Grant held up a palm. "No, nothing like that. It was more along the lines of questioning his ability to do business. The filer is a lawyer claiming he has a contract pending with O'Brannoch and he wants to be sure the old man's mentally competent to sign it."

Hawk stared at the deputy in disbelief.

"Mentally competent?" Rhiannon asked.

Grant gave her an oily smile. "Everyone's aware of Fitz's condition. The people who made the purchase offer on the ranch, I expect that's the origin of the petition."

"But why would they do such a thing?" she asked.

He shifted on his feet. "To force a competency hearing, I expect."

"They can do that?" Hawk put in, starting to suspect where all this was going.

Grant shrugged expressively. "If it involves lawyers, I expect so."

"What's the point?" Rhiannon said. "A judge will just appoint Redhawk or me as his conservator. And we both agree with Fitz about the contract."

"Are you sure?" he asked meaningfully.

"Of course we agree," Hawk practically snarled.

"Then there's no problem," he said. "Anyway, just thought I'd let you know."

"Thanks very much," Hawk said, hanging on to his temper by a thread.

With a mock salute, Grant strolled out of the bar.

"The little weasel," Hawk hissed under his breath. "I can't believe they'd pull something like this."

"I don't understand," Rhiannon said with a troubled expression.

He lifted his hand to her cheek, running his fingertips along her pale, satin-soft cheek. "They're counting on us to get greedy. Or one of us."

"Greedy?"

"Irish Heaven is worth over a million dollars. Control of that would be mighty tempting to a lot of broke-down cowboys and poor immigrant lasses."

Her chin went up. "I'm no poor immigrant lass."

He chuckled and kissed her temple, then grew somber again. "They're counting on us fighting over control of the money."

She looked at him for a long while, searching his eyes. He suddenly couldn't breathe, wondering what she was thinking. He knew what *he* was thinking. If they got married, it wouldn't be an issue. Whoever was doing this would have to give up and realize they were a united front.

But were they?

She was being awful silent.

"I see," she finally said.

"Well?" he demanded, a bit more harshly than he'd meant to.

"Well, what?"

"Is one of us going to get greedy?"

She leveled him a gaze. "I want exactly the same thing you want, Hawk. But I'll abide by Fitz's wishes. You know that already."

What the hell was *that* supposed to mean?

He clamped his jaw and made himself finish his beer before saying, "Let's get out of here. I've got work to do."

While Rhiannon fetched Fitz, he paid the tab and shoved away the temptation to put her in the truck, drive straight to Reno, and force her to marry him.

Why couldn't the stubborn woman see that was the best solution to *all* of their problems? That way they'd both get what they wanted, and nobody could split them apart through dissention and doubt.

Hell and damnation.

He was overreacting, he told himself firmly. She wasn't going to go against him. She'd just said so. And he trusted her.

Pretty much.

As it turned out, after reading the accompanying documentation and affidavits, the judge deciding the petition ruled that a full competency hearing for Fitz was in order. The estate was too extensive to leave the running of it to people with no legal standing. Fitz's lawyer testified he had no extant power of attorney, and his doctor confirmed he was unlikely to recover his faculties enough to legally execute one.

So it was up to the judge to choose a conservator.

While on the stand, Rhiannon and Hawk both suggested appointing the person who would inherit Irish Heaven according to Fitz's will. Unfortunately, the laws in their county prohibited his attorney from revealing the contents of the will before his death, without his signed authorization.

It was a frustrating catch-22, and Rhiannon felt completely wrung out, well before the proceedings ended.

She cringed when the judge called Fitz to the stand as the last witness. He'd been disoriented through the whole hearing, muttering about the IRA and the injustice of their British oppressors. She was afraid he'd appear so far gone the judge would take him away and put him in some awful facility. That would break her heart. He deserved to be cared for by the people who loved him.

"Do you know why you're here?" Judge Fernandez asked him.

"Aye," he said belligerently. "'Twasn't enough you got me brother, now you want me in prison, too.''

"For what?" the judge asked patiently.

"Bein' a patriot. Erin forever!" he called out, shaking a fist.

"Mr. O'Brannoch, do you remember moving to the United States?" Fernandez probed.

Fitz blanched, his whole demeanor changing. Suddenly he rose and grasped the railing in front of him. Rhiannon could see his hands tremble.

He turned a distraught gaze on Redhawk. "I'm sorry," he said, his voice rough with emotion. "I'm so sorry, lad! We didn't mean to—" His eyes flicked to her. "If I thought it would end this way, I'd never have asked you to take my mission that day."

Judge Fernandez looked puzzled but went on. "Mr. O'Brannoch, you are not obligated to tell us, but it would be a big help if we could know who you've named as your legal heir, in your will."

"And now they've thrown you in prison for life." Fitz covered his face with his hands. "Oh, Janet, Janet, what have we done?"

Shock froze Rhiannon to her chair. *Janet?*

The judge turned to Redhawk. "Do you know what he's talking about, Mr. Jackson?"

Hawk looked visibly shaken. "I assume it's something about his past. He—" He halted and swiped a hand over his mouth.

Rhiannon swallowed hard. She knew he wouldn't want to air Fitz's secrets in open court, but something told her this may be her only opportunity to learn this one. And it sounded big.

"He's talking about his brother, Jamie," she said. "Janet is my mother." Gathering her courage, she faced her uncle. "Uncle Fitz, were you and Janet together the day they arrested my father? The day of the bombing?"

For a second she saw lucidity in his eyes, saw the knowledge of what he'd done, the regret, and the anguish over it. "Aye," he whispered, then he broke down with a sob. "I'm sorry, love."

Instantly she was on her feet, rushing to him. "It's all right, Uncle." She knelt down, holding him in her arms, rocking him. "It doesn't matter. You didn't set that bomb, Jamie O'Brannoch did. My father chose his own fate. It's none of your doing."

"Ah, Janet, me love, you were never mine for the taking," he murmured, and she wasn't sure if he was there with her or back in the past. "What made me think I could?"

"She loved you, Uncle," she whispered, knowing it was true. Even if she hadn't found the letters, she'd always instinctively felt there was something missing in her mother's voice, in her expression, when she'd talked about Da. Rhiannon had always assumed it was because her mother couldn't forgive him for leaving the two of them all alone in the world, over a fickle thing like politics. Now she knew the truth. The politics were just an excuse.

"Why don't we adjourn for today?" Judge Fernandez suggested, clearing his throat. "I think I have all the facts I need for a ruling."

Hawk's gaze met hers and her heart skipped a beat.

Passion.

That's what had been missing in her mother's eyes.

Did she see it there in Hawk's?

Maybe. Or maybe it was just the love and compassion he felt for his dying mentor shining through.

"I'll have my decision tomorrow," the judge announced, and they all rose as he left the room.

She wished her own life could be decided as easily.

"Nervous?" Hawk asked as he opened the outside door for them and took her arm to walk to the truck, Fitz trudging along behind.

"Should I be?"

"I guess that depends on how much you want the ranch."

And suddenly she understood, deep in her heart, it wasn't the ranch at all that she wanted. What she wanted was the feeling of belonging. Of being a family.

Of passion.

And that was something she'd never get from 538 acres of Arizona desert.

Turning, she took Fitz's elbow so the three of them were walking arm in arm down the dirt sidewalk.

"What I want," she answered, "is to go home and forget about all of this. And finally eat our Christmas dinner."

The next day, Judge Fernandez named Rhiannon as Fitz's conservator.

As soon as he had his doctor's okay, Redhawk resumed his vigil with the cattle.

Rhiannon was worried sick. Pete lent him a small Arctic-weight tent, cot and pocket heaters that came in at the trading post, but she still thought Hawk was mad to risk his health in the bitter winter weather, and endanger his life with rustlers who'd already proven they were willing to shoot first and ask questions later.

She'd tried for the entire week, but couldn't budge him off his decision. Now he was packed and ready to go.

"They got away with six more steers last time," he said, sliding his rifle open and checking the chamber. "That means we only have seven left for spring market. One more attack and our entire income for the year will be wiped out. *Everything.* Do you want that?"

Apprehensively, she watched him drop a full box of shells in his duster pocket. "No, of course not. But—"

"And after spring calving, they'll no doubt start in on the cows and newborns. I have to stop them before that happens."

She understood all that. But in her heart she knew that wasn't the only thing driving him out into the cold, bleak night.

It was her.

He'd listened without comment to the announcement in her favor by the judge; he hadn't even blinked an eye. But he'd taken it hard. She'd seen it in his expression when he didn't think she was looking. He'd been very quiet ever since.

He'd also started to defer to her in all decisions, to the point where sometimes she'd wanted to throw something at him. He said he was teaching her the ropes. She knew better. His pride was hurting.

What she didn't know was what to do about it.

"For heaven's sake, be careful," she said, giving him a hug goodbye before he walked out the door. She hung on to him for a few more precious seconds. She missed him terribly when he was gone at night. Hated sleeping in the bed without him.

"I will." He kissed her, and for a moment she thought he was as reluctant as she to let go.

"Come home if the weather turns," she reminded him. It was the only promise she'd managed to wring from him—if it dropped below thirty degrees or started storming, he'd come in, as the rustlers were unlikely to be out then, either.

"Yeah," he said. And then he was gone.

Leaving her with empty arms, and an even emptier heart.

She watched him ride over the far ridge and sighed, not looking forward to the long, lonely night ahead.

Suddenly, there was a loud knock on the door.

Chapter 14

Rhiannon's head swung around and she glanced toward the sound of the knocking, then at the clock. Nervousness shimmered through her. It wasn't that late, but who could it be? Hawk was gone, and Fitz already asleep.

Biting her lip, she debated whether she should just ignore it.

It grew louder. Then a yell. "Rhiannon!"

With a chuckle of relief, she ran to the door, opened it and smiled. "Burt. What are you doing here this time of night?"

He grinned and leaned against the doorjamb, hands behind his back. "Oh, I was in the neighborhood…"

She laughed and waved him in. "I suppose being within fifty miles is considered in the neighborhood around here."

He winked. "Reckon so."

"Would you like some tea, or maybe a—" She halted in consternation. Were they out of beer?

From behind his back he produced a six-pack. "Since Fitz is

keeping you in these days, thought I'd invite myself on a date with you here."

"Burt," she chided, suddenly unsure of what was going on. "You know I don't go out on dates since Redhawk and I…"

He made a dismissive gesture. "Not a *date* date. Just to talk. No biggie."

Odd that he didn't ask where Hawk was. Almost as though—

"Wanted to bring you up to speed on the investigation," he said.

She motioned for him to take a seat at the kitchen table. "Has there been a new development?"

"Well, yes and no. We followed up on the truck," he said, and twisted open a beer for her. "Reinterviewed everyone at the Lost Man. All the alibis seem to hold up, and forensics didn't find anything unusual in the truck."

"Did you check their bank accounts? For the money from the stolen cattle? Or that restaurant deal?"

"Not without probable cause, we can't."

"So we're back to square one."

"Looks that way," he said, leaning back in his chair to take a few more pulls from his bottle. "So I hear you've been made Fitz's conservator."

She sighed. "Yes. I have."

"Will you be selling the ranch?"

Her jaw dropped. "No. Why would I do that?"

"It's no secret, Rhiannon. You guys are pretty well bankrupt." His brows rose at her expression. "You're actually thinking of keeping the place?"

"I have no intention of selling Irish Heaven," she said indignantly, and got to her feet. "And if you—"

"Hold on to your horses, there, doll. Just relax. I'm not suggesting you should. In fact, I think you'd be crazy if you did sell it."

Reluctantly she sat down again. "Sorry. I'm a little sensitive about the subject. Redhawk—" She stopped and shook her head.

"He what? Doesn't trust you?"

"Of course he trusts me, it's just—" She laughed and took a sip of beer. "Never mind. He's just worried about the rustling. I am, too."

He reached for her hands across the table and took them in his. "Rhiannon, I want you to know you can come to me, if you need help. With anything. Anything at all."

"Thanks, Burt. I appreciate that," she said, subtly attempting to extract her hands from his, but he held tight.

"I mean it, sweetheart. I know you're hurting for money now that you're not working at Jake's, and, well, I have a bit put away. Anytime, Rhiannon. Just give me the word."

"Burt, I'm not—"

Suddenly the back door swung open, and Redhawk strode in, duster flying, carrying his rifle under his arm. He halted in his tracks.

His gaze latched on to their hands, still joined over the table, and anger flashed from every pore. "Well, isn't this cozy," he said, his voice low but seething with hostility.

"Hawk!" She yanked on her hands, but only succeeded in freeing one.

The other, Burt brought to his lips before releasing. "The offer's always open, sweetheart." Then he turned to Hawk. "Evening, Jackson," he said, and rose to his feet with a false smile. "Thought you were out babysitting bovines."

Hawk's eyes narrowed. "How did you know that?"

Burt shrugged. "Stands to reason. Everyone figures the rustlers will show up again sooner or later. Besides, the sheriff is having a cruiser drive by a few times each night."

Rhiannon's eyes widened. "You've been *spying* on us?"

"Police surveillance," Burt corrected. "For an ongoing investigation."

"Why weren't we notified?" Hawk demanded.

Burt leveled him a flat gaze. "We generally don't inform suspects of our movements." At Rhiannon's gasp, he added. "Don't worry, we've ruled you out, since you weren't in the country when the rustling started."

"How convenient," Hawk muttered acerbically.

She stared at him, hurt cascading through her at his cutting remark.

"Nice boyfriend," Burton said, picking up his hat from the table. "You're right not to trust him."

"Get out of my house," Hawk growled. The muzzle of his rifle raised slightly. *"Now."*

Burt's brows flicked. *"Your* house?" He gave Rhiannon a pointed look. "Remember what I said, doll. Anytime." To Hawk he said, "Next time you threaten an officer of the law I'll have you arrested." Then he walked out the back door with a slam.

Neither she nor Hawk moved for a long moment.

"Did you invite him over?" he finally asked.

For the first time in her life she felt like slapping a man. Hard.

Instead of answering, she went to the sink and washed her hands, scrubbing them thoroughly. What she really wanted was to take a shower. *After* she smacked Hawk silly.

Gathering as much calm as she could muster, she leaned back against the counter and asked, "Could he be doing the rustling?"

It was Hawk's turn to stare. *"Grant?* What makes you think—"

"Nothing. I'm probably just being paranoid."

He snorted, setting aside his rifle. "Please. The man can't even ride a horse."

"Really?"

"His father was a deputy, probably his grandfather before that."

"Then why does he want the ranch?"

"What makes you think he does?"

"Why else would he come here offering help?"

Hawk crossed the room in two strides and grasped her behind the neck, fingers digging into her flesh. "The good deputy wants *you,* Rhiannon. Any fool can see that."

She gazed up at the hard, angry face of her lover. "And I only want you, Hawk. Any fool can see that."

After a second his eyes softened, along with his grip. He took a deep breath. "He was touching you. If he ever touches you again, I swear I'll kill him."

She slid her arms under his duster and around his waist. "He won't. It was a mistake to let him in. I'm sorry. It won't happen again."

"Promise?"

"Promise. Thank goodness you came home. What made you change your mind about going out?"

"I saw headlights. Got worried."

She tightened her hold. "Stay," she whispered. "Please stay with me. I hate it when you're gone."

Silently he held her close, the firm, steady beat of his heart pounding in rhythm with hers. He pushed his fingers into her hair and caressed her. She could feel his indecision, heard it in the short, jetted breath he let out.

"I don't want to go," he said at last. "But I have to." After a long kiss, he set her away. "Lock the doors. All of them. And don't let anyone in. I don't care who it is."

She nodded and stuck her hands under her armpits so he wouldn't see them shaking. "Be safe," she said, and again he was gone.

Redhawk galloped Tonopah to the top of the plateau overlooking the ranch road and watched Burton Grant's taillights bump along to the highway, turn and disappear toward town.

He didn't trust the bastard. Not within ten miles of Rhiannon.

But could he be involved in the rustling as she had suggested?

He mulled it over as he made for the canyons. Naw. Fitz didn't like Grant, but that was about something long ago having to do with Grant's dad. As far as Hawk could tell, the son had always been on the up and up. Other than having eyes for his woman.

Come to think of it, Jeremy Lloyd—Hawk's other main rustler suspect—also had roving eyes. Jeremy had asked Rhiannon out numerous times after their one dinner date, even when she kept turning him down.

Hawk tipped his head back and gazed up at the glittering swath of stars overhead. He needed heavenly inspiration to clear his mind.

What was he missing? Rhiannon couldn't be the reason all this was happening. It had started long before her arrival. He was just being a jealous lover.

There had to be something else about Irish Heaven that was attracting the rustlers.

But what?

He thought about it for the rest of the night as he sat bundled in his sleeping bag, rifle propped next to him, keeping watch over his tiny remaining herd. And realized he didn't know nearly enough about the history of Fitz and Irish Heaven.

That's where the key must lie. Somewhere in the past.

At least he hoped like hell it did. Otherwise, as clever as these guys were, if it was all random, he might never be able to figure out this thing and stop them.

He waited until an hour after dawn, then hoisted himself onto Tonopah and made for home. Sunrise had been spectacular, yellow and orange and violet blues blazing over the bright red sandstone cliffs. Now the birds and animals were out searching for food and greeting the new day with cheerful abandon. The desert air was crisp and clear as he rode, and he could practically smell the bacon Rhiannon would be frying up as he walked in the door.

But when he rode up to the ranch, the hairs rose on the back of his neck.

Lucky Charm lay dead in his pen.

The bull's thick throat was slit ear to ear and its once-powerful body pierced by a dozen cuts, now inert and surrounded by a frozen pool of blood.

* * *

Hawk found Rhiannon cowering in the hall closet.

"Baby!" he exclaimed, relief avalanching over him at seeing her safe. But it immediately turned to panic as she launched into his arms with a frightened cry.

"Oh, Hawk!"

"Darlin', are you all right? Did someone hurt you?" he demanded.

"No," came her muffled reply from the layers of his coat where she'd buried her face after bringing him to his knees. "We're fine. They didn't come in the house."

"Who?" he said, fury whipping through his blood, sped by the thundering of his heart. "Who was here?"

"I didn't see them. Only heard them. With Lucky Charm." She broke down. "Oh, God, it was awful."

He set his teeth to keep them from chattering with the force of his wrath. He literally vibrated with anger. "Did you call the cops?"

"The phone wouldn't work."

"All right. Shhh," he soothed, battling to stay calm himself. Wanting to find someone—anyone—and make them pay. "I'm here now. Nothing's going to hurt you."

She gave a little mewl and clung to him tighter.

"Baby, we need to get you out of this closet." Apart from anything else, his knee was burning like hell and he thought he might have sprung the stitches in his arm firing himself off Tonopah like a rocket and practically tearing the screen off its hinges in his haste to get the back door unlocked. Somewhere along the line he'd lost his arm sling. "Come on, now, help me up."

Mention of him needing help rallied her. She lifted her head and looked at him. The expression on her face made his heart break in a million pieces. So anxious and vulnerable. Yet she swallowed her fear and gave him a brave if quivery smile.

"Sorry I'm being such a ninny."

"Don't even think it. Let's get out of here and make sure Fitz didn't wake up in all the commotion."

They helped each other up from the closet floor, peeked in to check on Fitz, then went to the kitchen.

"I'll make some tea," she said, and he felt marginally better. If she was already making tea, she was coming around.

"No, I'll make it," he said, taking the kettle from her. He, on the other hand, needed to do something or he'd start smashing things. "You sit and tell me exactly what happened."

She folded her hands in her lap and stared at them while he filled the kettle, then tossed aside his duster and jacket. When he sat next to her and covered her hands with his, she started talking.

"It was in the middle of the night, maybe two or three o'clock, when I heard something stirring up the animals in the barn. I thought it was you coming back, and I looked out the bedroom window. But there were two horses tied to the fence. So I knew it couldn't be you."

She stopped to swallow. He felt the muscle below his eye tick madly. "Go on."

"Lucky Charm's stall door opened and a man stuck his head out. He looked up at the bedroom window, right at me." Her voice caught.

"Did he see you?" he asked, keeping his tone carefully even. He didn't want her to know how close he was to losing it.

"I don't know. It was dark and I jerked back behind the wall, but—" she lifted her shoulders "—I don't know."

"What happened then?"

"I ran downstairs to call the police, but the phone wouldn't work. I dialed and dialed, but it was dead." She put her hand over her mouth. "And all the while I could hear how they— Oh, how the poor thing bellowed!"

She choked on the words and he hauled her into his arms, ignoring the pain that sliced through his injury. "I'll kill them," he muttered in outrage. "I'll hunt them down and kill them slowly for putting you through this."

Her breath hitched. "No. I'm fine. Really. Let the sheriff find them and put them in jail. I don't want you hurt again."

"Did they do anything else? Anything at all?"

"I'm not sure. When the phone didn't work, I ran and hid. I'm sorry."

"Hush, now. You did exactly the right thing. Here, drink your tea."

He managed to get her to sip the soothing brew. He needed to get out to the barn. He was deathly afraid of what else he might find. If they'd hurt the other horses, he wouldn't be responsible for his actions. But he had to know.

"I need to take care of Tonopah," he told her. "And check the other animals."

"No!" She jumped up from her chair, crashing it onto the floor behind her. "Don't leave us alone. Please!"

He held her when she pressed into him. "Just to the barn. You and Fitz will be fine. You can watch me from the window, okay? If I don't tend to Tonopah, he'll catch cold. He's all lathered up."

She drew away reluctantly. "You're right. I'm sorry I'm being such a coward. It's just…it all reminds me of when I was a child in Belfast and the British would harass us after my father—"

She stopped, and he could see her visibly pull herself together. "But that's all in the past. You go now. I'll be all right."

He hesitated a moment, astonished at how she was able to shake herself out of her inner terrors. The woman was amazing. If only he could do the same thing with his anger.

"Are you sure?"

Her spine straightened. "Positive."

Fetching his rifle, he pressed it into her hands. "Watch me from the window. If anything but me moves, shoot it."

Her mouth gaped. He knew she'd never held a weapon before in her life. He also knew if she tried to shoot anything, he'd better duck quick. But that wasn't the point. The point was empowerment.

A lone tear trembled on the edge of her lashes when she looked up at him. With his thumb he wiped it away. Then strode out the door to see just how bad these bastards were.

He almost fell over from relief when he found Jasper and Crimson nervous but unharmed in their stalls. He rubbed down Tonopah and gave them all an extra ration of oats, opened the Dutch doors to let in the sunshine, and ignored their protests when he left them confined instead of leading them out to their corral.

"Sorry, guys. Don't want to mess with the crime scene," he muttered, giving them each an ear rub.

He deliberately avoided going anywhere near Lucky Charm. He didn't have the heart. He'd leave that to the cops.

"I have to drive to a phone and call this in," he said to Rhiannon when he was back in the kitchen, after giving her the relative good news.

She gnawed on her lip as she nodded. "Take us with you. I don't want to stay here by ourselves."

"Yeah." He wasn't about to leave them, anyway.

"Can we wait until Fitz wakes up? I'd really like to lie down for a bit," she said apologetically. "I'm still shaking."

"Of course."

They went upstairs and he tucked her into bed, showered and slid in next to her. Immediately she snuggled up close, wrapping her shivering body in his willing embrace.

He was still livid with rage over what had been done to them…to her. Because whoever did this had known damn well she'd been alone on the ranch with a helpless old man when they'd struck. They'd deliberately terrified her.

Why?

The only explanation he could come up with was, they also knew she was the conservator for her uncle, and therefore responsible for all his financial decisions—including selling the ranch.

"You can't let them intimidate you into selling," he murmured.

"I know," she answered, shocking him that he'd spoken the words out loud. "I won't."

He gathered her precious body tight to his chest, suddenly vividly cognizant of what might have happened....

If any harm came to her, ever, he didn't know what he'd do.

Actually, he did. He thought of his cousin sitting in prison on an eight-to-fifteen attempted-murder charge, and for the first time understood what the man must have gone through. Someone had hurt his sister. He'd gone after the guy. Hawk knew he would have done exactly the same thing himself. There were just some things a man couldn't tolerate others messing with.

For Hawk, it was his ranch and the people he considered family.

That's when cold reality hit him. The way things sat, he couldn't protect them both.

He'd have to choose.

The herd and the solvency of the ranch...or the safety of those he loved.

He couldn't do both.

If he was with the herd, they could get to his family. If he was with Fitz and Rhiannon, they could destroy the herd.

Hell and damnation.

He tried to figure a way out of it. So he could be in two places at once. But there was no way he'd bring Fitz and Rhiannon with him up into the canyons at night. And there was not a chance in hell he'd ever leave them alone on the ranch at night again. That was plain old not happening.

Not until these sickos were behind bars.

But how could he catch them if he couldn't be out hunting them?

The whole thing was impossible. He felt as frustrated and helpless as a roped and trussed rodeo calf.

"We'll have to bring the cattle down from the canyons," she said, as though reading his mind. "It's the only way."

"Can't," he said. He'd already considered that. "They're more sheltered against the cold up there. Besides, there's not enough grass to feed them down here."

"We could buy hay and feed, same as you do now. Just more."

"With what?"

"Hawk, does the ranch owe anyone any money?"

"Hell, no. We've always dealt in cash only."

"Maybe it's time we made an exception."

"That's a slippery slope, Rhiannon. Half the farms in the Midwest went under because they started thinking that way."

She was silent for a moment. "Would you rather sell the cattle in the spring and pay off an honest debt to the feed store, or let the rustlers just take the herd without a fight?"

He dipped his head and looked at her. He couldn't believe she was showing this much spunk after what she'd just gone through. Amazing didn't come close.

"You up for a fight?" he asked.

"Oh, yes," she said, meeting his gaze. The green of her eyes flashed like emeralds.

"It could get ugly."

Her brows hiked.

"Right." Okay, so it was already as ugly as he dared imagine. These men had to be stopped before it got even worse. "We'll report the attack and buy feed this afternoon."

"And tomorrow we move the herd."

He gave her a hug. "Tomorrow we move the herd."

The dream was gone for him. He had to accept that he wouldn't be raising his rodeo horses, or anything else, on Irish Heaven. Bringing the cattle to the corrals would keep them safe, but he could also kiss the Cattlemen's Association reward goodbye. And with it, the ability to put the ranch back on its feet.

This was the end of the road for him.

It was a good strategy for saving the property, but it also ensured there would be no need for a cowboy on the ranch after spring calving. No cattle meant no one to care for them. And there wasn't much else for a man like him to do around a ranch with no herd or horses. Rhiannon could get another job and just live there. He had no other skills. No one was going to hire him as a bookkeeper or sales clerk or even a bartender. He was useless without a horse under him. This was it.

But he'd be damned if he'd let anyone take Irish Heaven away from Rhiannon. Not when she so obviously wanted to fight for it. He'd stay and help her. Until spring calving.

Then he'd go.

Yeah, it was about time he put his troubled past behind him and struck out on his own, forged a real future for himself. His mother's problems and his old rodeo injury had been crutches long enough. He would never fulfill his dreams clinging to a life based on guilt over the past and a fear of failure in the present.

Sure he had a bum knee and worse luck. But he was a good horse trainer. He'd find a job that paid actual money, and save every penny until he could buy a place of his own. It might be just one acre, but it would be his. And it would be all legal, on paper. Not just a pipe dream or a promise.

It was the right thing to do. Rhiannon was Fitz's blood kin. She deserved to have the ranch. He'd known it all along, he just hadn't been able to admit he'd wasted eleven years of his life on an impossible dream. He should have known better.

Now it was time to fix past mistakes.

Get on with his life.

The woman in his arms stirred, and his heart squeezed so hard in his chest he had to bite his tongue to keep from groaning out loud.

How would he ever find the strength to leave her?

How would he be able to walk away from all this?

But how could he stay? Even if she married him, he'd have no way of supporting her after the herd was sold. Besides, she'd made it very clear she had no interest in being his wife.

She wouldn't marry him. And he couldn't stay.

End of the rodeo. Come springtime, his eight seconds were all used up and he'd have to limp away from this one the loser.

But this time, instead of a banged-up knee, he'd be leaving with a broken heart. And he doubted if he'd ever recover from that.

Chapter 15

Fitz was having a good day, and Rhiannon didn't want to spoil it. She kept her smile firmly in place as she puttered in the kitchen and he chatted on about an old Celtic dolmen he and her da had discovered on the family farm as boys. He was speaking as if it had happened just yesterday, excited as boys get, and worried that his archrival Lloyd Collins would hear wind of it.

"There's treasure buried beneath them stones!" he declared. "Silver and gold! He'll steal it—I know he will."

Rhiannon felt guilty ignoring Fitz, but she was too preoccupied by Redhawk's troubling behavior to concentrate.

Hawk had taken the attack a week ago badly. He hadn't been the same since. He was even broodier than when she'd first arrived at Irish Heaven. And had avoided her nearly as much as when she was still convinced he disliked her.

"He's a snake, that Lloyd Collins is! Gotta watch him every minute, I do."

Of course, she knew Hawk didn't dislike her. The few nights they'd spent in bed together since moving the herd down to the corrals had been…wonderful. He'd been attentive and giving and sweetly devoted. He'd held her endlessly, just silently stroking his strong, callused hand over her skin. When they made love he was so achingly tender it brought tears to her eyes.

"Him and his boyo Burton Grant. What a pair," Fritz went on.

But something was wrong.

Very wrong.

She could feel it.

And it terrified her.

"The two of them are cookin' up something together, you mark me words! They'll steal everything if I let 'em!"

The attack had galvanized Hawk, turned his determination to steel, to save the remainder of the herd. But it had also turned him away from her. Except for in bed, he was slowly, subtly withdrawing from her.

She didn't know what to do.

She walked over and gave Fitz a hug. "Don't worry, Uncle. Hawk is watching the treasure carefully. He won't let anything happen to it."

"Aye, he's a good lad." He gave a laugh and looked up from his lunch. "So, Bridget, what's this I hear about you and Patrick Callahan? Have you decided to give me over, then?"

For a moment she was so surprised at being called by a name other than Janet, she didn't understand what he was—

"Uncle! I thought you said you and Aunt Bridget weren't an item."

He seemed momentarily confused. "Sometimes you look so much alike I forget who I'm talking to," he said, shaking his head, confusing her even more. Who? Janet, Bridget or herself?

"Did you mean you and Aunt Bridget were involved?"

Fitz blinked, and gave her a sad smile. "Now that Janet's with

Jamie, you better tell that Patrick Callahan I'll give him a run for his money."

Her lips parted, and suddenly she couldn't help asking on Bridget's behalf, "Why should I wait for a man who doesn't love me?"

"He could learn," he said seriously.

She stared for a second, then shook herself mentally. That was never going to happen. Not with Fitz and Bridget, not with Hawk and her. And this was a vivid reminder why giving Hawk her heart had been the most foolish thing she'd ever done in her life.

She placed a kiss on Fitz's head. "Ever think about moving to Arizona?" she asked, grasping at anything at all to change the subject.

"And move away from Ireland? Not unless me very life depended on it. Everyone I love is here."

She sighed, reminded of what the doctor had said about taking him back to Ireland. Too bad there was no possibility.

She also remembered his outburst at court that day, and she wondered what life-threatening event had sent him fleeing his beloved homeland to America when his only brother had just been arrested and the woman he desperately loved left alone and terrorized with a child to raise.

"What happened, Uncle Fitz?" she asked. "What made you flee Ireland?"

He leaned in conspiratorially. "It was Lloyd Collins and Burton Grant," he whispered. "They got the treasure. I had no choice but to leave."

Rhiannon settled Fitz in his favorite easy chair to watch the telly, which she tuned to a children's show with short segments he could follow, then she went back into the kitchen to watch Hawk from the window. He was out in the corral putting Crimson through his paces, as he did every day warm enough to let the horses out of the barn.

After that he'd probably sit on the rustic split-rail fence and stare out at the herd until the sun went down. Then he'd come in for supper and go out again and stare some more. As he'd done for the past week.

Well, not if she could help it.

She bundled up and walked out to where he and Crimson were working.

"He looks good," she said with deliberate cheerfulness. "Think he'll be ready for spring?"

"Should be," Hawk said, glancing up. "Still needs work weaving barrels, but that'll have to wait till the ground is less icy. Don't want to risk him slipping."

She wrapped her arms around herself, already chilly after two minutes. "When should that be?" She was really looking forward to warmer weather.

He glanced up at the sky, which over the course of the day had filled with dark, menacing clouds. "Not anytime soon, looks like."

"More snow, you think?"

He gave the tongue click for Crimson to come stand next to him. "Tonight, I'd say." The horse trotted up and accepted a half carrot, munching noisily as Hawk rubbed his neck.

They looked good together, the man with the copper skin and his red pony. Their dark eyes so composed and genuine. So hardworking. So honest in their affection for each other. One pair so guileless. The other so…deceitful.

It was as obvious as the chiseled nose on his face.

Hawk was hiding something.

"Is there something you'd like to tell me?" she asked.

He turned away to uncinch Crimson's saddle. "Like what?"

"Like why you've been avoiding me."

His movements slowed for a heartbeat, then he threw her a smile that tried to be wry. "Darlin', every time I look at you all I think about is how to get you naked. We wouldn't get a whole lot done around here if I didn't try to steer clear."

He was lying. And yet it was true. It never took him long to get her down to bare skin when they were alone together. Her cheeks heated thinking of the blazingly sensual caresses he bestowed upon her every chance he got.

All right, maybe he wasn't lying.

Could the explanation really be as simple as that?

It didn't feel quite right, but for the moment she'd have to accept it. She approached and leaned against his back, putting her arms around him as he grasped the saddle and removed it.

"Who needs work, anyway?" she whispered to the back of his neck. To be honest, she was as mad for making love as he was. She wanted to experience it with him as often as she could, so when she went back to Ireland she'd at least have those breathtaking memories to pull out and relive. The more she had to savor, the less heartbroken she'd feel at his loss.

He wasn't the only one hiding something. Her decision to return to Ireland had solidified in the days since they moved the herd. But in the meantime she wanted every precious minute with him.

He turned, still holding the saddle, and gave her a lopsided smile. "Fitz still awake?" he asked.

Putting aside her melancholy, she reached up for a kiss. "Afraid so."

His lips were icy cold and a little stiff, but it didn't take many seconds for them to heat up and become soft and pliant against hers. They parted, and his hot tongue invaded her mouth, tasting musky and exotic, setting off a chain reaction of heat in her whole body.

Need bubbled up from deep within her. "I want you, Hawk."

There was a crunch as the saddle hit the snow a few feet away, and then she was in his arms. Their coats were bulky, and as his hands grappled to get under the thick layers he made a frustrated noise. "This isn't working."

His tongue clicked the signal for Crimson to stand steady, and the next second she was sandwiched between the solid warmth of the horse's side and Hawk's broad chest. She felt a giant tug and the front snaps of her coat gave way, leaving one less barrier between them. Her pulse skyrocketed.

He was wearing leather gloves. She shivered as his cold hand closed over her breast, and under her sweater she felt the erotic scrape of his supple, leather-clad thumb across her nipple. She moaned in pleasure. And heard the grate of a zipper.

"What are you— Oh!"

He pulled her jeans and panties down. Just a few inches. Enough to slide his hand between her thighs. The air was frigid on her bare skin, but suddenly she was on fire. His mouth came down on hers, swallowing her loud gasp.

His heavy boots shoved hers apart and she wantonly gave herself up to the deliciously carnal sensations he was wreaking upon her. She began to tremble, sucking in breath after breath as his wicked gloved fingers brushed and circled the very center of her sizzling need. One finger entered her, and she shook with want of him.

"Hawk," she pleaded. Needing *him* inside her.

But he was relentless in his sensual assault. He continued to coax, with his hands and his tongue and his words, without letting up.

"Give it to me," he said, low and rough in her ear. "I want it all, Rhiannon. Come on, baby. Show me how much you want me."

His finger slid over her again and she cried out, her body suddenly exploding in a violent, glittering climax that went on and on.

He grabbed her as she dissolved into throbbing weakness, the cold forgotten, her worries eclipsed, through hot sensual oblivion.

Then he turned her and bent her over against the horse, yanking her jeans down further. She squeezed her eyes shut as he came into her, hard and thick, with a growl of possession that she felt to the innermost reaches of her soul.

She grabbed Crimson for purchase, and felt the stiff scratch of horsehair against her cheek as Hawk hilted inside her. She gasped in blinding pleasure. She'd never touch or smell a horse again without thinking of this moment.

Hawk held her in an iron grip, his gloved hands wrapped around her thighs, keeping her right where he wanted her—right where she wanted to be—as he thrust into her over and over. Until he roared out her name in completion, and his arms banded around her middle as though he'd never let her go.

"You're mine," he rasped between gulping breaths. "Don't ever forget you're mine."

Hawk hated himself for deceiving Rhiannon. She might not think he was husband material, but she cared for him. He could see it in her eyes when he made love to her. When he caught her looking at him while they worked side by side on some everyday chore. And in her smile when she woke up in his arms every morning.

She was looking at him like that now as they relaxed in the living room, and he felt so guilty he had to turn away and hide his face.

Only a jerk would betray that kind of trust. How could he just up and leave her come spring?

Hell, it was her own fault! Her continual refusal to marry him was driving him away. He would never be what he wanted to be in her life, so he had to go. Now...before the need for her killed him. Make a new life for himself somewhere far away. And hope someday he'd forget her.

He gave a silent snort. Like that was ever going to happen.

The phone rang and she picked it up. Her face went stony and she extended the receiver to him.

"It's for you. Teresa."

He ground his teeth. Of all the stupid times for that woman to call. She knew he was a lost cause. Why did she persist in hounding him?

"Hey, sweet thing! You coming out to Jake's tonight?" Teresa asked brightly.

"Sorry, can't make it. Listen—"

"But sugar, it's New Year's Eve!"

His annoyance ground to a halt for the split second it took to add up days. "Well, I'll be," he muttered. "Must have lost track."

"You can't be having *that* much fun," she said, a pouty edge to her voice.

He glanced at Rhiannon, still rosy and disheveled from their afternoon's activities. "As a matter of fact…"

"You're gross, Redhawk Jackson. And even *you* need to come up for air sometime. You can bring her, too, I guess." She gave a huff.

"Sorry, can't leave Fitz," he said patiently. There was no way on God's green earth he was spending New Year's Eve anywhere but Irish Heaven, and he said as much when Teresa protested that he could give the old man a sedative and lock the doors.

"You're getting real boring, Hawk," she sputtered as her parting shot and hung up.

He replaced the receiver and glanced at Rhiannon, who had her nose buried deep in a book, pretending not to listen.

"That was Teresa," he said.

"I know. I answered the phone," she reminded him primly, nose still buried.

He didn't know why it delighted him so much when she got jealous. A totally irrational pleasure. But there it was.

"She wanted me to go to Jake's. Invited you, too."

"Generous of her."

"I'll bet Burt will be there."

"Good. He can keep her company."

He chuckled. "She said it was New Year's Eve."

The book dropped slightly. "Really?" The look on her face told him she'd been just as unmindful of time as he'd been lately. "I don't suppose we have any champagne?"

He gave her a sardonic look. "How about twelve-year-old Irish whiskey instead? I think there's still some left."

She finally smiled. "I suppose that'll have to do."

At midnight they polished off the rest of the bottle, with Fitz's help. There wasn't that much remaining in it—just enough to put a cheerful slant on things, and stir the embers left over from the afternoon.

Which is probably why none of them noticed that night in the early hours when the rustlers sneaked into the corrals and stole the rest of the herd.

Rhiannon took one look at Hawk's face when he walked into the kitchen just after dawn New Year's Day and she knew something was horribly wrong.

He didn't stomp. Didn't yell. Didn't even swear. But the look in his eyes would strike a man dead in his tracks.

"They're gone," he said, and she knew instantly what he meant.

She whipped her gaze out the window to the pasture, but it was impossible to see anything. As predicted, snow had just started coming down in blankets. "How many?" she asked.

"Nearly all the steers. They generously left the cows for us to take care of until spring." His voice was rife with anger and disgust.

She slapped the towel in her hand down on the counter and spun on a toe toward the laundry room. "Let's go after them."

"Are you nuts?"

She grabbed her coat. "They couldn't have moved them before it started getting light. It's slow going out there. They can't have gotten far."

He grabbed her arm. "Rhiannon. These guys are dangerous. They tried to *kill* me, if you remember."

"So we should just let them get away with it?"

She knew she wasn't being entirely rational. But the blood of a thousand years of rebellious Celtic spirit flowed in her veins and she was *not* giving up without a fight. "Get your rifle, Hawk. And if you have an extra, get one for me, too."

With that, she flung open the door and stalked out into the flying snow, pulling the hood of her coat up and slamming the old Stetson Hawk had given her on top of it.

After a few moments she heard the door close, and Hawk's boots crunched swiftly after her. "I only have the Winchester. We'll need to stay together."

"Where do you think they're headed?" she asked as they saddled the horses.

"The highway, I expect. I put in a quick call to the sheriff. He's going to send his men to check from that side."

She pressed her lips together. "Good idea." She should have thought of that. She had to calm down so she could think straight. But she was just so incensed. The idea that someone would go to these lengths to deliberately hurt Fitz and Hawk, and now her—the unfairness of it made her blood boil.

As she spurred Jasper into the sea of frigid white, determination drove her on and fury kept her warm.

"Can you see any sign of their tracks?" she asked Hawk as they criss-crossed the pasture where the steers had been penned.

"Everything's been covered up by the new snow," he said, studying the ground with a scowl.

"They planned that," she said with a frustrated sigh.

"Yep. Our bad luck it happened on New Year's Eve while we were distracted."

"You think?"

Something in her tone must have made him look up. "You mean they planned it, like on Christmas?"

She reined in Jasper and clamped her teeth. "What I think is, it's a pretty strange coincidence Teresa called last night to stir up trouble between us."

Redhawk's jaw went slack. "How would that have helped them?"

"She knew it would cause a fight. But being New Year's Eve and all, she also knew you with your romantic streak would make things right before we went to bed, even if you'd been planning to guard the herd. She knows you very well."

She'd rendered him speechless.

Good. They could ride faster if they weren't talking.

She spurred Jasper. "Which way to the highway?" she called.

Tonopah jumped to catch up. "This way," Hawk said, and took the lead without further comment on her theory. Which was fine. It was another thing she hadn't really thought out. "Just follow my trail," he told her.

Which was easier said than done. The snow was coming down faster now, big puffy flakes the size of tea biscuits, making it impossible to see more than five feet in front of her. She did her best to keep Tonopah's swishing tail in sight, but then the snow would swirl up and he'd disappear for a minute or two.

This time it had been about five minutes. She'd relied on Jasper to instinctively know where the other horse was, but maybe that was wishful thinking.

"Hawk?" she called loudly, praying he was still in front of her. She tried not to panic when he didn't answer.

Hawk had always told her to stay put if she ever got lost or anything happened to her out in the desert. He said it was a lot harder to find and rescue a moving target than one that stayed in one place and made itself conspicuous. But how did you make yourself conspicuous in the middle of a snowstorm?

She shouted his name again. And was answered only by the deafening sound of silence.

It was eerie how silent it could be in the wilderness. Of course, there was usually some wind, the call of birds soaring high in the sky, the scurry of small animals over the ground and the rustle of sage and grass and piñon needles.

But today, it was as though she and Jasper were floating somewhere deep in the vast silence of outer space; that's how little sound there was. The world was muffled and cloaked, as if nothing else existed in the universe but the two of them.

"Rhiannon!"

Thank God. "Hawk! I'm here!"

Out of nothingness he appeared, black duster whirling behind him, riding out of the white void like a primitive god from the mists of time.

"Damn it, woman!" He galloped around her, Tonopah rearing as he reined him in. "Tighten this around your saddle horn," he ordered gruffly, and flung her the lasso end of a long, coiled rope.

She gladly did as she was told. "Any sign of the cattle yet?"

"Nothing. Not that I can see anything in this mess. The highway should be that way, though." He might as well be pointing at the moon for all she was turned around.

"I'm right behind you," she assured him, more than grateful for the impromptu umbilical cord connecting them.

It took over three hours to make it to the highway, since they went at a snail's pace, searching for any indication of the herd's passage. But there was no sign. They didn't even find a broken twig.

On the bright side, by the time they arrived at the barbed wire fence and the shiny black ribbon of asphalt bisecting the endless white, the snowstorm had slowed to a fine dusting of ice crystals sparkling in the little bit of midday light.

They trotted along the road's verge up to the far property line and back, hoping to find where the steers had been loaded into trucks.

"Maybe they used the chute on the ranch road," she suggested. That's the one they'd used the day she arrived at Irish Heaven, when Redhawk had mistaken her for one of the rustlers.

"Maybe," he said, but his tone was doubtful. "Let's ride back to the ranch that way and check it out. It'll be easier on the horses anyway."

A few minutes later they ran into one of the deputies the sheriff had sent out to patrol the fence. Hawk flagged him down.

The cruiser pulled over, and the deputy rolled down the window. Rhiannon didn't recognize him.

"You spot anything, Jackson?" he called.

Hawk eased Tonopah up to the vehicle. "No trace of them. You?"

The deputy shook his head. "Barely a car on the road today, even after the plow came through. No trucks. No cattle."

Hawk jetted out a breath. "I just don't get it."

"You sure those steers were stolen? Maybe they just wandered off in the storm..."

Frowning, Hawk pushed his Stetson back on his head and leaned down to brace his forearm against the saddle horn. "Not unless one of them learned how to unlatch a gate and open it while I wasn't looking."

"It was left open after they'd gone?"

"Closed, actually."

Rhiannon figured that had been a slap in the face. The tossers had wanted them to know it was no accident.

"Sheriff's got a deputy watching the Lost Man, too. If he sees anything suspicious out there he'll bring 'em in for questioning."

"But I thought he'd ruled them out as suspects," she said, pulling Jasper up alongside Tonopah.

The deputy shrugged. "There's no solid evidence it's them. But the sheriff's been around these parts a long time. He's got a pretty good nose for who's trouble. I guess there's some history there."

"What kind of history?" she asked, suddenly alert.

"Dunno, exactly," he said. "Haven't seen the file, since it's not really my case. I'm just putting in some overtime today."

"That was interesting," she said excitedly, after the deputy had resumed his patrol and they'd turned their mounts onto the dirt road leading back to the ranch. "I wonder what he meant by history?"

"I'd guess probably someone at the Lost Man has an arrest record," Hawk said, stretching his knee out and rotating the shoulder of the arm he still had in a sling.

Rhiannon watched his painful movements, her anger spiking.

He must be hurting like crazy. He shouldn't be out in this cold weather or even riding a horse at all, not with his injuries. He should be at home, curled up by a warm fire drinking hot chocolate and watching college football on the telly with Fitz, like every other male in America was doing on New Year's Day.

Suddenly she gasped. "Oh, no!"

"What?" Hawk said, lifting his head from scrutinizing the sides of the road.

"My God! We left Fitz by himself. All this time!"

Hawk's eyes clapped onto hers and he said one succinct swearword.

"How could we have forgotten?" she said, guilt swamping over her in a deluge.

"I'm sure he's fine," Hawk said, nevertheless looking worried. "He was still asleep when we left. It's only about noon now. He probably stayed in bed, after the drinking we did last night."

"I hope so," she murmured, and urged Jasper into a trot. She sent up a fervent prayer that her uncle was fine and hadn't wandered off in the snow in a lapse of common sense.

But alas, that prayer wasn't answered. When she and Hawk galloped up to the ranch house twenty minutes later and ran inside, Fitz was nowhere to be found.

Chapter 16

"This is all my fault," Rhiannon lamented when Hawk met her in the kitchen after she'd combed the house and he had searched the outbuildings.

The empty stall he'd discovered in the barn had made Hawk's heart quail.

"He's taken Crimson," he told her. "God knows how far he's gotten by now."

She put her knuckles to her mouth and made a choking noise. "What are we going to do?"

"You wait here in case he comes back," he told her firmly. He wasn't taking a chance on losing both of them in this weather. "I'm going out after him."

She jumped to her feet. "I'll go with you."

He put his hands on her shoulders and squeezed to get her attention. "No. You won't. I need you here in case he returns. If I'm not back in two hours, call the sheriff to get Search and Rescue out here. Can you do that?"

Reluctantly she nodded. "Find him, Redhawk. Please find him."

"I will." Or he'd die trying. It had stopped snowing, but was still bitterly cold. The old man wouldn't survive a night out in the open, and that was one guilt Hawk couldn't live with.

Swiftly he gathered a few emergency supplies and a couple of blankets, which he tied onto his saddle as Rhiannon made him a sack of sandwiches and a thermos of hot coffee. He grabbed them, gave her a kiss and jumped on his horse.

Last time he'd wandered off, Fitz had headed toward the mountains. Hawk figured that direction was as good as any to start with.

Again he crisscrossed the wild, open territory between the ranch house and the canyons, hoping to pick up the old man's trail from after it stopped snowing. An hour later he found a wandering string of hoofprints he immediately recognized as Crimson's distinctive gait. With a heartfelt prayer of thanks, he turned Tonopah's head to follow the tracks.

After a short time he came to with a start of realization. *Crimson's weren't the only furrow and tracks in the deep snow.* He hadn't noticed before because he was concentrating so hard on not losing the trail while steering Tonopah clear of dangerous obstacles under the snow as they hurried across the plateau.

But for a moment the angle of the sun and shadow changed, and a wide cluster of parallel ruts became clearly visible, even under the thick layer of new snowfall.

The herd!

Fitz had found the stolen cattle! And along with them, no doubt, the rustlers.

Instinctively, Hawk reached for his rifle, terrified of what he might find ahead. But mindless of the dangers, he spurred Tonopah into a gallop. *This time he had them.*

And it was one fight he didn't intend to lose.

Rhiannon forced herself to eat, though the sandwich and tea tasted like sawdust and dishwater. And it took all of fifteen minutes to accomplish.

Now what?

She was so frightened for both Fitz and Hawk she was literally shaking. Maybe she should stoke the fire so the house would be warm and toasty when the men returned.

Because they would return soon. *They must.*

She went into the living room and stuck several more pieces of wood into the stove, carefully closing the glass door afterward. As she knelt on the floor, she suddenly spotted something sticking out from under the sofa. Some sort of papers?

She pulled them out. It turned out to be a manila file with some sort of legal contracts in it. Contracts for…the sale of Irish Heaven!

Her heart stopped as she searched for a date. When could this have—? Her eyes widened. *Wait.* The contract was dated over twenty-five years ago! With a sigh of relief, she caught sight of the selling price. Wow. Fitz had gotten a real bargain on the ranch. It was a long time ago, but still, the price seemed a pittance for the size of the property.

She sat back on her heels, taking it all in and wondering what would have made Fitz seek out the old record of sale. Living in the past must really have—

That's when she noticed the name of the seller. *Collin Lloyd.*

She frowned. Why did that name sound so familiar? Lloyd… Could Collin Lloyd be Jeremy Lloyd's father? Or—

All at once she remembered where she'd heard it before. Not Collin Lloyd, but Lloyd Collins! That was Fitz's archrival back when he and Rhiannon's da were boys. In the story he'd told last week about the dolmen treasure…

Suddenly the breath froze in her lungs.

By the saints!

Could he have been trying to *warn* her by telling that story? Even in his deteriorating state of dementia, had Fitz been desperately trying to communicate something? But what? Had he confused the name of a real childhood rival with a present enemy who was also trying to steal something from him?

But Jeremy Lloyd was *already* one of the prime suspects for the rustling.

Then it struck her.

Motive.

She looked down at the contract in her hands and realized that Fitz had wanted to show them the *reason* for the rustling. Jeremy Lloyd must have felt his father was somehow cheated when he sold Irish Heaven to Fitz. As it indeed appeared from the price.

That was why this particular ranch had been singled out by the rustlers—Jeremy Lloyd was calling the shots. And that was also why the attacks had gotten so vicious and personal.

It *was* personal.

And she could only guess to what lengths the younger Lloyd would go to reclaim his inheritance.

Could that include murder?

The answer was obvious. He'd already shot Redhawk and left him to die of exposure. What would stop a man capable of that from murdering a helpless old man in a snowstorm? He wouldn't even have to shoot him. Just make sure no one found him before he froze to death.

She cried out at the horror of the thought. *"No!"*

She had to do something! Quickly!

She sprinted for the phone and rang the sheriff's office, getting the dispatcher.

"Is the sheriff there, please?" she said frantically.

"I'm sorry, he's out on a call. Can—"

"What about Burton Grant?" she interrupted. "Is he there? He has to call Search and Rescue. Fitz O'Brannoch has wandered off from the ranch and is lost somewhere out on the plateau."

The dispatcher made appropriate noises as she dialed Burt's

extension. "I'm sure Deputy Grant will see a search party is put together right away."

When Burt came on the line she anxiously explained the situation, and her suspicions about Lloyd.

"Don't worry," he assured her. "Arizona has some of the best Search and Rescue squads in the country. I can have a team out there within an hour or two."

"Tell them to hurry," she said, and hung up.

Making a quick decision, she grabbed her coat and gloves and headed back out to the barn to resaddle Jasper. Hawk wasn't going to like it. He got really tetchy when she disobeyed a direct order. But someone had to warn him—so he didn't walk right into a trap.

And she was the only one available.

It shouldn't be too difficult to follow his trail. It had stopped snowing completely, so Tonopah's hoofprints should be clear as day, leading her right to him. And with any luck to Fitz, as well.

She just prayed she'd reach them before it was too late.

Hawk followed Crimson's tracks all the way up to the cliffs. The rustlers must have sought shelter in one of the many canyons when the blizzard blew up. It was a little out of their way, but it made sense. If the truck couldn't get through because of weather, they were sure to be caught if they held the stolen cattle anywhere near the highway. In the canyons, they could hole up as long as needed, in relative safety. After all, who would think of looking on Irish Heaven itself for the rustlers and their booty?

As he followed Fitz's trail, it was joined from either side by two other horsemen. Hawk's pulse doubled. There were no overt signs of a struggle, but that didn't mean they hadn't hurt the old man, or threatened him. He gripped the reins so hard Tonopah jumped.

"Sorry, boy," he soothed in a low voice, stroking the horse's neck. Poor devil was all out of breath. They'd been going non-stop since dawn. If they didn't get to rest soon, he'd fall over.

The furrows in the snow led Hawk right to the mouth of what he knew to be a sizable box canyon. But the entrance was fairly inconspicuous. Which told him the rustlers were pretty damn familiar with Irish Heaven territory if they knew how to find it.

Grabbing his rifle, he left Tonopah to rest amidst a small group of junipers and went on foot to find the animal trail leading up the cliffs. There always was one. He found it and climbed a ways up, then crawled on his stomach to the edge of a ledge that looked down into the bowels of the box canyon.

What he saw made his blood boil.

Jeremy Lloyd. Talking and laughing with three other men, one much older than the others. Hawk's stolen cattle were milling and lowing at the far end of the canyon, about fifty yards away. Fitz was nowhere to be seen.

Hawk scooted back and took several deep breaths, battling the urge to just lift his rifle and shoot the bunch of them. However, besides the obvious downsides to killing, dead men couldn't tell him what they'd done with Fitz. Aside from which, with his arm injured as it was, aiming accurately would not be so easy. He might shoot an innocent steer.

He took a last cleansing breath and crept a bit further down the ledge. Maybe he could overhear some of their conversation. Maybe they'd let everything slip, and *then* he could shoot them.

His desire to do so only increased as he lay very still and listened.

"What a chump. Let's just knock him in the head and let the cattle trample him, like they did with Rudy," Jeremy said in a nasty tone.

Hawk came alert. So they *did* have Fitz. But where was he?

"We'll do no such thing," the older man said. "Rudy's death was an accident. I'll have no part of murder."

Hawk snorted silently and watched as the three younger men exchanged looks.

"I don't know how you can say that after everything he's done to you, Dad," Jeremy said in a petulant whine.

So the old man was the jerk's father. The Lloyd patriarch. Hawk felt sorry for him with such a sniveling rodent for a son.

"The only mistake Fitz O'Brannoch made was not selling Irish Heaven back to me after I got back on my feet," Lloyd said sternly. "I warned him. But he wouldn't listen. We had no choice but to bankrupt him same way *we* were. But I've gotten no pleasure from doing it."

"The land is more important than some dumb old man," Jeremy ground out. "He's senile. Nobody'll miss him when he's gone."

Hawk almost didn't see the swift cuff on the head Jeremy received from his father, he was so stunned by the news that the escalating bad luck on Irish Heaven had been due to years of deliberate, systematic sabotage. He thought of the countless accidents and seemingly random disasters that had befallen the ranch and men over the past half decade. They all took on a different light now.

This had started long before the rustling ever began.

Deep breaths weren't helping. Hawk was about to leap over the ledge and pummel the bastards to bits when Fitz came wandering up to the assembled men at the fire. Hawk halted in midmovement.

"How long does it take you to piss, pops?" one of the young men said with a snicker. "Thought you'd passed out somewhere."

"A lot o' brew in the bladder," Fitz answered with a grin, an exaggerated sway and a slur to his words. He plopped down on a tree stump close to the fire. "Ah, it feels lovely."

Hawk clamped down on his outrage as one of the cowboys handed Fitz a can—obviously another beer. They were getting him drunk! Hawk could only imagine what they planned to do next. One way or another, Jeremy would see Fitz didn't survive long enough to be found alive. Of that, Hawk had no doubt.

Trusting and guileless, Fitz was sitting there with the very men who had caused his downfall, half-frozen and oblivious to the fact they were taking his cattle and plotting to steal his ranch right under his nose.

No. This wasn't going on another minute.

"What'll we do about the niece, Rhiannon?" Jeremy asked, freezing Hawk in his tracks as he began to crawl backward. "Everything would have been so much easier if she'd just fallen for me. But that no-account half-breed foreman has her scared to look twice at any decent man," Jeremy said disgustedly. "She even told Burton Grant to take a hike."

The father's head shot up. "Grant? What the hell is he doing hanging around her? I told him to keep a low profile!"

The two other young men chortled. "Seems his *profile* had a mind of its own."

"Yeah, it kept getting bigger!" They laughed uproariously.

"That's enough," the older Lloyd snapped. "She won't be a problem. With the herd gone and no income, she'll have no choice but to sell out. She knows squat about ranching. Grant's idea of forcing that conservatorship was a stroke of genius."

Heartsick, Hawk glanced at Fitz, who was ignoring the conversation, tipping his beer back to drain it. The old guy didn't have his heavy winter coat on, just a hip-length jacket over his blue jeans. He must be freezing. Except the doctor had told them that eventually, even if he felt things, he'd immediately forget feeling them so he wouldn't realize he was cold, hungry, hurt or whatever.

Maybe the physical stress of the raw cold had shocked Fitz's illness into further decline.

"God damn it!" Hawk muttered.

He'd meant to keep his voice low, but apparently he'd put more oomph into it than he'd intended because the four men below twisted their heads toward him as one.

"Hey!" Jeremy yelled, jumping to his feet.

But the older Lloyd was cooler and grabbed the shotgun at his side before calmly standing—and pointing the muzzle right at Fitz's temple.

"Whoever you are, get your ass down here right now," he shouted. "Or I'll blow Fitz O'Brannoch's brains out."

A loud shout rent the winter stillness.

Voices! And they didn't sound happy.

A startled flock of birds took flight from the cliffs just ahead of Rhiannon. Anxiously she reined in Jasper. The tracks she'd been following led straight to where the sounds of a scuffle were coming from.

Were Hawk and Fitz in danger?

Spurring Jasper to a gallop, she closed the short distance to the cliffs, and suddenly came upon Tonopah standing at alert among some trees. He nickered and shook his head at seeing them, but didn't leave his spot, letting them come to him.

Quickly dismounting, she examined him, finding no blood or anything else out of place. Except Hawk's rifle was not in its sheath. A single set of boot tracks led from the copse up into the cliffs.

Giving Jasper the signal to stay put, she matched her steps to the boot prints and followed them as quickly as she could. If Hawk was hurt again…

No. He was fine. She hadn't heard any shooting.

The trail was steep, rough and difficult to follow, especially in winter gear. It looked like it led to a vantage point up above a narrow canyon. Along with the shouting, she heard the unmistakable sound of restless cattle lowing, all coming from the canyon below.

Suddenly she almost stumbled over Hawk's Winchester. It was lying on the ground, just above a ledge which overlooked— By the saints! *It was the rustlers' camp.*

She swiftly ducked down so the men below wouldn't see her, snatching up Hawk's weapon.

Where was he? And why had he left it up in the cliffs?

Frantically she searched the ground around the gun. Again, no blood, no signs of a fight. Just boot prints leading out onto a ledge. Carrying the rifle, she followed them, and found depressions in the snow where he'd lain on his stomach observing the activity in the camp below. She did the same.

She stifled a gasp. Both Fitz and Hawk were surrounded by four arguing men—one of whom was holding a shotgun. Hawk looked wet and bedraggled, like he'd been dragged through the snow. She gripped the rifle in her hands, wishing like hell she'd learned how to use it.

All at once Hawk leapt at one of his captors, grabbed the shotgun and whacked him on the head with it. The man went down and a melee ensued. Arms flew, legs kicked, men cursed and she could hear the solid *smack* of fists meeting flesh. The shotgun had been thrown aside, but now one of the men rolled from the fracas and crawled toward it.

Throughout, Fitz had been left standing in confusion, but when he saw the man making for the weapon, something in his mind must have clicked.

"No, you don't!" he shouted, and fiercely kicked the man's outstretched hand. "I'll take that." Swiping up the shotgun, he yelled, "Stop! Let 'im go or I'll blast the lot o' youse."

Instantly there was a pause in the fighting. Eyes darted to Fitz, who looked like he meant business. Rhiannon prayed he'd stay lucid enough to pull this off.

"How do you know that gun's loaded, pops?" one of the rustlers challenged, panting from exertion.

"I'm feelin' lucky," Fitz said with a smirk. "Are you?"

"As a matter of fact—"

"Hands up!" Fitz ordered.

When the rustlers hesitated, Rhiannon scrambled to her feet and raised Hawk's rifle. "Do as he says!" she yelled down. "If he doesn't shoot you, I sure as hell will."

All heads turned toward her, stunned at her sudden appearance. Hawk's expression was the most shocked of all.

"Tie them up, baby," she called to him. "Before I pull the trigger by mistake. This gun's awful heavy."

Two minutes later they were trussed up like the pigs they were. With a sigh of relief, she lowered the shaking rifle and sent Hawk a triumphant smile before turning to rush back to the horses and join him in the canyon.

But as she hurried to grab Jasper's reins, she ran right into Burton Grant.

"Burt!" she squeaked in surprise. "What are you doing here?"

"I believe you sent for me," he said with a smile. But his eyes looked grim.

She glanced around and saw a big bay mare. "I didn't think you could ride a horse."

His brows hiked. "Sweetheart, my family's lived here for three generations. Of course I ride. I own three horses."

"Oh." Suddenly she was nervous, but couldn't think why. He was there to rescue her, after all. Well, Fitz.

"Did you find him?" he asked, casually glancing at Tonopah.

"Um. Yes. We did. Hawk's with him." She pointed. "In the canyon."

"Canyon?" His eyes narrowed on the spot she indicated. "Oh, I see. Is he all right?"

"Yes, he's fine. Thanks. You can call off Search and Rescue. Thank goodness."

For some inexplicable reason, she hesitated to tell him about the rustlers. There was just something not right about the way Burt was looking at her. She started to back up.

He pulled out his cell phone and punched in a number. As he spoke to the dispatcher, Rhiannon slid the Winchester into its sheath and mounted Jasper.

When he hung up she said, "Thanks for coming, but we'll be fine from here."

Burt regarded her for a brief second. "I don't think so," he said levelly. He caught hold of her bridle and relieved her of the rifle. As her pulse scrabbled, he tugged the reins from her hands, reached over and grabbed Tonopah's, too. Then he walked them to his bay and swung into the saddle, settling Hawk's rifle across his lap.

"What are you doing?" she demanded. "Let me go this instant!"

"Can't do that, Rhiannon. Sorry." He turned the bay toward the canyon. "I know who and what's in that canyon. And we have a little something to settle first."

Her heart sank. She'd been right. He was involved in the rustling!

Even though it had been her suggestion, she still couldn't believe it. Not so much because he was an officer of the law, but because he'd seemed so…forthright.

As he towed her in to the rustlers' camp, her stomach knotted. Fitz was lying on the ground and Hawk was bent over him.

"Jackson," Burt said, lifting the rifle.

Hawk spun. "What the—"

"Step away from O'Brannoch and untie these men." He pointed the muzzle of Hawk's gun at Fitz, who looked like he was unconscious.

"Fitz!" she called, and leapt off Jasper to run to his side. "What's happened?"

"He passed out," Hawk said, eyes never leaving Burt. "I can't get him to come to."

A choking noise escaped her throat. "Oh, my God." She knelt at his side, hardly paying attention to what else was happening. She was too concerned with her uncle. "He needs medical help!" she cried desperately, after trying unsuccessfully to revive him. She looked up to see Hawk untie the last of the four rustlers under the careful scrutiny of Burt, who now held the rifle aimed at her. Hawk's expression left little doubt what he'd do to Burton if given half a chance.

"Mount up," he told the men. "You, too," he said to Hawk.

"I'm not leaving them," he growled.

"You'll do as I say," Burt growled back. "Or I'll shoot them both right now."

Her jaw dropped, more in shock than panic. "You'd do that?"

He had the grace at least to look uncomfortable. "I wouldn't want to," he said. "But unless Jackson does exactly as I say, I'll have no choice."

"You'll leave my horse, at least?" she managed.

He turned away. "No." He stuck the rifle under Hawk's chin. "Don't make me use this."

Hawk gave a single nod. She could see he was seething, but he obeyed and swung onto Tonopah.

The rustlers ran and fetched their horses, then rounded up the stolen steers and were ready to move out. Rhiannon quickly dragged Fitz to a place out of the path of the pounding hooves as they went by.

Cradling her uncle's head in her lap, she couldn't help the tears that crested as she watched the man she loved being taken away, probably forever.

There was no way any of them would get out of this alive. They knew the rustlers' identities, and worse, that one of them was a sheriff's deputy.

This would be the last time she'd ever see Hawk.

But before she could say a word, or even meet his gaze, Burton had forced him to ride on, galloping away under the threat of his own rifle.

A sob worked its way up her throat as she saw him disappear through the mouth of the canyon.

Oh, God.

She was alone in the bitter cold, without shelter or food, miles from home or any means of communication, with an unconscious man to care for.

And they were all going to die.

Chapter 17

There was no way in hell he was going to die like this.

No damn way.

Redhawk banked his fury and concentrated on how he could get out of this mess and back to Fitz and Rhiannon. To hell with the cattle. They could take them, and Irish Heaven, too, for all he cared. The only thing he wanted was to save the lives of those he loved.

"Hey, Deputy!" Jeremy shouted to Grant as the men got the herd moving in the direction of the highway. "You better cuff that renegade's hands!"

Grant snorted loudly. "He's practically a cripple! Don't tell me you're afraid of this guy?"

Hawk lifted his slitted gaze to Grant. Cripple, eh? He'd show him—

"He's a savage. Don't matter if he's injured or not, he's vicious. We're no match for that," one of the young guys—the one he'd slammed in the face with his fist—said, touching his bruises.

The little wimp. Hawk felt a spurt of satisfaction.

"Okay, fine," Grant said disgustedly. "But I'll have to tie him. I didn't bring handcuffs."

Grant trotted his mount up to Tonopah so they rode side by side. He glanced over, his face inscrutable. "Cross your wrists," the deputy ordered. "And let me have them."

Oh, he'd let him have them, all right. Just as soon as he got close enough. Meanwhile, Hawk did as he was told.

To his shock, Grant looped a length of rope loosely around his wrists, letting the ends dangle. "Complain about how tight it is," he said under his breath. "And just follow my lead."

Momentarily stunned, Hawk could only stare after him as he galloped away. What the hell was that supposed to mean?

"Gee, you think you could have tied this any tighter?" he shouted sarcastically after his retreating back.

Was he supposed to believe this was some kind of undercover set-up to catch the rustlers?

"Shut up, Jackson, and I might let you live," Grant yelled back over his shoulder.

It had to be. There was no other explanation for Grant leaving him the use of his hands and lying about it.

Well, hell.

But what about Rhiannon and Fitz? They'd been left with nothing. They'd die of exposure if they weren't rescued before nighttime.

He glanced at the sun, estimating that it must be midafternoon. They'd be fine for a few hours. Especially if Rhiannon kept the fire going.

He clenched his teeth. Rustler trap or no, he was going to kill Burton Grant when they got these bastards in handcuffs. Endangering the lives of innocent bystanders was inexcusable.

It wasn't easy playing possum, but Hawk managed to appear ornery yet appropriately defeated for the two hours it took them to slog their way through the deep snow to the highway chute.

The elder Lloyd had phoned ahead as soon as his cell phone got a signal, so the truck was waiting for them.

Along with Hawk's unknown fate.

He definitely didn't trust Grant. He'd gone along solely on the supposition that a guilty man wouldn't have left Hawk's wrists untied. But that was a giant leap of faith.

One that could cost him his life, if he'd been outfoxed.

His heart beat double time as he waited with Grant for the others to load the stolen cattle onto the truck. Their horses stood side by side and his own Winchester pointed at him from where it lay across Grant's lap. His mind worked furiously, trying to figure out how to overpower five men and live through it.

After the last steer was secured, the truck gate slammed shut and Jeremy Lloyd pulled the handle to lock it. "What do we do with him?" he asked Grant, flicking his thumb at Hawk.

"What do you want me to do with him?" Grant answered with a nasty sneer. The implication seemed obvious. Hawk's nerves screamed. If Grant was legit, he didn't want to mess up the plan. But if he wasn't... *Hell and damnation.*

Jeremy chuckled. "You must want her real bad, man."

Grant's white teeth flashed. "I do."

"Then kill the renegade."

"Whatever you say." With a look of triumph, he turned to Hawk. "Get off your horse, Jackson."

"Wh-what?" Even though part of him had been expecting it, the betrayal still caught him by surprise. His mind reeled. *He had to get—*

"You heard me!" Grant shouted, then mouthed, Trust me. He raised the rifle and indicated the snow-covered berm between the highway shoulder and the fence. "Walk up to the top of the rise. Hurry up! We don't have all day."

Conflicted but all out of ideas, Hawk snowshoed up the hill. He'd have to dive over the top and— Suddenly, a loud rifle rapport rang out. A shot whizzed by his ear. Instinctively he turned and froze. *Crap.*

After a second Grant darted him a look of consternation and silently mouthed, Fall! Then rolled his eyes.

Hawk let fly a swearword, grabbed his side in mock pain and fell dramatically over the top and down the back side of the rise. Praying the slight time delay hadn't made the rustlers suspicious.

He held his breath. A split second later the elder Lloyd cursed harshly. "What the *hell* did you do, you idiot? Are you *insane?* I told you I wanted no part of murder!"

"Come on, let's get out of here, Dad," Jeremy said, then there was a slamming of truck doors and the engine was revved.

Hawk dared a peek over the rise. Grant was letting them get away!

Suddenly lights flashed and sirens wailed, shattering the snowy peace of the plateau. Sheriff's cruisers were everywhere, coming from every direction. They pulled out from behind nearby trees, screamed up the highway from both sides, roared down the road from the ranch.

Hawk vaulted to his feet, watching in relief as the two Lloyds and the others were dragged from the truck and slapped in handcuffs.

"Hawk!"

He whirled, and caught Rhiannon as she leapt into his arms. "Baby! You're safe!" He hugged her close, never so glad to see anyone in his life. "Fitz?"

She nodded happily. "Cold and disoriented but basically fine. They took him to the hospital to check him over."

He covered her lips with his, needing to taste her, to feel her warmth, to know she was truly safe. After a long kiss, he let out the breath he had seemingly been holding since being taken from her. "Thank God you're both okay. How did you get back?"

"The search and rescue team came and got us just after you

rode off. Apparently the sheriff was watching the whole time. I was so worried about you!"

"I'm no worse for wear. Grant managed to let me know it was all a setup."

"And you trusted me?" Grant stood at the top of the rise looking down on them with a wry smile.

Hawk managed to smile back. "Hell, no. But I didn't seem to have a lot of options. Gotta say, I'm pretty relieved you turned out to be one of the good guys."

"Yeah, well. I may be good, but you're the lucky one."

Didn't he know it. He hugged Rhiannon tighter. "You think?"

Grant sighed elaborately. "The reward *and* the girl. How lucky can one guy get? It's downright depressing."

The reward and the girl. He liked the sound of that.

The Cattlemen's Association reward!

In all the commotion, he'd forgotten about that. "Oh, man," he said on a long, elated breath. "Looks like Irish Heaven is saved, after all."

Rhiannon gazed up at him, her smile radiant. "You did it, Hawk. I'm so proud of you."

Hawk's happiness slipped just a little. He whisked her up into his arms and started walking toward the warmth of the nearest sheriff's cruiser so she wouldn't notice the sudden stab of sadness that seized him.

With the substantial reward, Irish Heaven would be solvent again. Rhiannon would now have money to live on and wouldn't have to work more than part-time. She could sell the remaining cattle and not have to worry about that end of things anymore. She'd be free to do whatever she wanted.

And he would be free to leave.

Because there was no longer any need for him on Irish Heaven.

He'd take his horses and a small slice of the reward money as back wages and strike out on his own, to make a new life for himself. It was time.

The lucky one? Yeah.

Grant was sure right about one thing.

It was downright depressing.

"My saints!" Rhiannon exclaimed when she saw an envelope from Ireland among the other mail that evening.

After making their statements at the sheriff's office, they'd stopped for fixings for a celebratory meal, complete with two bottles of champagne. Hawk had grilled steaks to perfection, and they'd shared one bottle over dinner with Fitz, saving the other for later. After dessert, she'd finally remembered about the pile of mail they'd fetched from the post office box.

She stared at the letter, wondering what had prompted Aunt Bridget to write. With sudden horror, she ran to the mantel and frantically searched for the letter she'd written to her aunt and uncle a few weeks ago when she'd felt so depressed about everything. To her dismay it was nowhere to be found.

"Did you see a letter sitting on the mantel?" she asked Hawk.

"Yeah, a while back. I mailed it for you."

"Oh, dear," she murmured apprehensively, balancing the letter in her hands.

"Something wrong?"

She planted a smile on her face. "No, not at all." But she didn't move.

This was what she'd decided was best, to return to Ireland. So why was she so reluctant to hear their answer?

"Are you going to open it?"

Her face started to smart from keeping the smile in place. "Of course." She swallowed, and carefully tore open the envelope. What had her aunt and uncle thought of her desperate plea to come back to the farm? Would they generously take her back? Or would they tell her she'd chosen to leave and wasn't welcome there any longer....

As she read through it, her eyes widened and her disbelief

grew. It was an apology. A poignant confession of how guilty
Aunt Bridget felt about inheriting her father's farm instead of her,
how badly she felt about the way Rhiannon had been treated during her years of living there, and a heartfelt plea for Rhiannon
to return to Ireland, and to bring Fitz with her.

> I've always carried a huge burden of responsibility and
> shame for your uncle's departure for America. It was I who
> told him the British had come looking for him with an ar-
> rest warrant the night your father was caught and put in
> gaol. That wasn't true. But I knew he'd go to America, for
> he'd spoken often of what he'd do if John Bull came for
> him. And I foolishly thought he'd take me with him.

Rhiannon was gobsmacked. It had been *Aunt Bridget's* fault
Fitz had left Ireland so suddenly? Unbelievable. And now she
wanted Fitz to return, so she could take care of him as he de-
scended further into forgetfulness.

> You've already done your share, my love, so dutifully
> nursing your dear mother, my sister, through her illness.
> Please give me the chance to make amends, in small part,
> for the unhappiness I've caused, by caring for the man I
> so wronged. You say in his mind he's already returned to
> Ireland. What better place to end his days than where he
> started?

"What is it?" Redhawk asked her, his voice tender and filled
with concern. He reached out and gently wiped the trail of moisture from her cheek. "Bad news?"

She hadn't realized she'd been crying. She gave a watery
laugh. "No," she said softly. "It's the answer to our prayers. How
would you like to take Fitz to Ireland?"

* * *

It took just over a month to arrange everything for their trip to the Emerald Isle.

Rhiannon had already made the most difficult decision of her life—not to return to America after taking Fitz home to the farm. So before their departure she put all the paperwork in order with Fitz's lawyer for Hawk to take over the responsibility for Irish Heaven, as well as Fitz's conservatorship. It wasn't easy, because she didn't want Hawk to know anything about those arrangements. She had no idea what his reaction would be when he finally found out she would not be returning with him, though she had a feeling it wouldn't be pretty.

But she had no choice.

Ever since her appointment as Fitz's conservator, he'd grown more and more convinced that she would inherit Irish Heaven. True to his word, he hadn't asked her to marry him again, but she'd known he'd wanted to. She'd seen it written plainly on his face more than once, and had only headed him off by changing the subject before he could get the words out. What he didn't know was, if she did inherit Irish Heaven sometime in the future—which she still wasn't convinced of—she planned to turn it all over to him, anyway.

She loved and wanted Hawk, but he didn't return her feelings—he wanted her, but it was the ranch he loved. She knew he'd devoted every minute of every day for eleven long years to its upkeep, sacrificing his life, taking nothing for himself. He should have this land. It was only fair. He'd earned it far more than she.

In the bank account, she left most of the reward money for him, taking only enough for airline tickets and a bit to make Fitz comfortable in his new home. Once her uncle had settled in with Bridget and Patrick, she would leave the farm and find a job and a place of her own in a nearby village.

It was time to get on with it. As difficult as it would be to leave Hawk behind, she couldn't spend her life taking second place to a piece of land.

She needed to be loved. She *deserved* to be loved.

"You'll never guess," she said one evening as they were packing, a few days before they were to leave, "who volunteered to take care of the horses while we're gone."

"Who?"

"Burton Grant."

Hawk grimaced. "Still trying with you, eh?"

"Don't be silly. He feels awful about having to point a gun at us. He promised to take good care of them."

.A grunt was Hawk's token objection. "He better."

"Speaking of horses…" Rhiannon had been wanting to bring up an idea she had. "What about buying a couple while we're in Ireland?"

At his surprised look, she explained, "Well, now that we've sold the cattle and the bad guys are in jail so we know there'll be no more disasters on Irish Heaven, you can do what you've always wanted to do. Raise and train rodeo horses."

In his expression she read a mix of hesitancy and pure temptation. "Irish Thoroughbreds aren't used for rodeos," he pointed out logically.

"I know. It's just, well, you could buy a stallion and use him in your line somewhere. For speed and heart. And maybe buy a mare, too." She tipped her head. "You could raise a Thoroughbred colt every once in a while like Fitz wanted to do. They're worth a lot of money over here, aren't they?"

He shook his head. "Yes. But that would eat up a lot of the reward money. Not sure that's smart."

"All right. Just the stallion, then," she conceded. But she was determined Hawk leave Ireland with at least one perfect horse. She could see how he wanted to say yes. He was just too practical sometimes.

"We'll see," he said, and turned back to packing boxes.

She'd wondered how to pack all her things without him becoming suspicious, so she'd suggested they move downstairs into Fitz's master bedroom after returning from their trip. He'd jumped on the idea, because of his knee. It had been aching worse than usual because of the cold and his injuries.

But it was strange and unsettling, seeing him pack his things, separate from hers. Almost as if he knew....

She shook herself mentally and forced herself not to think. About never sharing a room with him again. Or her bed. Or her life. Because if she broke down now and started to cry, she feared she'd never stop. She was barely holding it together as it was.

The day of their flight came all too soon, but at the same time it was exciting knowing she'd see her homeland again. Fitz did well on the plane, and Hawk was like a little kid he was so enthralled by the view from so far above the earth. They held hands the whole trip over, and were still holding hands when Aunt Bridget and Uncle Patrick picked them up at Shannon Airport. She never wanted to let go.

She liked how everyone stared at her with her handsome cowboy. It wasn't every day one saw a full-blood Paiute in Ireland. Hawk looked deadly in his boots and jeans, wearing the shirt she'd embroidered for him under his lambskin coat—and his Stetson, of course. He looked about as Wild West as it got. People actually cleared a path as they walked arm in arm down to the luggage carousel.

She wanted to shout, "He's mine!" to every pretty girl who tossed him a flirtatious smile along the way.

It was the hardest thing in the world to know that with a single word she *could* be his, forever—and the hardest choice she'd ever make not to say that word. Oh, how she wanted to. But she had to be tough.

"You made the right choice," Hawk whispered in her ear.

Shocked, keeping the devastation locked inside, she glanced up at him. "Look at Fitz," he said, tipping his chin at the trio of Fitz, Bridget and Patrick, none of whom had stopped talking since they'd tearfully greeted each other just outside Customs. Fitz was visibly thrilled to be here.

It took all her strength to keep a smile on her face. "Yes," she said around the lump in her throat, "it all worked out brilliantly. This is truly best for everyone."

A hint of a frown passed over his forehead. "What—"

She turned toward the carousel. "Look. Here's our luggage."

She knew she'd have to tell him eventually. But not yet. For just a few more days, she wanted to see him smile at her in that special way. And pretend she was his.

Just a few more days before she let him leave her far behind.

Redhawk had never seen so much green in his life. Or such beautiful horses. It was an incredible place, this country.

He wrapped his arms around Rhiannon and pulled his hat down against the chill wind. The temperature might be above zero, but it felt like eighty below because the air was laden with moisture. Colder than a banshee's curse, as Bridget would say.

"What's he doing?" he whispered to Rhiannon as they watched from afar as Patrick spoke with the sellers at the giant equestrian auction where they hoped to pick up their new Thoroughbred stallion.

"Working his magic," she whispered back.

Hawk might have the gift of picking out good horseflesh, but Patrick knew all the players, and he had the Irish knack of striking a good bargain. Hawk had given Patrick his first three choices and monetary limits, then trusted Rhiannon's uncle to pull off a miracle. The prices of these two-year-olds were making Hawk's hair stand on end.

"All bluff," Patrick had assured him.

He hoped that was right. Otherwise Hawk'd be going home empty-handed. He'd love to have a fine stallion to start his breeding program with, but refused to leave Rhiannon's coffers depleted.

"This will probably take hours," Rhiannon murmured, turning in his arms. "Let's go for a drive."

"I wouldn't mind that."

They'd had a good trip so far, but they'd hardly been alone together since arriving in Ireland. Naturally they hadn't been able to share a bed; he'd had to bunk with Fitz in the spare room, and Rhiannon had taken her old spot on a futon in the living room. It had been more than frustrating.

But beyond that, it seemed like Rhiannon was withdrawing from him. Even on the rare occasions they found themselves alone in a room, she hesitated to get physical, shying away from his kisses and embraces more often than not.

Yeah, all this should be a good thing. Because when they returned home and he left Irish Heaven, he wouldn't have her close anymore. He might as well get used to it.

But he didn't want to. Not yet. He wanted to squeeze every bit of closeness out of every single minute they had left together. Before he had to let her go.

They walked out to the car they'd borrowed from Bridget, and Rhiannon slid behind the wheel. He didn't like driving on the wrong side of the road. Especially when he was this preoccupied.

"Where are you taking me?" he said, waggling his eyebrows. He hoped to some cute bed and breakfast with a huge fluffy bed, a fireplace and room service. He squirmed in his seat, already anticipating it.

She took his face between her hands and gave him a far too chaste kiss. "Not where you're thinking," she said, smiling, but her eyes looked sad. "There's something I want you to see." Her gaze drifted gently over his face. "And I have something I need to tell you."

His heart skipped a beat. He didn't like the sound of that. He had something to tell her, too, but serious discussions could wait until they got back to the ranch. They were supposed to be having fun on this trip. "Rhiannon—"

"Shhh." She put a finger to his lips. "You're going to love this place I'm taking you."

It was farther than he expected. They drove for about an hour, which wouldn't get you to the nearest big city in Arizona but was incredibly far by local standards. They followed the shoreline for the last half of the trip, hugging the wild, sea-splashed rocks of the western Irish coast.

"I'm glad Fitz is happy," he remarked as they passed an old man walking with his dog along the side of the road, whistling.

"Me, too," she agreed. "I'll admit I was feeling a bit guilty passing on that responsibility. But it seems to be what he wants."

"He never stopped loving Ireland, or talking about it."

"And Bridget is so good with him. Even Patrick seems to enjoy having him here."

She lapsed into silence again. Hawk was uneasy about why she was so moody. He felt the walls dangerously close to closing in on them. Or maybe between them. He was desperate to stop that from happening. *Not yet.*

It was a terrible thing to discover you were in love with someone only to find it was too late and you'd lost her.

The thought was so quiet, he almost didn't notice it forming in his head. But suddenly it was there, big as the Atlantic crashing against the cliffs, and just as insistent.

He loved her desperately.

He'd loved her all along.

So what was he going to do about it?

He gazed out the car window at the cold gray ocean, where it wore against the solid rock of the shore, washing over it, wearing it down grain by grain.

That's what he'd tried to do with Rhiannon. Wear her down. Keep making love to her and asking her to marry him until she finally said yes. But it hadn't happened. She'd seemed happy with him, happy when they made love. But she still didn't want to marry him.

Unrequited love was hell.

Maybe he'd give it one last try. Here, wherever it was she was taking him.

He realized she'd pulled over and was getting out of the car. He followed suit and went after her up a steep path to the top of a grass-covered hill overlooking the sea.

The view was spectacular. They were high on the point of a narrow peninsula, surrounded on three sides by water. Above the cliffs the green of the grass stood in stark contrast to the black rock and the wintry blue sky. Rugged and beautiful, yet soft and soothing in a savage way. Sort of like Arizona. But very different.

She took his hand and led him right up to the top of the hill, to a strange formation of stones, about fifty feet long and twenty feet wide. The stones were quite large and looked like granite, and were set in a configuration that looked kind of like…the outer outline of a pair of lips, without the upper dip.

"What is this?" he asked, amazed how anyone could have managed to move those giant boulders an inch, let alone into a specific arrangement.

"Most people think it's a druid stone circle, like Stonehenge. But it's really a boat grave. They're pretty rare in Ireland. Mostly you find them in Scandinavia."

"They buried a ship here?" he asked, incredulous.

She laughed. The lilting sound carried on the wind like an ancient melody. He loved the way she laughed. "No. It's a person, or persons. But they arranged the stones in the shape of a small boat. See, the two ends are the bow and the stern? It's thought to carry the dead to the afterlife. The grave sites always overlook the water."

He peered out over the crashing waves. "A dead sea captain, maybe?"

"Viking."

"Ah. Longing for the homeland. Like Fitz."

She smiled wistfully. "Maybe. Some people, the UFO types,

think it's a radio transmitter for contacting outer space. They say if you whisper something at one end you can hear distinctly what's said at the other end."

He chuckled. "What a bunch of fruitcakes."

"Yeah. No doubt." She turned to him, but stared down at the ground, folding her arms across her midriff. "Redhawk, I'm not going back."

At the abrupt change of subject, he stared at her uncomprehendingly. Suddenly his pulse took off at a gallop. "What?" Surely, she hadn't said—

"I'm going to stay here, in Ireland."

He gaped. "For how long? You can't leave Irish Heaven on its own for—"

"You'll be there to take care of it."

He shook his head. "No. I'm not—"

"I know it's a lot of work for one person, but you could hire—"

"You don't understand. I *won't* be there. I'm leaving the ranch."

Her face was a portrait of shock. For a moment she was speechless.

Damn. He hadn't meant to tell her yet. Not until after he'd proposed one last time.

"You are?" she finally asked. "Why?"

On second thought, her intention to stay in Ireland told him loud and clear what her answer would be.

She was leaving him. The fact that he'd planned to leave her, too, was irrelevant. He felt sick.

She was leaving him.

"Why?" he echoed, putting out a hand to steady himself against one of the ancient stones. "Because…because it's time for me to move on. Irish Heaven is yours by blood. I have no right to take it away from you, and I don't have the heart to try anymore. It's yours, Rhiannon. You belong there."

And that was the God's honest truth. For a while he'd thought they might belong there together, but…well, that obviously wasn't going to happen. He'd been willing to fight to stay, to stay with her, willing to throw in his lot with hers even when they hadn't been lovers, or even friends. Now that they were both, it was killing him to let go of the dream. But she wasn't interested. She'd rather stay here in Ireland than be his wife. So be it.

She was staring at him like he'd lost his mind.

"How can you say that?" she accused. "Irish Heaven is so *yours* I've felt like an intruder from day one. No. I can't take that land away from you. You said it yourself, it's what you live for. Your heart is filled with Irish Heaven, and I'd never forgive myself if I made you rip it out."

It was his turn to stare at her.

Did she have no clue? That it was *her* in his heart? That by staying here, she was ripping it out more completely than if he never saw Irish Heaven again?

He was having a hard time forming words. "I don't want it," he rasped. "Not without you there."

He saw her blink and swallow heavily. "I can't, Hawk. Not like—" She swallowed again. "Sell it, then. I've arranged for you to be conservator when you get back. You can buy a place of your own, somewhere you'll be happy…."

"Will you be happy here, Rhiannon?" he asked. "Is this what you really want?"

She gazed at him, her eyes moist with the mists of the sea, green as the grass of her native land, her skin pale as porcelain and her expression desolate as the wild and rocky cliffs below.

"My offer of marriage still stands," he said, reaching for her. "Please, Rhiannon. Say yes."

Her hand lifted to meet his, but stalled before he could catch it, or even touch her. Her lips trembled, and he was sure she wanted to say something…but she didn't. She remained silent for a long time before at last tearing her gaze from his.

"I'm sorry," she murmured, banding her arms around herself, looking everywhere but at him.

His heart felt like that rodeo bull had crushed it instead of his knee. Sharp pain razored through his whole body so raw he had to breathe deeply to keep from crying out.

What would he do now?

What *could* he do?

Get up and go on. Alone. Like he always did when life knocked the legs out from under him. It hadn't beaten him yet. This time, though, he wondered.

He nodded once, pulled his hat down over his eyes and stuck his hands in his jacket pockets. Then he walked away. He had no idea where he was going, but he had to be by himself.

Behind him a muffled cry sounded, but he didn't let himself look back. He kept walking. Until he reached the farthest stone at the bow of the boat grave, then he slid behind it, leaning his back against the cold granite for support while he sucked in several deep lungfuls of frigid air to keep his knees from buckling.

Suddenly he heard a sound. At least he thought he did. Like a whispered faerie song, sweet and magical, as though the words came from the very stone itself.

"I love you," the faerie whispered, so low and soft it could have been the wind soughing through the grass.

He held himself absolutely still, straining to hear it again. But there was nothing save the wind. His mind was playing tricks on him.

Closing his eyes, he cursed his imagination. "I love you, too," he whispered back, unable to stop himself.

This time he heard a soft gasp.

Rhiannon!

He spun around the giant stone to peer down the length of the formation. And saw her. Standing at the other end stone, hand over her mouth peering back at him with wide eyes.

"Was that you?" he demanded, starting to walk back toward her.

"Is it true?" she returned.

"Is what true?"

"Do you love me?"

He halted in the middle of the boat and planted his hands on his hips. "Of course I love you! Why do you think I asked you to marry me about a hundred times?"

Her hand slipped from her mouth. "To get the ranch, of course. You never said a thing about—"

He ripped off his Stetson and flung it to the ground, drilling his hands through his hair. Hell.

Hell and damnation. So *that* was it.

"Come here," he said. And waited patiently for her to make up her mind to come to him. She looked skittish as a colt, shifting her weight from one foot to the other.

What an idiot he'd been. An utter, complete fool. He'd been so busy worrying about how *she* felt, he'd never bothered telling her how *he* felt.

He stretched out his hand to her. And willed her to take a step.

She did. Finally. Then another. And another.

By the time she reached him, she was running. She ran into his arms, and he folded her into his embrace, holding her tight so she could never get away from him again.

"I love you, baby," he whispered in her hair. "I loved you from the first moment I saw you in that stupid wool skirt in the hundred-degree Arizona heat. I loved you when you were chasing that silly pig and pulled me into the mud. I loved you when we were fighting. I loved you when we made love. I love you so much I don't know what I'll do if you really mean to stay in Ireland. I guess I'll just have to stay, too."

She went so still in his arms, panic started to crawl through his limbs. Okay, maybe he was wrong.

"Of course…if you don't love me, it's—"

Her hand clamped over his mouth. "I do love you," she whispered. "You have no idea how much. I just thought—"

He kissed her fingers. "Nothing's more important to me than you, Rhiannon. Not the ranch. Not money. Nothing. Please, darlin', if you can stand being the wife of this banged-up, hard case cowboy, please put me out of my misery and marry me."

She tipped her head up to him and smiled. A lush, beautiful, promise-filled smile that spun his heart in his chest.

"Yes," she simply said. "I will."

And that's when he knew his hard-luck days were over forever. He'd found the one thing more precious, more worth fighting for, than anything else in the world.

Love.

Epilogue

"You look deadly."

Rhiannon beamed at her old friend and returned her fierce hug. "Thanks, Maureen." Maureen was the tenth girl in the receiving line to tell her that. The Irish-lace wedding dress she and Aunt Bridget had put together on the old farm treadle machine had turned out stunning.

"And your new husband," Maureen confidentially whispered in her ear, fanning herself dramatically, "he looks even deadlier." Maureen was the *twentieth* girl in the receiving line to tell her *that* and then ask, "I don't s'pose he's got a brother somewhere, by any chance?"

Rhiannon grinned, and gave Hawk's arm a squeeze. "I'm afraid Redhawk Jackson's one of a kind, Maureen."

Her friend gave a mock sigh. "And just my luck you found him first."

After another hug, Maureen gave Hawk a starry-eyed handshake then joined the other wedding guests on the short walk from the village church to the vestry rose garden, where the reception would be held.

They were lucky. The April weather was glorious, a rare warm, sunny day for an Irish spring. The entire village had turned out for the celebration; all of her own friends, and many of Fitz's old childhood cronies from growing up on the farm were there.

"When can we get out of here?" Hawk murmured suggestively, nuzzling her neck after the receiving line finally wound down.

Maureen and the others were right. Her husband did look deadly. The combination of dove-gray morning suit and cowboy boots was unusual, but set off his dark, exotic looks to perfection.

And he was all hers.

"As soon as possible," she murmured back.

It seemed like forever since they'd been on their own together, let alone able to steal a kiss—or anything else. Aunt Bridget and Uncle Patrick had gleefully seen to that. "A couple should look forward to their wedding day," they'd said with a twinkle in their eyes. What they'd really meant was their wedding *night*.

Rhiannon had never looked more forward to anything in her life than she did to tonight's simple room in a bed and breakfast down the road.

No, that wasn't true. Even more than tonight, she looked forward to their new life together on Irish Heaven.

Hawk leaned down and gave her a lingering kiss. "I love you, Rhiannon Jackson," he whispered.

"I love you more," she whispered back, and took his arm for the stroll to join their friends and family.

The reception was endless, but wonderful fun, filled with laughter and music, dancing and a feast of epic proportions, topped off by a colossal wedding cake made from several tiers of Uncle Patrick's famous custard-filled layer cake in both chocolate and vanilla. It was a little lopsided but tasted heavenly.

Fitz had a huge grin on his face the entire time. He danced and flirted with all the girls, drank whiskey with his boyos, and even sat in with the band, playing a set of lively tunes on the penny whistle that had the whole congregation clapping and dancing a jig.

"He looks happier than I've ever seen him," Hawk remarked afterward, as they sipped champagne. "The doctor was right. I can't believe the difference bringing him back here has made."

"I'm so glad," Rhiannon said softly. "He's such a special man."

"That he is," Hawk agreed, and they clicked glasses. "Now, can we please get out of here? I'm feeling a strong need to be alone with my wife." The loving look in his eyes was spiced with desire.

She shivered and smiled up at him. The celebration would go on until the wee hours, but Rhiannon knew they weren't expected to stay. Thank goodness. "I'll fetch the car keys."

"No need." Hawk took her glass and set it with his on a nearby table. Then he gave a loud whistle, making everyone look up. He bowed and swept an arm toward the path. "Your carriage awaits, my love. Well, sort of."

Suddenly there was a clattering noise, and the crowd erupted in oohs and aahs, opening a path for—

Hawk's new stallion!

The Thoroughbred was a beauty, purest black with white socks and a streak down his nose. But today he was decked out in a multitude of white ribbons and flowers—roses, lilies and daisies—braided through his flowing mane and arranged around his saddle in a blanket over his withers and rump reaching all the way to the ground.

"Oh, Hawk!" Rhiannon exclaimed in awed enchantment as the stallion cantered regally toward them. "He's absolutely gorgeous! But how…?"

"While you've been sewing, we've been training," Hawk said with a heartstopping smile. "What do you think?"

She threw her arms around him. "I think it's the most romantic thing I've ever seen."

She kissed him, and the onlookers laughed and clapped in delight. He whirled her around and around and then up onto the stallion, sidesaddle, amidst cheers and applause. Swinging up behind, he grabbed her around the waist and spurred the horse through the crowd and away from the merry feast.

They were soon ensconced in front of a roaring fire in their own private room on the top floor of the quaint village inn, champagne glasses in hand.

Rhiannon didn't think it was possible to be any happier than she was right at this very moment. Wrapped in the arms of the man she loved with all her heart, the present—and the future—just couldn't be any brighter.

"Come here, wife," he whispered, and gave her a long, loving kiss. "You look good enough to eat," he murmured.

Just then there was a light knock on the door.

"Ignore it," she said, wrapping her arms around his neck.

Something slid under the door.

"What on earth…?" Hawk muttered and went over. He returned with a large envelope. From America.

"Should we open it?" she asked, curiosity getting the better of her.

"Why not." Hawk tore it open. His grin faltered as he glanced at the papers it contained, and his eyes grew wide.

"Hawk?" she asked, pressing into his side, peering over at the top document. It looked official. Sort of like a—

"Jesus, Mary and Joseph," she whispered. "That's—"

"I c-can't believe it," Hawk stuttered. He handed her the cover letter with a shaky hand. "This is dated over three years ago!"

Stunned, she read aloud, "As pursuant to the instructions of our client, Fitz O'Brannoch, who has decreed that the enclosed deed should be turned over to Redhawk Ivan Jackson—" She choked and darted him a shocked look. *"Ivan?"*

He made a face. "Don't start. Just read."

"—Ivan Jackson and Rhiannon Margaret Sophia O'Brannoch, either upon the death of Fitz O'Brannoch, or the legal marriage of said Redhawk and Rhiannon, whichever should come first—"

Her mouth stopped working as the meaning sank in. Her eyes filled with tears. "Oh, my God." She must be dreaming. *It was the deed to Irish Heaven.* "He's given us the ranch!" she cried.

And cried. And launched herself into Redhawk's waiting arms.

He rocked her back and forth, kissing her hair and cheeks and eyelids and lips. "How did he know?" he murmured at last. "Before we even met…how did he know we'd fall in love?"

Taking Hawk's hand, she led him to the bed, her heart filled with a joyous, overwhelming certainty. "Fitz knew you, knew what kind of man you are. How could I not fall in love the moment we met? You're everything a woman could ever want."

He looked at her with melting tenderness, his eyes glowing with so much love it filled her soul with light. "I'll make you happy," he promised, his voice rough with emotion.

And as they lay down on the bed together for the first time as husband and wife, she kissed him and whispered, "My dearest love, you already have."

* * * * *

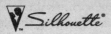

SAGA

National bestselling author
Debra Webb

A decades-old secret threatens to bring down Chicago's elite Colby Agency in this brand-new, longer-length novel.

COLBY CONSPIRACY

While working to uncover the truth behind a murder linked to the agency, Daniel Marks and Emily Hastings find themselves trapped by the dangers of desire—knowing every move they make could be their last....

Available in October, wherever books are sold.

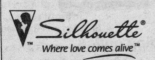
Where love comes alive™

Bonus Features include:

Author's Journal, Travel Tale and a Bonus Read.

If you enjoyed what you just read,
then we've got an offer you can't resist!

Take 2 bestselling love stories FREE!

Plus get a FREE surprise gift!

HARLEQUIN®
Next™

COME OCTOBER
by *USA TODAY* bestselling author Patricia Kay

Victim of a devastating car accident, Claire Sherman couldn't bring herself to face the perfect fiancé and perfect life she'd lost. Starting over with a brand-new identity seemed like the best way to heal—but was it?

Available this October

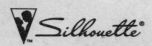
#1387 RIDER ON FIRE—Sharon Sala

With a hitman hot on her trail, undercover DEA agent Sonora Jordan decided to lie low—until ex U.S. Army Ranger and local medicine man Adam Two Eagles convinced her to find the father she'd never known and the love she'd never wanted.

#1388 THE CAPTIVE'S RETURN—Catherine Mann
Wingmen Warriors

During a hazardous mission in South America, Lieutenant Colonel Lucas Quade discovered his long-lost wife, Sara, was alive and that they had a daughter. As they struggled against the perils of nature and the crime lord tracking them, could they reclaim their passion for each other?

#1389 ROMANCING THE RENEGADE—Ingrid Weaver
Payback

Timid bookworm Lydia Smith had no idea she was the daughter of a legendary gold thief, but sparks flew when dashing FBI agent Derek Stone recruited her to find a lost shipment of gold bullion. Together they uncovered her secret past…and a chance for love worth treasuring.

#1390 TEMPTATION CALLS—Caridad Piñeiro
The Calling

As lives went, both of hers had sucked. At least when it came to men. But that was before New York City vampire Samantha Turner met detective Peter Daly. His passion for life, for justice—for her—was enough to tempt her out of the darkness and into his embrace, but would the temptation last when she finally revealed her true nature?

SIMCNM0905

INTIMATE MOMENTS